THE NOVEL AS AMERICAN SOCIAL HISTORY

RICHARD LOWITT, GENERAL EDITOR

HAGAR'S HOARD

HAGAR'S HOARD

BY

GEORGE KIBBE TURNER

INTRODUCTION BY

JOHN DUFFY

THE UNIVERSITY PRESS OF KENTUCKY

LEXINGTON 1970

INTRODUCTION

by John Duffy

In the nineteenth century two great pestilences period-
ically swept through America, terrorizing the population and
leaving thousands dead in their wake. One of these, Asiatic
cholera, visited the United States only three times during
the century. On each occasion it struck the port cities first
and then quickly spread through the country via the inland
waterways. The second, and most devastating, of the great
killer diseases was yellow fever. This disorder is a viral
disease transmitted by a specific mosquito, the *Aedes egypti*.
The incubation period is quite short, usually four or five
days or less. The first symptoms are a flushed face, in-
jected eyes, scarlet lips and tongue, and a high temperature.
Nausea, vomiting, and constipation are often characteristic
of this stage, and the patient suffers a prostration greater
than the degree of fever warrants. On the second or third
day the temperature temporarily falls and jaundice appears.
Throughout this whole period the patient suffers from
muscular pains, headaches, restlessness, and an extreme
irritability. Coincidental with the jaundice, the second
characteristic of yellow fever appears, the so-called black
vomit. Gastrointestinal hemorrhages lead to the vomiting of
partially digested blood, usually dark brown or black in
color.

While the course of the disorder ordinarily runs much
longer, many of its victims die within the space of two or
three days. The case fatality rate, particularly in a non-

endemic area, may run as high as 80 or 90 percent. To add to the grimness of this disease, the period of convalescence is long, and those patients who arise too soon from the sick-bed often die from massive hemorrhages.

The prospect of dying from this ghastly pestilence was bad enough in itself, but until the end of the nineteenth century nothing was known of the disease nor of its means of transmission. It often eluded the most rigid quarantine, struck its victims down by the hundreds, and then with the advent of cool weather, mysteriously slipped away. Medical opinion was sharply divided as to whether yellow fever was spontaneously generated in putrefying filth or whether it was a specific disease introduced from the outside. Quarantine often seemed to work, and yet at other times the contagion found its way into a city despite all precautions. Although it was generally recognized that filth and crowding were conducive to epidemic disease, in the nineteenth century few cities could boast of their cleanliness. Yet the filthiest of cities sometimes escaped the infection while a relatively clean one might be attacked.

The public, confronted by a medical profession which was bitterly divided both on the issue of disease causation and on the correct form of medical treatment, disregarded the theoretical arguments and usually favored quarantine measures. Unfortunately, the establishment of a strict quarantine had a devastating impact upon commerce and trade, and many businessmen were happy to support those physicians who argued that yellow fever was engendered by local conditions. Since commercial groups usually dominated local politics, quarantines were often imposed too late or enforced too laxly. Without a knowledge of the role of the mosquito, however, even the best of quarantine systems could not be completely effective.

Yellow fever was no new disease to America in 1878. It had first appeared in the American colonies late in the seventeenth century, and it plagued the Atlantic coastal cities from Boston to Charleston throughout much of the eighteenth century. Shortly after 1800 it left the port cities of the Northeast for good but intensified its attacks on the Gulf Coast and South Atlantic towns. The epidemics in these areas increased in number and intensity until the 1850s and then tapered off. The last yellow fever outbreak in the United States occurred in New Orleans in 1905. Although the number of epidemics declined after the Civil War, improvements in transportation enabled the disease to spread far into the interior. The great epidemic year of 1878 saw yellow fever gain footholds along the entire Gulf Coast and then push up the Mississippi as far as St. Louis. As was the case with every outbreak in the Mississippi Valley, New Orleans was the port of entry. Its appearance there caused apprehension in every town and city up the river, an apprehension that steadily mounted as the contagion seemed inexorably to make its way upstream.

Memphis, far removed from the Gulf Coast, had already experienced three yellow fever epidemics prior to 1878, all of which were traceable to outbreaks in New Orleans. The first one occurred in 1855, when the town was still small, and only a few casualties resulted. The second came in 1867 at a time when New Orleans was once more undergoing a serious outbreak. The disease traveled slowly upriver from New Orleans and did not reach Memphis until late in September. Nonetheless, in the few weeks remaining before cool weather reduced the mosquito population, 1,500 cases with 250 deaths were recorded.

The intensity of this brief epidemic led to the formation of a Howard Association in Memphis. These organizations existed in a number of American cities, and although their precise origin is not clear, one of them was founded to combat the ravages of yellow fever in New Orleans as early as 1837. The New Orleans group consisted of thirty young businessmen who established themselves as a chartered organization dedicated to looking after the health and welfare of their city during the recurrent epidemic crises. The association became active only when it was clear that New Orleans was beset by a major epidemic disorder. The usual practice in times of emergency was for the association's members to divide the city into administrative districts, with each member taking responsibility for a particular area. The first task was to raise funds, both locally and from outside sources. The association then hired physicians, nurses, pharmacists, and whatever other personnel were needed. Over and above providing medical care for the sick, the association established food depots, infirmaries, and temporary hospitals, and operated a complete welfare program to take care of widows, orphans, and those workers made jobless by the epidemic. The organization and operations of the New Orleans group generally set the pattern for associations in other cities.

The Howard Association organized in Memphis in 1867 consisted of 25 members. During the 1867 epidemic two of the original members succumbed to yellow fever. The next outbreak, in 1873, was much more severe. On this occasion, when almost half the townspeople fell sick, the Howard Association recruited a total of 37 members. Surprisingly enough, only five of them caught the disease and all recovered. Considering that the association members spent their entire time among the sick and dying, visiting them in their homes and in hospitals, this casualty rate was amazingly low.

The severity of the 1873 epidemic resulted from two factors: a large increase in the city's population and the appearance of the disease earlier in the summer. During this deadly summer and fall, 2,000 residents succumbed to yellow fever. To appreciate the significance of this figure, one must bear in mind that the total population during the outbreak was only 15,000, of whom approximately half were

Negroes. Almost half the population—7,000, or 47 percent—
caught the fever, and the case fatality rate was about 29 percent, or 13 percent of the population.

The starkness of the casualty figures for the 1873 epidemic scarcely begins to show the horror and fear engendered by this terrible fever. It was not so much the
actual death rate nor the sufferings of the sick as it was the
unknown origin of the disease. In the nineteenth century,
when many diseases debilitated and killed all age groups,
death was common enough, but yellow fever was an un-
explained pestilence which struck in random fashion. A
yellow fever victim might be nursed by his family and not
give his disease to anyone, or it was possible for the entire
family to be swept away in the course of a few days. Under
these circumstances, the citizens of Memphis and other
Southern cities watched the approach of yellow fever with
a mounting sense of horror and the first rumor of its
presence was enough to send shock waves of panic throughout the city. Entire families immediately piled their belongings into carriages, wagons, and any available vehicle and
fled from what they thought might be the doomed city.
Steamboats and trains were jammed with fleeing residents,
and before the exodus was over, the city would be largely
depopulated of the upper and middle classes. In New
Orleans, where the disease was a more familiar evil and the
native population had developed or acquired a high degree
of immunity, a larger percentage of the upper classes tended
to remain in the city. In the early days, physicians and
ministers were often found among the refugees, a fact which
led to some bitter comments in the local newspapers. As
the century progressed and a greater social conscience developed, those professionals who avoided the responsi-
bilities of their callings were the exceptions.

Having experienced the horrors of a major yellow fever
epidemic in 1873, the residents of Memphis were justly
alarmed in 1878 when yellow fever was rumored to be in

New Orleans. City officials and health officers in that city repeatedly had been accused of concealing the presence of yellow fever until the situation was completely out of hand, and the accusations were not without some justification. On the other hand, in the prebacteriological days, it was not easy to make a positive diagnosis of yellow fever on the basis of the first few cases. Moreover, to admit the presence of even a single case was enough to cause quarantine barriers to be raised on every hand, thus effectively isolating the infected city. Every port would promptly close its facilities to vessels from the suspect area and nothing could be shipped in or out of the port. All railway lines and roads leading from the besieged city would be barricaded, and its economy would soon grind to a halt. Under these circumstances, it behooved physicians and health officials to be chary of conceding the presence of an epidemic disease until there could be no question as to its nature. In practice this often led city officials, under strong pressure from newspapers and businessmen, to deny the existence of any threat to public health until the number of deaths reached a point where the epidemic could no longer be concealed.

Aside from the fact that the New Orleans officials were usually reluctant to concede the existence of yellow fever, Memphis had other reasons for apprehension. The impact of Civil War and Reconstruction, political corruption, and a lack of social consciousness on the part of the business classes had reduced the city to a deplorable state. Although the population had doubled over the pre-war years, a large part of the increase consisted of thousands of illiterate Negroes who had fled from their masters and who eked out a miserable livelihood by begging, stealing, and doing odd jobs. The city itself was literally bankrupt. The inability of its citizens to pay their state taxes had led the state to take possession of one-third of the city's taxable resources, and the remainder was drastically reduced in value. The streets were barely passable. There was no organized system for collecting garbage and rubbish, and much of the sewage from the city's water closets and privies poured directly into a bayou which flowed through the center of the city. Stagnant pools filled with dead animals and refuse of all kinds abounded. Since it was generally accepted that epidemic diseases were invariably associated with filth and crowding, the residents of Memphis had ample reason to worry about the invasion of yellow fever.

Early in May news was received of the presence of epidemic yellow fever in the West Indies. Since this information often presaged an outbreak in New Orleans, the Memphis City Council was petitioned to institute a quarantine. Its members, however, refused to take action. The Board of Health, provided with some funds by popular subscription, then began an attempt to clean up the city's forty-year accumulation of dirt and filth, a task far exceeding its limited resources. In the meantime, rumors of yellow fever continued to arouse alarm and trepidation among the townspeople. Around the middle of July news came that yellow fever had broken out in epidemic fashion in New Orleans. Quarantine stations were immediately established on the two railway lines coming from the South and another on the Mississippi River just below Memphis. While it was felt that these measures should protect the city, rumors continued to fly and an uneasy spirit pervaded the town. On August 9 the disease was said to have reached Grenada, Mississippi. The answer to a telegraph inquiry to Grenada officials was paradoxical: an emphatic denial from the officials but at the same time an urgent request for nurses and physicians. Two members of the Memphis Howard Association volunteered their services. Shortly after arriving in Grenada, one of them telegraphed the Memphis *Appeal* reporting 100 cases, "none of which had so far yielded to treatment."

As excitement rose in Memphis, the trickle of panic-

stricken citizens leaving the town widened into a growing
stream. In the meantime, the report of a death from yellow
fever in the city itself greatly increased the tension. When,
on August 15, twenty-two new cases were announced, the
stream of refugees became a mass exodus. Stores, businesses,
and industries rapidly began closing their doors, and every
type of transportation was swamped with fleeing citizens.
Within a ten-day period, an estimated 25,000 people fled
Memphis. Within another two weeks the population was
reduced by 5,000 more, leaving less than 20,000 to face the
yellow fever. By the end of August the panic was over, and
those who remained grimly faced the prospect of a major
epidemic. They had little choice. Every road and pathway
leading out of the city was closed by barricades manned
by vigilantes from neighboring villages and towns, determined to prevent the spread of yellow fever into their
domains.

There is a widely accepted myth that people confronted
with catastrophe lose all sense of morality and try to lose
themselves in debauchery and licentiousness. During some
of the great New Orleans epidemics, occasional news stories,
based on the flimsiest of evidence, were carried by distant
newspapers. These stories described the complete break-
down of society with an accompanying spirit of reckless
abandonment. The truth was almost the exact opposite.
Once a feared pestilence materialized and the crisis was at
hand, every American city reacted in an amazingly orderly
fashion. A sense of responsibility and a spirit of brotherhood
infused the entire population; caring for the sick, burying
the dead, and providing for those impoverished by sickness
and the economic disruption became the major preoccupa-
tion. Every voluntary association, including churches,
fraternal orders, militia companies, business associations,
and labor unions, gave its utmost on the city's behalf. Despite the deadly reputation of yellow fever, physicians and
nurses from all sections of the United States volunteered

for duty in the stricken city, and money and relief supplies came pouring in.

Those citizens who remained in Memphis at the end of August 1878 lived up to the best of American traditions. The Howard Association assumed the major task of providing medical care, and a Citizens' Relief Association was organized to handle the vast quantities of money and supplies flowing in for relief purposes. New York City alone sent over $48,000. Volunteer nurses and physicians came from all sections of the country. Those from Southern cities were welcomed, since many had acquired an immunity to the fever. Despite the desperate need for assistance, Dr. R. W. Mitchell, medical director of the Howard Association, conscientiously warned those arriving from the North of the greater danger they faced. Even knowing the situation, however, most of them elected to stay.

By the beginning of September the epidemic was in full tide and the number of deaths per day was steadily moving upwards. The peak came in the middle of the month when the daily death toll reached 200. In the succeeding weeks the fever gradually burned itself out, and on October 29 an end of the epidemic was officially proclaimed. In the space of three months 17,600 cases of yellow fever had occurred among the 19,600 inhabitants left in the city. Of those who fell sick, 5,150 died, giving an overall case fatality rate of 29 percent. In terms of the white population, the figures are catastrophic. Of the nearly 20,000 inhabitants left in the city, approximately 14,000 were Negroes. Only 946 of the latter succumbed to the fever, whereas 4,204 of the 6,000 whites died during the outbreak. To summarize, within a three-month period almost 80 percent of those remaining in the city caught yellow fever, of whom 29 percent died. The deaths included almost 70 percent of those whites who did not flee the city that dreadful summer. Approximately sixty physicians served during the outbreak, of whom no less than forty-five fell victim to yellow fever. This figure included seventeen local physicians and twenty-eight volunteers. While several Protestant ministers disgraced themselves by fleeing at the first sign of the fever, the vast majority of clergymen stayed at their posts. The Catholic church suffered heavily, losing ten priests and eleven nuns. Only two of the resident priests survived the epidemic. Among the Protestant clergy, ten ministers died. In addition, four out of seven Episcopalian nuns who served during the outbreak lost their lives. As might be expected, the Howard Association took heavy casualties. Of the original twenty-eight members recruited at the beginning of the epidemic, no less than nineteen were sick or dead by the middle of September. An appeal for new members drew in eleven more, making a total of thirty-nine who served during the epidemic. Of this total, thirty-two were attacked by the fever and twelve succumbed to it. Only seven members escaped, five of whom had already suffered from yellow fever in previous epidemics. It is quite likely, too, that the others had undergone mild and undiagnosed cases.

Despite an inordinate amount of sickness and death among its membership, the Howard Association collected and spent over $500,000 to relieve the sufferings of the plague-stricken residents. In the process they employed 2,900 nurses and provided medical care and supplies to over 15,000 people. As the city hospital filled to capacity, the association opened up three infirmaries to care for the sick. Early in October, when it was clear that the Memphis outbreak was waning, the association organized relief trains and sent physicians, nurses, medical supplies, and provisions to those neighboring towns and villages suffering from the pestilence.

The great yellow fever epidemic of 1878, which spread death and sickness far and wide along the Gulf Coast and in the Mississippi Valley, had a profound effect upon the United States. As mentioned earlier, yellow fever always generated fear and horror far beyond its real danger to the American population, and the 1878 outbreak brought a popular outcry for action against the fever. An immediate result was the creation of the National Board of Health, the first effort by the federal government to create a central health agency. In New Orleans, Memphis, and other Southern cities a sharp impetus was given to the public health and sanitary reform movements: a yellow fever commission was dispatched to Havana to study the disease; and the entire nation became concerned with public health problems. Occasional yellow fever epidemics continued to break out in New Orleans and in the Southern section of the United States after 1878, but the intensity and virulence of the attacks steadily declined. The final yellow fever outbreak occurred in New Orleans in 1905. By this date the role of the mosquito was well known. A concerted campaign against mosquitoes by national, state, and city health officials brought the epidemic under control, but not before 452 residents of New Orleans had lost their lives. When George Kibbe Turner's novel *Hagar's Hoard* was first published in 1920, there were many Americans, particularly in the South, who could recall the terrors engendered by yellow fever. Even the youngest generation must have heard their parents describe incidents or tell stories of the great nineteenth-century killers. For all of his readers, Turner's novel must have recalled the disturbing anxieties and the ultimate panic aroused by the threat of yellow fever.

The author, George Kibbe Turner, was born in Quincy, Illinois, in 1869 and entered newspaper work in 1891. From 1906 to 1917 he was a staff writer and editor for *McClure's Magazine*. His first novel, *The Taskmasters*, was published in 1902. Between this date and 1927 he published seven other novels, including *Memories of a Doctor, White Shoulders,* and *The Girl in the Glass Cage.* He also contributed a number of short stories, articles, and poems to various magazines.

With a newspaperman's eye for the sensational, in 1909 he began investigating the connections between prostitution and politics in New York City. *McClure's Magazine,* for which he was staff writer at the time, was delighted to publish these exposés. In his articles Turner attacked such notorious figures as "Big Tim" Sullivan, "Monk" Eastman, a prominent gangster, and a host of Tammany Hall political leaders. In 1910, Turner was one of the chief witnesses before a grand jury investigating vice and corruption in New York. Yet, unlike many of the muckrakers, he was not a social reformer; rather, he was a man with a keen sense of what would attract public attention.

Hagar's Hoard created only minor ripples in the publishing world. Although it was reviewed in both the *New York Times* and the *New York Evening Post,* the two journals gave it only brief and unfavorable notices. There were no enthusiastic reviews, and by and large the book quickly disappeared from sight.

By any literary standards, it is certainly no great novel. The characters are stilted, the plot can scarcely carry the weighty narrative, and the Negroes are a stereotype. Yet Turner does manage to convey the vague anxiety, the feeling of oppression and near panic as the disease came ever closer and closer to the city. He gives some idea, too, of the sheer horror of the epidemic itself—the omnipresent hearses and wagons carrying the dead, the gloomy palls of smoke, and the silent and deserted streets, which kept each individual in a constant state of anxiety, wondering where the fever would strike next. The great killer diseases—smallpox, bubonic plague, yellow fever, and Asiatic cholera—have plagued mankind for centuries and have evoked a great mass of literature. With the advent of bacteriology, the major epidemics of earlier days have been virtually banished from the Western world. It may be that *Hagar's Hoard* represents the last contribution to plague literature.

CHAPTER I

I WAS reading a piece in the *Commercial Appeal* the other day about their finding $60,000 in greenbacks in an old miser's house, some of it in those little old green shin-plasters that go back to Civil war time. And I showed it to my wife, and we smiled a little, and then grew sober right away again; for it set us thinking of my Uncle Athiel Hagar, the miser, and the Yellow Fever Year of 1878.

It was on a Tuesday that the Fever came. I remember it because it was the day after rent day, the last Monday that my Uncle Athiel ever gathered up his rents from his negro tenements. I can see him now, driving into the black alley that still August evening — his high, frail, old, mud-stained buggy swaying and lurching on that old wretched roadway; and Dolly, the old horse, wet and soapy from the hot weather. And my Uncle, there on the worn and shiny seat, in his linen duster; and the little old brown satchel for his collections in between his feet. Every man and boy and nigger in the town knew the rig — the clay-stained, old, high buggy, with its paint checking off, and the little clay-colored man, with his bright, black eyes, and his lame leg a little extended; and the battered little handbag that brought back his nigger rents on Mondays. "Old Grum," they called him, or "Grummit"— behind his back, but never to his face.

I went to take the horse and unharness it. I did a good

9

lot of that kind of work around that place — nigger's work, that other people had their niggers do. But my Uncle Athiel had no more niggers about his place than he had to. For he said that every nigger was a thief at heart. And so, when I came, he had me do it; and he was mighty pleased to have me — a lot more than I was, I want to tell you. I was good and tired of it. And if it hadn't been for Vance, I wouldn't have stayed there for one minute.

" It's been right hot," I said to him, for it certainly had been a wicked, old hot day.

But my Uncle paid no more attention to me than to the horse. He just turned and lifted out the little satchel of small change from the negroes' rent, and when he had got it:

" This town is ruined," he said, in a tiresome voice, half like he was speaking to himself; and walked on toward the house. And I stood there looking after him.

He had been getting worse all summer — down and depressed one day, sharp and ugly the next one — cross as an old dog on a chain. But I had never seen him just like that before.

" Some more money trouble," I said to myself, " or something about the rents."

So then I unharnessed the old horse, and spanked her into her stall — slapdash, like a boy does things; for in spite of what I thought about myself, I wasn't much more. And my uncle moving so slowly, I wasn't very much behind him into the side hall. He stepped up stairs to leave his bag of change in the great Purple Room where he slept, and to wash himself; and pretty soon I heard the key turn when he locked up the Purple Room again as he came down to supper.

At supper time, too, he had very little talk for us. And

it seemed to me he was way down deep in one of his gloomy fits when he used to fret about the poorhouse.   He was a little deaf, my Uncle, and usually, if he was going to talk at all, he started it.   But if he didn't care to, he sat there silent, the way he did that night, looking away into that country a thousand miles off, that old folks build up for themselves out of their thoughts and memories.

Yet that night he was different than he ever had been. And both Vance and I remembered, and spoke afterward, of the way that finally he looked up and said to me a second time: "This town is ruined," in that tired monotonous way that deaf men talk, and went on eating.

It came out afterward, like I expected, that he had been short in his collections.   His nigger tenements were about all his property he hadn't sold now, except that great house we lived in.   But they always had given him more trouble, in spite of the big interest they brought in on his money, than anything he had ever had.

And now, it seemed, the niggers were getting restless, like the white folks, over all this talk of Fever; moving around, getting more shiftless and trifling and excited every day — not from fear of the Fever, for they weren't supposed to have that then, but from something else; from God knows what new crazy notions — like they always do at times like that.   And five families of them had suddenly disappeared from the tenements since just the week before.

Yet that wasn't it entirely, either.   Both Vance and I have said so since a hundred times.   It didn't quite account for the way her father talked to us that night, after he had finished up that last round of collections on his tenements, nor for the way that he turned and said to me a third time:

"This town is ruined; and we're ruined with it!"

It came out of him like a groan; more like an involuntary sign of some deep, old, inward trouble than common ordinary speech. And he didn't even start that talk he used to make, when he was like that, about how we all of us were bound out to the poorhouse. He just sat silent.

I saw Vance watching him out of those deep eyes of hers, stiller and more anxiously than she usually did. She was pale, paler than ever that night — the heat probably, I said to myself. Her lips were parted, and I knew that she was tired. But then, of course, I didn't know that other thing that was really bothering her.

Vance tried to talk with both of us, tried to talk and make him laugh, but it was too hard for her. She was tired, and her voice was faint; and her father didn't hear and wouldn't hear, and didn't want to talk. And so we sat and finished supper, without talking. And the room went still, and the daylight started dying down, and there was no noise from outside through the windows; for the whole world was just exhausted and tired out, at the end of another scorching day. And about the only sound we heard in that great high room where we sat was every now and then when some fly, caught in on the paper wound around the chandelier near the ceiling, started its fine, high singing, and then got still again.

" Come on out now, Beavis," said Uncle Hagar, getting up from the table.

I knew then right away what was coming. He was going out to give the yard and barn another going over and inspection for fire and thieves. Once in so often, when he got more than common nervous, he started out on those searching expeditions of his. But there was never one that I remembered so thorough, and so long as this.

He went ahead across the yard — I can see him so much plainer than anything I saw yesterday — in his

linen duster, and his wrinkled linen trousers, and his old-
time boots, covered with that old, reddish-yellowish clay
dust; and his great old hickory cane, smooth from twenty
years of wearing in his hands. And I can see his clay-
colored face, and his bright black eyes, and his smooth
straight hair, still black; and his close mouth, cut like a
bluish gash across his old yellow face.

I was of no special use. He had to see everything for
himself. He went through the shed and small barn where
Dolly was, around the servant's room — everything; even,
at last, the great empty barn, that we never used and
opened.

We unlocked the side door, and stepped in; and the
dust, and the silence, and the still dry air of the place,
stood around us — hot as an old oven; choking full with
the dusty smell of an unopened stable — pine wood and
hay, and horses, and leather — all baked together.

We stood there for a minute, looking around; and then
my Uncle Hagar started looking through it. For he always had an idea that there might be some thief hiding
there, some tramp or nigger. And more especially that
summer, when he had that suspicion that there were some
particular niggers hanging around and staring at the
house. Some particular niggers, and among them that
new half-nigger he had been seeing several times lately.

He started hunting around, through all that heat, himself. And I did like he told me to, and stood below and
watched and waited while he did it. Old, lame a little
from that strain he got when wrestling when a boy, going
sidewise up the stairs but walking right along ahead, his
thin mouth shut, stern as the wrath of God descending
on the Israelites in the Old Bible — the old man was a
figure, in spite of all his years, that no thief would want
to see coming headed toward him, I believe. And es-

pecially when he was carrying that great hickory cane of his, and carrying, too, somewhere in his clothes — his linen duster probably — that little old-time Derringer pistol of his that he always wore on him; that once, they said, he had shot a man with.

Day and night he had the two of them about him. At night, I knew, there stood his hickory cane, set up at the head of his bed — of his great canopied bed in the Purple Room; and there underneath his pillow, always ready, lay that curious little Derringer of his, which he bought first when he was a boy in this rough, new Mississippi River country. Just a raw country boy, come down here from that hill country to the east, where they raise and send away the kind of man he was.

You've seen them, I expect — those lean, leathern, clay-colored men, with small round heads, and bright eyes, they raise up there — hungry folks from a hungry soil, that went south and west, and still go, for that matter, looking for more food. You find the Southwest full of them — these small-headed men from the hills — with only room enough in those little heads of theirs for a few ideas and feelings, but those few fierce and strong. The best pioneers, the best soldiers, the best enemies — and the best murderers, I believe, the world has ever seen!

"Nothin'," said my uncle, going out and locking the barn door after us. "Nothin'!"

Lord, what a relief it was coming out of that place! Even the air outside seemed cool and juicy for a little while after that old oven.

My uncle stood a while and mopped his forehead with his old, red handkerchief.

"Come on," he said then. "Let's go out and see if there's any air stirring out on the bluff."

There wasn't any. The river lay there under us, in the

twilight, sleek as a new glass bottle — not a breath stirring.   And yet it was cooler there always; and I was always glad to be there.

We sat there, he and I, side by side, on that old clay bluff, looking over the Mississippi.   I liked it there. Coming from back up inland, I never got tired of it — the long, snaky river, disappearing both ends into the woods; the everlasting flat line of tree-tops over in Arkansas; and the big white steamers with their white filagree woodwork, like great wedding cakes, upon the brown colored water.

My uncle sat there several minutes silent, like he generally did; took out his tobacco, and cut off that little tiny sliver that he always took to chew, hitched his old lame booted leg over the other, and sat sideways, looking down, staring at the levee and the city.   After a while his mouth twitched at the corner.

" It's come," he said.   " It's here finally."

" What? " I asked right away.

But before I spoke, I knew already what he was going to say; or I thought I did.   As hot as it was, a cold flash shot over me.

" The Fever," said my Uncle Hagar, still looking from me toward the town.

" I was down in there to-day," he went on talking. " It's here now; and I know it.   They can lie all they want to."

I had never seen the Fever; I wasn't there five years before, the last time they had it there in town.   All the dread I had was from what I heard and saw — the fear of other people's fear of it.   For I saw that everybody stood there all that summer through — all the white folks — stood and watched and listened for it like a man at night, out hunted by a sheriff's posse.

They said they died like flies in autumn that time before — poor people mostly. They said they buried them
in trenches. A tropical disease, come up the river from
the South, in the air. There was nothing you could see;
just this old poison in the air you breathed. One day you
were perfectly sound and well. And all at once this blind
headache took you. In three days after you were dead;
and in three hours more a coffinful of black jelly — your
flesh dropping from your bones out in the graveyard.

"They can't fool me," my Uncle Athiel went along.
"It's there right now. They can't fool me with their
lies, and the other fancy names they give it. I've seen
it too many times. It's smoldering down there in a dozen
places now.

"Right there," he said, and pointed with his cane.
And as it turned out afterwards he was right. It was
right there, just where he pointed.

"Yes, and half a dozen people," he went on, "are dead
already, though they won't admit it. They won't say it
was the Fever that killed them."

His eyes shone, his mouth worked at one corner. The
fear of the Yellow Fever, which lay twitching at the nerves
of every white man in the town, had touched him. I could
see it. And I was quite a lot surprised. For he had always said it was nothing to be scared of.

"That ends it," said my Uncle Athiel, letting his cane
drop back to the ground again; "that ends it! This
town is done for!"

I sat silent — thinking of the Fever, of the death in
the air, which we had been watching for and fearing all
that summer. I was wondering if he really knew; if in a
week or two it would be all around us.

And as I thought, my Uncle Athiel cracked out that old

common oath he usually gave when he had used up all the rest.

" By Judas H. Iscariot," he said.   " Done for! "

And after a while he went on, speaking out his thoughts. " I've seen property go down and down year after year. Down, down! It's down already next to nothing. And now this ends it."

I woke up from my own thoughts then, and looked at him. For he talked in such a dead, old, doleful voice, I had to. And I saw right away, what I ought to have known at first. It wasn't the fear of Fever that was scaring him at all. It was that same old fear he always had, about his money. " His property," he always called it.

Everybody to their own mind, of course, even to the things they are scared of. I thought that to myself as I sat there, looking at him.

I sat there, a stranger almost, in this new country — thinking and wondering about that Fever, and what I had seen and heard of it, and what it really was. I didn't know one thing about it; I had never been where it was in my whole life. I only saw the fear of it around me, in other people's eyes.

But I knew that all around me those folks were standing nervous, jumpy with fear — of that danger that was coming from the South; touched with the fear of death. And even I myself was not free from it now.

And here beside me sat this man, shaky and sharp-voiced too — but not at all from what was scaring all the rest — not a particle from fear of death. After him, as I know now — though I did not then — was a more ceaseless, monstrous, hounding fear, that, once set on men's trails, comes driving them faster and faster as the years go by — till finally it drives them shivering out of life itself: The money fear; the fear of loss and poverty. And we all get it following us, more or less, all of us, I believe, in our old age.

But naturally, I didn't understand it then. You never do when you are young. So I sat and watched him from the corner of my eye, curious; his yellow face, his straight hair and the big old waxen yellow ear that was toward me — thinking then how strange he was. For it was plain enough that he was just swept out of himself with excitement.

" All the summer," he went on, " I've seen it coming up. All this summer, long before I sold my block.

" I sold it out, and took my loss," he went on talking to himself. " Five thousand dollars — five thousand under what I paid for it.

" Five thousand dollars," he said over to himself underneath his breath, and called out his old Iscariot oath again.

" I'm glad I done it. I'm glad I took it now," he said suddenly and stiffened up. " That's five thousand dollars more than anybody'd give for it to-day. No, sir, you couldn't get rid of it this minute — no, not for love nor money."

I sat looking at him corner-wise, wondering where his excitement was going to take him to. Never once in all the time that I was there had he talked to me so direct and straight about his money. Complaints and groans, and prophecies of the poorhouse — plenty; but never once such clear and open talk of any sums of money he might have.

But then, for several minutes after that, my Uncle Hagar went on talking about the ruin of himself and of the city.

The place was ruined utterly, now and forever. Ruined, busted, done for. No bus'ness, nothing. No one to buy and no one to sell. " Two weeks from now," he said, " there won't be one merchant solvent in this town."

And the banks, he said, were sure to go. And he was damned glad of it. He always cursed the banks, and those that ran them.

" For do you know what's going to happen here? " he asked me.

I told him that I didn't, though I expected that I really did.

" Everybody's going to leave this town at once," he said; " all the white folks. They're all going out of here together like a flock of lunatics.

" And then," he said, his voice rising up; " then, do you know what will be left here? "

" What will? " I asked him.

" Thieves and niggers — that's a'l," said my Uncle Athiel. " Thieves and niggers — in an empty town! "

I'd never seen him anything like that before. There was color in his old yellow face, even in that tallow-colored ear toward me. I saw the blood come up into it and turn it lifelike. He swung suddenly and stared with his bright eyes into my face.

" This town is full of thieves! " my Uncle Hagar said.

I started back a little — he put his face so close up to mine.

" Full of thieves," he said to me, and I sat, saying nothing, waiting.

" Lemme ask you something," he said, talking on. " I want to ask you somethin'. Do you imagine we're the only ones that's talking and whispering in this town — right now! "

And I didn't know what to say to him.

But he didn't care at all, I expect, whether I talked or not.

"Look yonder, look down there," said he, pointing north again with that great heavy cane of his, to that long ragged line of old brick blocks — that rendezvous of niggers and thieves — the bad niggers, and the murderers and the nigger thieves.

"What do you think — what do you think they're talking of to-night?" asked my Uncle Athiel, pointing. "All those hungry fellows over there?"

You know what the levee was those days — snack houses, and bawdy houses, and sudden lights opened into the darkness; and dead niggers in the alleys in the morning. A desperate place.

"Lemme tell you somethin'," said my Uncle Hagar, answering himself. "They know it's coming. They know it's here. They're down there just waitin', watchin'. They're all waitin', watchin'— all over town — waitin' for it to break loose!"

I thought then — of the negroes especially — while he was talking. For I knew he was thinking mostly of them himself. The niggers and the way they acted. Their bowing and scraping; and underneath it all, their watching ways — their great brown eyes forever following you around. All just standing there, and watching you always, and more than ever when your back was turned — standing, watching, saying nothing. I was raised out to the east, where they didn't have so many. I never could get used to them — to that great black herd of them in Memphis, especially.

"You see those paths?" my Uncle asked me, suddenly jerking out toward them with his cane.

The things went in and out; up and down and crisscross, twisting and turning and going around to their unseen endings down the bluff.

"Judas!" my Uncle said, "an honest man never stepped in one. Every one of them was beaten by the feet of thieves."

He stopped and turned and looked at me.

"Niggers and thieves," he said. "Niggers and thieves, watchin' and waitin'— and whisperin'. This town is full of thieves — right now," he said again, and his voice grew every minute sharper.

"Right now!" he said again, and jumped up on his feet.

"Come on now," he said. "Come on along. It's gettin' late,"— and started out toward home.

He had only gone a rod or two when he stopped and stared at me again.

"We got to keep our eye peeled," said my Uncle Hagar. "We got to keep our eye peeled from now on!"

He turned, and I came after him, knowing just exactly how he felt, feeling it myself. For if they were talking down there, like he said they were; if they were talking of anybody, they certainly were talking about us — and about my Uncle's house.

CHAPTER II

COUNTING the thoughts of everybody — black and white together — I expect my Uncle Athiel was the best-known man in Memphis those days — and the most talked about. The negroes stopped and watched him, and the boys, as he drove around town in that high old rickety buggy of his; Mondays especially, after his collections, with that little old brown satchel between his feet. And they whispered after him that name they gave him; Grummit, old Grummit, and of all the money he had hidden away. For everybody said he was the worst old miser in Memphis.

I expect most folks, from other sections of the country, don't believe there are any more old misers now, outside the story books. But it is different with us down South, or it was until here just a few years ago. For there was a plenty of them in that country I came from when I was a boy, and all through Tennessee everywhere — and in Memphis, too. Every litt e town and cross-roads village had one, just as much as they had their town drunkard. And the miser and his house were known just as well as he was.

And now, when you stop to think of it, this was all perfectly natural and to be expected. All during the war time, nothing was safe in our country. The thieves from the North and the thieves from the South were all turned loose on us by war. And so all kinds of folks got into

22

the habit then of digging their money into the ground,
or hiding it around the house to save it. And then right
after the war came the banks failing. There were a
great number of banks failed — and some of them in the
most scoundrelly kind of way And one natural result
of all this, like I said, was to breed these old misers with us.

It was one of these bank failures after the war, I know,
that turned my Uncle Athiel to his habits, more than any
one of his other losses; and gave his house — that great
brick house of his — its curious name and reputation.

I never knew all the story. But I do know he was
caught in this big bank failure a little after war time —
the smash of the great Mr. Bozro's bank. And from that
time on he never spoke of banks without cursing them.

" A bank," I heard him say a dozen times, " is a place
where they take your money and keep it."

And bankers, so he said, were the only men on earth
who got the Saviour mad enough to strike them.

" He knew what he was about," he said with a great
common oath. " He only knew how much they deserved
it."

And for ten years he had never set his foot inside a
bank, except when he had to when he went to change
money there; to change his silver and little bills for big
ones. I wondered sometimes how they did it for him,
after what he said of them. And he never would leave one
dollar there.

Now everybody knew all this and talked about it. And
everybody knew that he had money. They saw him gathering all those years and never spending. And they knew
it must be somewhere. And it was for that reason, I
expect, that after a while that great house of his got its
name. For everybody — when I was first there — called
it Grummit's Bank.

There had always been stories about that great house since its building — since Mr. Bozro first built it. For he was a great man in his day, and very much talked about. But all the older ideas were lost and half forgotten now in that last one which gave it that new name that it was known by.

In a way, if you wanted to think about it so, it did look a little like a bank from the outside — more than like a dwelling — or, anyhow, I got to think so. Very big — as big almost as a Main Street block was those days, and very solid. Thick heavy walls of brick, lumpy trimmings, standing out beneath the eaves, all brick; and brick eyebrows over all the windows; and blind windows — blind empty niches, built for statuary that was never made, they said; but looking more, it always seemed to me, like they were just made to show how thick and heavy those brick walls were. And a slate roof, French style; and an eight-sided, sloping tower, covered with gray rounded slates, and two round eyelike windows — for all the world like an old gray owl, sitting up there over the front door. And it seemed to me, like I told you, and does now, more like an old bank than a house.

Anyhow that's what they call it, Grummit's Bank, and they had all manner of stories about it. But the chief one — that was in everybody's mouth, the one all the rest started from — was that somewhere, hidden away in it, my Uncle Athiel Hagar had a hundred thousand dollars in greenbacks.

Just where that tale of Hagar's Hoard of Greenbacks started from; just why it was a hundred thousand dollars always; and why it was always greenbacks and not gold — I didn't know. And nobody could tell me — or could have told me — if I had had any one to ask. But it was something everybody believed and talked about so common, that we heard it ourselves. Even my Uncle Athiel heard it.

And when he did, he was always in a great hurry to deny it. It always excited him and made him mad. It was about the only thing I knew of that ever set him talking. But it always did.

" A hundred thousand dollars," he said to me more times than once in those few months that I've been here; " I wish to God I had a hundred thousand cents. So I could be sure I wouldn't spend my last days in the poorhouse."

For even then — in those first months that I knew him — he would now and then, when he grew excited, or things had gone against him, start up that talk of poorhouse and poverty. Bitter and angry, generally, but sometimes down-hearted and depressed. But so earnest always, that it seemed he almost believed in it himself.

More generally he would talk and go on about the poorhouse. But there were other things he turned to sometimes, especially to the losses he had, and once or twice, I remember, he got started talking of all the money he had lost in that old Confederate currency.

" A hundred thousand dollars, huh! " he said. " I expect they mean Confederate money."

And starting then, he railed and cursed the war, and both the North and South. Grant for attacking and Lee for surrendering — anything that made all that old Confederate money worthless.

For he had got great quantities of it, so Vance told me once, toward the end of the war; bundles of it — holding on to it, thinking it might after all be worth a little something. It made him very bitter talking of it.

Sometimes he would deny that story one way; sometimes another. But he would always deny it some way; I

couldn't help but notice that myself. That old story of
a hundred thousand dollars — the faintest mention of it
— would get him mad and excited almost any time. And
sometimes he would even bring it up himself.

"I wish I could catch the tom fool that started that
a-going," I've heard him saying. And if he could have,
there would have been plenty of trouble for somebody.

But nobody started it, I expect; it just grew. Yet no
one could be got to doubt it either. That hundred thousand dollars was just as much a fact in the minds of everybody, and a hundred times as well known, as the money in
the safe of any bank in town.

Now, ready money was scarce in the South those days,
you may remember, and a hundred thousand dollars in
cash, right there, made Rothschild, whom we used to talk
about when I was a boy, instead of Rockefeller, look
mighty thin and far away. And so, in spite of all our
pinching, and all our small and shabby way of living,
that house of ours — old Grummit's Bank — stood up
there on a bluff like the city on a hill that could never
be hid, in the New Testament.

Everybody knew it; everybody talked about it. The
boys in the street even used to whisper of it, resting after
play.

"A hundred thousand dollars! A hundred thousand
dollars! If you had it, what would you do?"

They couldn't imagine, any of them. Poor ragamuffins
— poorer than Job — most all of them. They didn't see
a two-bit piece once a year. And they would say all
manner of wild and foolish and extravagant things about
it. It was like a story to them, I expect, and our old
place the ogre's castle in a fairy tale. They walked by
very serious; and whispered, looking out the sides of their
eyes at the tower and the closed windows, and drawn

shades. For the house was so big, we kept a good share of it closed continually.

It was funny to me when I thought of it. I had been there for months now and I knew just nothing at all about my Uncle's money business. But the boys and niggers knew it all — how much it was, how it was in greenbacks and not in gold, and why — and a great lot of other information.

But the most curious idea of all to me — that all the negroes and the children had — was the story of where he kept this hoard of his. Having it there, I expect, they had to know just where it was and how he watched it. So they said he had it in the tower. I heard that story several times myself.

I sat once, I remember, in the darkened saloon parlor, beside a window opened in the front. The blinds were shut, and through them I saw and overheard these boys, two boys, one ten or twelve perhaps, the other maybe eight — looking up, and talking of our tower.

" I wonder if he's shut up there now," said the bigger boy, looking.

" Who? " said the little spring piping one.

" Old Grummit."

" What's he doing there? " said the little one after a long while — and gazed up wondering.

" He sits there; he sits there counting it," the bigger one went on telling him, as certain as Revelation. And they stood there, both of them, quite a while, looking, silent — and I listening to them, trying not to laugh.

But that idea about the tower I knew was common, all over everywhere. And the ridiculous part of it to me was, in all the time that I'd been there in the house, I'd never known my old uncle to go up into the old tower once. And yet all that time, that was the commonest and

most talked of all the stories of that house of ours among
the boys and niggers.

For it wasn't only boys that talked about all this.
There were plenty of others besides boys who talked of
Grummit's Bank. We knew that, all of us. There wasn't
a thieving negro in the town, who didn't lie and dream
about that house of ours. It was thieves' talk in the dens
along the levee. And the rousters on the steamboats
leaned over the rail and stared at it, going by on the
Mississippi. It was as prominent in the minds of that
low class of population as the Louisiana lottery. And we
knew it.

A hundred thousand dollars! There it was, in there
somewhere! If you could find it and steal it. There it
was — just for the reaching out of hand and taking it.
And then, thieves' paradise, eating and gambling and
drinking and women forever!

We knew all this, I say, or enough of it anyway. And
it had, I know, its influence upon us every day in our
lives — on all three of us. And yet I can say right truth-
fully, that on that day — the last day before the Fever
came, I, on the inside of the house, knew less than everybody seemed to know from the outside. There was money
there, I believed. How much, I didn't know, nor where it
was.

But I had been there only a few months then; it was
less than a year that my mother died; and I didn't know
for certain, anything to speak of. All that I did learn
was from what little I might hear about my Uncle's business — which was as little as he would let me; and what
I couldn't help but see of his curious actions about the
house — that great old house; the way he hated it, and
cursed it, and watched it.

He hated, in the first place, the very mind that conceived it, and the way it was brought forth. For it was built, a monument to himself, by that great Southern financier, Mr. Bozro, that they talked about so much, till his great bank failed after the war; the man whose failure had robbed my Uncle Hagar of so much money.

I never saw the man; he was dead long before I got there. And all I knew is what they said of him. A little man, very spic and span and dressy; and monstrously conceited.

"He looked just like Napoleon," they used to say about him — and laugh. For they said they really thought he did.

Now, that great house of his he had built to be the finest in the land, taking the patterns of it from great houses he had seen abroad — especially in France, they said. But he didn't get to use it long, before it ruined him — it and all the other grand manners he had given himself. And they found him shot one morning — dead by his own hand in the great canopied bed of the Purple Bedroom he had built for himself. And his bank and all his other enterprises, blown sky-high — all gone.

It was in this grand smash of Mr. Bozro — bank, property and all — that my Uncle had been caught, as I told you — not once but all around. He lost this big lot of money in the bank to start with; and then in the ruination of Mr. Bozro's personal business which came with it, my Uncle Athiel had been caught again — twice caught. For first he had to take this house over on a mortgage, for a personal debt, the house and all its furniture, and secondly, he had to keep it. No one could use the thing. It was too big. There was no sale at any price for it. So at last we three, my uncle, his daughter, Vance, and I, when I first came there, were forced to occupy this great place to save it. And the monument which the great local financier had built to draw the forefingers of all passers-by to it, and exalt his name forever, now kept his memory green in one mind only — my Uncle's; and that in a manner it was scarcely worth while building houses to secure.

" I wish that I was God for twenty minutes," I've heard my Uncle say — a number of times. " I'd fix him."

He didn't say it often. It broke out of him, principally, when there were repairs to be paid for, on the house, or when the tax bills came. For the taxes were monstrous those days.

" I'd see him fry in Hell a million years," he said, " and this thing with him! "

For never, I believe, when he once fixed his hate upon a man, did he forgive anybody anything. Forgiveness wasn't in his blood.

It was this hate, I noticed, first, like I said. It came principally, of course, from the money that old place had cost him. But then I noticed, right away, how, with all his hatred of the house, he guarded it: The locked door to the Purple Room, which he slept in; his fear of fire; his rule against all niggers in the house as far as possible — for all but that one, that one religious darkey, Arabella. And always, his great care in locking and keeping that great house locked up day and night. And that perpetual warning he had given me ever since I came there to keep my eye peeled — keep my eye peeled for fire and thieves.

And now, since the Yellow Fever had started up the river from New Orleans, the fear and anxiousness of my uncle for that house had grown continually; and naturally his growing fussiness had its effect on us. He was very shrewd at seeing things. He had told us from the first that the disease was surely coming; and when it did come crawling up towards us, nearer and nearer, his mind dwelt more and more, not so much on the danger of death, as the disorder and loss and thievery that was coming out of it. And it all naturally had its effect on us.

I know that all those weeks the sense of watchfulness, and the feeling of being watched, too, grew upon us. Every now and then we got an idea that some one, some particular person, was watching us. You couldn't help it — especially when my Uncle was continually noticing these folks, folks that were watching us, or that he thought were.

There was an old nigger that started coming to the back door I remember — an old shambling nest of rags with a big veined coarse skinned, black hand stretching out of it; and the tiresome mumbling whine of those old time nigger beggars.

" Please give th' ole man a nickel, boss. Please give th' ole man a nickel? "

He had two trips for nothing; and the third my Uncle sent him off a flying.

Then there was later on that half nigger, whom my Uncle saw several times — that big half nigger on the bluff behind us whittling with his great cotton knife — looking. That made more of an impression on me. I never saw him myself, but I heard my Uncle talk of him a number of times. And I kept looking out for him and never finding him.

You understand that river was an ugly place those times. We were nearer pioneer days then. There was violence and murder, free and open in those river towns. And I remember their saying that down town in Memphis there wasn't one street corner but what some one had been murdered on.

For that matter the Mississippi was always a kind of

thieves' highway and is to-day.   But nothing to those old steamboat times.   Thieves and murderers, local and imported too, moved South and North, searching, finding, trading and escaping on the river.   And we sat there on the edge of this ugly path of secret travelers.   And down on the levee were their well known haunts and stopping places.   We could see them from our upper windows. And all over that town was the poverty that came after the war.   The thousand hands of poverty — of negroes especially — stretching out; begging and picking and stealing.   I never could get used to them — that black herd of niggers there in Memphis.   Ragged, limping, consumptive; laughing, crying, gorging, and starving by turns, like savages; but everlastingly on the edge of want.

So it is little wonder to me now, when I think of it, and know all I do to-day, that my Uncle was so careful watching his house and property — night and day — and especially those days of the coming of the Fever.

CHAPTER III

SO then my Uncle Athiel turned and went back home; and the great house loomed up before us, dark and ugly as a great old mausoleum in a grave yard. And just before we came to it — across the alley, and into the back yard — the only light that we could see went out, and Arabella, the negro servant, came out and locked the door; and started down the path to the great servant's room by the alley, where she spent her nights alone — her two dogs walking with her.

"All locked up?" asked my Uncle.

"Yassah," said Arabella, not even looking at him.

She was one of these sanctified niggers. Nothing ever troubled her. Her face was just as round and smooth and peaceful as an apple; not an expression in it, only that faint old smile those religious niggers have — the kind that know they're sanctified, and sure of going to Heaven. Curious acting things, when you see them first, but the most honest of the lot. And I know for a fact my Uncle hired this one for just that reason. She was the only nigger he would have in his house. And he had her just because he knew that she was a sanctified nigger. He told me so.

"Look here," said my Uncle to her; "you're lettin' those dogs loose in the yard every night, now, ain't you?"

"Yassah," said Arabella, walking right along ahead. Her voice was just as smooth and calm and peaceful as her face.

" Look out you do," said my Uncle.

Arabella and her two dogs went straight along ahead down the path toward the alley. Belle, the black and tan, before her — a little dancing nervous thing, up on the tips of her toes. And behind, slouching at Arabella's heels, General Sherman — the great old yellow dog she called General Sherman — naming him, the way the niggers do sometimes, after celebrated folks they want to honor.

God knows what wicked mixture of mongrels there was in that dog. There was hound, I expect; and some mastiff, for he was a great high beast; and plenty of other kinds, for certain. He was so old and worn out, and lay around so much that there were callouses on his front legs, made from lying on them. And when he went following along after, like he did now, with his old red eyes looking down at the bottom of Arabella's dress, he lurched and sagged and looked like he might just stop anywhere and fall to pieces in the path.

My Uncle stood a minute, looking after them.

" You can't trust a nigger," he said. " You can't trust any of them. She ain't half so human as that dog."

Then we went on, and through the side door into the house.

Vance was standing there. I saw her before we went in — standing looking out from the window, playing with the curtain cord, thinking. She looked mighty frail and delicate, watching out that way into the dusk, from that great arched window, like I saw her so often evenings. For they wouldn't let her out much after supper. They said the night air wasn't good for her. Folks were different then; they had just the opposite notions from what they do now about the night air.

My Uncle walked in the sitting room, and I after him.

And I heard him, just as soon as he got there, call to Vance and give her that curious unforeseen order.

" Shut that window," he said right loud to Vance.

" What ! " said Vance, surprised.

" Now ! " said my Uncle Athiel.   And she shut it like he told her to.   He treated us both like children, for that matter, and we both just had to take it.

" Now lemme tell you something," my Uncle said to Vance, " and you, too," he said to me.   " From now on every window on this floor goes shut at sundown."

" Here, where we sit, too ? " asked Vance.   For the others were all locked anyhow.

" What I said was every window," he told her.

" Why ? " I asked.

" Why," he said after me.   " Don't you know why yet ? "

" No," I said.   " I don't."

" I'll tell you then," he said to me.   " I'll tell you. It's because this town is full of thieves ! "

And then for a second or two we all stood silent, Vance and I swapping glances.

" We'll roast to death," I said.   " We'll just choke up and die.   We can't breathe in here."

" It's time you got to learn how then," said my Uncle, and his voice was getting ugly, the way it did when he was crossed in anything.   " For it won't be long now before you'll have to know, anyhow.   You'll have to if you want to keep on livin'."

I didn't get what he meant that night.   I didn't catch it.   I wasn't even sure I heard him right, so I didn't say any more.

And after that he started out himself and went around, closing everything that was open, and looking over all the rest.   And Vance and I stood staring at each other.

" Can't I help you? " I said to him once, trying to make up, and be friendly. But he didn't want me.

" No, I'll help myself," he answered me, and went along. He went through the whole floor, we heard him stamping — through the Crystal Room, across the Hall; the dining room, the kitchen, and even in the cellar.

" I don't like this," said Vance to me.

" Neither do I," I told her.

" Did you notice him — his eyes? " she whispered.

" Yes," I said.

" I'm awfully worried — lately," she told me. " I'm awfully — anxious." I looked at her then, sharp. For it seemed to me then — though I wasn't sure — that she shivered a little.

" He hasn't slept at all," she said — and stopped. For he was coming back again. There had been nothing much for him to shut up, excepting that one room where we all were — that sitting room in the front.

He was back again and stood looking in through the doorway at us. I've often wondered just what was in his mind then; just how the world looked through his eyes.

" Don't sit up too late," said Vance, going toward him to say good-night. " You've got to have your sleep."

" Lemme tell you something," said my Uncle, looking past her to me. " After this — from now on, you want to keep your eye peeled — more'n ever."

Vance kissed him good-night.

" Keep your eye peeled! " he said to me, hardly noticing her — and turned to go upstairs.

And then, as if he had an after-thought, he stopped and turned again.

" We're bound out to the poorhouse," he said, in that old miserable voice he talked in when he felt blue and down hearted. " They'll get us all there finally. But we'll give 'em a good hard fight doing it."

And then he went upstairs alone, and we waited there without talking, and listened to him till he reached his Purple Room again and locked the door. We just stood listening to him going — that little common man, trudging up through the dark corridors of that great old mansion that Mr. Bozro, the banker, built to be a monument of his elegance and power; that little old yellow man hunted by fear and poverty, that common terror that old folks have, which seems to follow them, no matter how much they have — the fear that some one will get their money away from them.

" Vance," I said, when he was gone. " This ain't going to do." For he certainly did not look right.

" He'll feel better to-morrow, maybe, if he gets some sleep," she said. " He hasn't slept any lately hardly," she told me.

" But are there really any thieves around here? " I asked her. " You haven't seen a one, have you? "

" No," said Vance, " but there's always somebody acts like they might be watching."

" Yes," I said, thinking —" yes." For that was true enough. " But what's started him going now? "

Vance didn't know.

" You haven't ever seen that half nigger he keeps talking of, have you? " I said to her.

" No," said Vance. " No. Not for certain. But once I thought maybe I had."

" I haven't; and you haven't," I said, and shook my head. " I believe sometimes that he imagines half these things."

But Vance was very certain that he didn't.

" That isn't the real trouble," she said. " You know

that. It's what's back of it. It's his losses. One after
another — year after year, for twenty years now. Till
every year he gets scareder and scareder for fear he'll
lose it all."

There was a good lot in that too. In his younger days,
they said, my Uncle Athiel had been a man who took as
many chances as the next one — especially in money business. He was a fighter and an ugly one. And I know
I've heard my father saying to my mother that he just
found out where money was, and went there after it.
And it didn't make much difference to him just how clean
or dirty the place was where he found it.

That was in the old days. But now for twenty years,
one thing after another had gone against him; and they
said he'd lost his nerve. I expect he had. For it'd been
enough to break any man's faith in his luck — what he
had been through.

Lord, but it was hot in that old sitting room, with those
windows closed!

"We can't stand this," I said to Vance.

"Let's go into the Crystal Room," said Vance.
"Maybe there'd be more air there."

So we went across, under the dim gas light in the hall,
to the great saloon parlor.

Almost all the rooms in Mr. Bozro's house — on the
first and second floors anyhow — had special names of
their own — mostly for their colors. They were mostly
all copied, like the whole house was, as I told you, from
some special room he had seen in his traveling abroad —
especially in France.

The Crystal Room of ours was the biggest and finest
saloon parlor that I ever saw. It was forty or fifty feet
long, I believe, and from its high ceiling there hung down
these two great crystal chandeliers, all glass chains and

prisms, that sparkled and tinkled and shone when they were lighted up, like a baby rainbow. Besides this, at either end, were two great black-and-gilt framed mirrors. And so they called it the Crystal Room — for the whole place seemed full of glass.

I lighted up one faint gas jet in the nearest chandelier, and it shone out in the dim circle of green and red in the great bank of glass above it. But the rest of the great room was dim.

" There, this is better," said Vance, " isn't it? "

" Yes," I had to admit it was.

" It won't be so bad shut up here evenings, when we're used to it — not in this great house," she said. " And there's another thing," she said, " if you stop to think of it. We won't be bothered with mosquitoes."

She always made the best of everything that happened. That was one thing I always noticed about her — even that year when she had her sickness — that Yellow Fever year when she was so delicate.

I didn't pay much attention to her. I was thinking about my Uncle and his fears and queer actions. I might have spoken to her that night about what he thought about the Fever coming. But I didn't think I would; I didn't think I'd worry her till I had to.

We sat there talking for a little while — in that great half-lighted room with its great furniture, and its big black piano, and its great mirrors — everything in the grand manner. And the old yellowish-brownish figures in the two high oil paintings — the paintings of Pocahontas' wedding and De Soto's Discovering the Mississippi — looked down on us from the wall. They were copies from those two celebrated paintings made especially for Mr. Bozro, by one of the finest oil painting artists in the South.

She looked slenderer than ever — Vance — in that old room — and frailer. She wasn't any invalid, but she was a fine, delicate thing — delicate as a cape jessamine — and full of ideas and excitements and impulses, that were too much for her. I watched her slight, thin hand on the arms of the chair, lying listless. And all at once it clenched itself and unclenched. She moved a little and sighed.

"What is it, Vance?" I asked.

"Father," she said, and stopped, her big eyes staring out before her. And suddenly I looked and I saw her shudder. This time I was sure. I saw it quite distinctly.

"What is it?" I asked her a second time. And I kept on asking till she told me.

"A dream," she said, at last — not wanting to.

"A what?" I said.

"Oh, I had the most monstrous dream," she said, and shuddered a second time.

"What about?" I asked.

And finally I got her to tell me:

"About my father."

I burst out laughing when I heard her — louder than I need to have, I expect.

"What next?" I asked. "What next? You certainly are sensible, Vance!"

She was always full of strange notions; and I was always having to laugh her out of them. They were strange and crazy and different from other people's — and they didn't do her any good.

"What was it?" I asked finally. "What was the dream about?"

"I'm not going to tell you," she said. "You'll never find out from me," and started turning it off with a laugh.

She wouldn't, either. She never would, when she didn't want to. That was what aggravated me so continually. She looked so frail, you'd never believe how obstinate she could be. When she didn't want to tell you anything or do anything, she wouldn't; she'd laugh it off or escape you someway.

But the real trouble with her was always that she took life so hard. Now this thing had bitten into her, I could see that, underneath it all, right away. Her voice showed it and her deep eyes looking out from her pale face beneath her great crown of black hair; and her thin delicate hand gripping when she spoke of it, on the chair arm, till the nails went white under the pressure. And now I thought I understood why her eyes had gone following her father around that night so steadily. It was this foolish idea about a dream. And it made me mad, like a lot of her ideas.

" You go to bed," I said, " and sleep — that's what you need. This weather's been too much for you."

" I expect so," she said.

" I know it," I replied.

" Yes, maybe I'll forget it," she said then, going. And I stood watching her as she went.

They say delicate women are that way sometimes — so sensitive and full of imagination, and quick to catch things about the other folks around them, that they seem sometimes to be taking information through the empty air, like they had a sixth sense almost, they say. I never took much stock in that myself.

But certainly Vance was delicate enough, and she had imagination plenty. Far too much for her, I believe. She had been alone a lot — even before her mother died — and still more afterward; and she had too, like the rest of our women folks here, the bringing up by the niggers, when they were children. And that makes a difference, I believe.

I remember now how she looked to me, as I stood there watching her go out — how frail and delicate and slim;— thin wrists and slender ankles; and a body I could more than span around with my two great hands. She looked more delicate to me, maybe than she really was — in comparison to myself. But there was hardly body enough to her, I used to think, to rightly clothe her soul.

I smiled to her when she went out, and she to me. And I heard her go along into her room upstairs — the Ivory Room, and close the door. And then I started out to follow her upstairs. And almost by the time I put out the gas and left the empty Crystal Room, her notion, her talk about that dream of hers had gone clean out of my mind. For I was certain it would be all gone from hers that next morning.

I put the light out in the glass chandelier in the Crystal Room; and my dim shadow in the great pale pier glasses passed out with me into the hall. Then I turned out the flicker of light in the bronze gas fixture in the lower hall-way, and went on up the long black walnut stairway to the second floor.

My Uncle, as I told you, had the Purple Room, the great bedroom of Mr. Bozro; Vance had the Ivory Room in front, where Mrs. Bozro had slept; and I was in the Red Room toward the rear; and in the " L " above the dining room, was the Turkish Room, unoccupied. Then upstairs, besides, on the third floor, were all those other bedrooms — six more of them — all closed and vacant.

I went into the Red Room and closed the door — lighted up the gas. And I sat down like I always did at night, to read my law books. That next year, thank God, I was to take my examinations to the bar. I was going to be my own man. No more like that last six months for me. I saw myself already sitting there, with my framed certificate from the State of Tennessee on the wall; and the steel engraving of Henry Clay, with that old parchment smile of his looking down on me from the wall; and a round top black walnut desk, and a cane-backed swivel chair; and a library of sheepskin law books closed in a book-case with glass doors. And after that some clients, and a dollar or two in my pocket I could call my own. And let me tell you I thought that time would never come.

I was twenty-one; and time goes slower then when you have to wait around to get what you're after. My folks had both died, and left me — with that little old red clay farm up in the hills. And I had made my mind up right away to get out of there — out of the mud and mire of that God-forsaken country; and go down to Memphis and be a lawyer. I had heard the lawyers hollering and speechifying once or twice on court days in the county seat. And it fired my blood, I expect.

And so, as soon as I was able, I came down to Memphis, and my Uncle Athiel was glad enough, as I said, to take me, when I told him what I could do around the place. I was a big husky boy, and I could see in his looks, as he eyed me, that he knew I would not be a bad thing for him to have around that great place of his.

That was all right; I was willing to do it, and I did. But there was no great love lost on either side, between him and me, I expect. There wasn't on mine anyway. For I knew before I came there, that, though I always called him Uncle Athiel, and he'd been brought up by my grandparents like their own children were, he really was no blood kin of mine at all. He was just a young boy from a poor family that had lived next to ours once, whom my mother's folks had taken in and cared for and adopted, when his people died. And it was a funny thing — the way things sometimes happen in this world — that this one poor boy we'd taken in, was the only one of us all that had property and money now. And here was I, at twenty-one, living under his roof, without a cent in the world, except two hundred dollars that I had gotten finally out of the old farm above the mortgage — and that pledged to this gamble of mine at getting started in the law.

So I sat there for an hour or two one night, trying to read my law book — without any luck at it. I sat there, slapping mosquitoes, for they came in the open windows to the light, eating me alive; and I tried to read — and my eyes slipped off the pages of the law book just as soon as they went on. I was thinking that night of something else.

I got thinking of the Fever, and whether it would really come; and of my Uncle and his fears; of his thieves and his fires, and whatever he had hidden in that old house of his, that made all that talk; that made him have those ideas about fire and thieves which were always uppermost in his mind.

Then after that I got thinking of Vance — how delicate she was, how delicate and high strung; and the strange ways and notions she had — different from other folks, men and women too. She was as distinct from the other women I had known — the common, wiry farm women I had been accustomed to in the country — as if they had been bred on different stars.

I sat there worrying about her that night; about how careful she had to be since her sickness that last spring; and how that hot summer had worn upon her; and now about this Fever thing, that seemed to be right down upon us.

" She'd have to get out anyhow, if that comes along," I said to myself. And tried to think of it that way; and did get the feeling that it would go right finally. And then I felt a little easier.

By and by, I thought it was a little cooler, so I put out the light and undressed myself in the dark, to save shutting down the shades, and keeping out the air. And I crawled in under the old mosquito bars on the bed, and, inside there, naturally, it was hotter than ever. I turned and sweat, and rolled and twisted the sheets up into ropes. I lay there restless, hot, worrying, without sleep.

The town seemed restless to me, too, I remember. There seemed more noises on the street. My Uncle moved around the Purple Room. And Arabella's dogs — the big one and the little one — went around the house patrolling. I saw them once or twice; and once or twice they got barking.

There was a song on the street, some drunken man was going home singing. And every half hour, I think it was, I heard, from the main street down under the hill the tinkle-tinkle of the bell of the little old bobtailed mule car that went by those days — passing by all night long, at intervals as regular as the striking of the clock.

And then, after a while, those old alley dogs got hollering — those nigger dogs out in the alleys. There never was such a place for dogs, I believe, as Memphis. I hadn't grown used to them yet.

Every time one started up, it set the whole pack yelling. The alleys were alive with them — those nigger dogs, those old tramp dogs, that came and went and loved and multiplied till the back alleys swarmed with them. Mongrels, crawling mongrels, afraid of their own shadow, the hands of every man against them. And at night time, when once the cry was started they all awoke and yelled together with idiot fear.

I remember lying there that night, half sleeping, and hearing that old miserable wail of crying dogs start near, and go shuddering out through the alleys of the sleeping town — waking, dying, fading out at last in the far distance, where the alleys ended in the empty pastures at the borders of the town.

The city seemed restless somehow — uneasy in its sleep. But maybe it wasn't so. Maybe I just thought so afterward when I remembered.

For it was that next day that the Fever came.

BOOK II

THE TERROR BY NIGHT

CHAPTER IV

THAT next day we knew the Fever was in town. And not a one of us who saw it come, I believe, is ever going to forget it. I know I never shall — not if I live to be a hundred.

I sit here now and talk of it, and right away I'm back again in that hot August afternoon on old Main Street; and I see the smudge of that first Fever fire on the street; and smell the taint of that old carbolic acid in the air. I never smell that, never, to this day, but I got a little sick and numb, and I say to myself:

" Here it is! It's come! " Thinking of course of that old Yellow Fever in the air.

What struck me first, I remember that first day I saw it, was the strangeness of it all. I'd never been where they had had the Fever before in my life. I just stood and watched and listened.

And after I'd looked down the road, at the place where the woman died, and the yellow spots of acid on the road-way, and the street roped off, the next thing I noticed was the queer way folks behaved. Everybody acted queer, it seemed to me — hurried, and got out of one another's way. And some were drunk, for they said at first that drinking gin would protect you. But the most of them, I could see, weren't drunk at all. They were something else.

There was one little man, I remember, a dapper dandy little man in a linen suit walking straight down the middle

49

of Main Street, directly in the white shine of the sun.
And everybody that passed him, going across the street,
he wheeled away from, and went way around. And if
they didn't go far off enough to suit him he waved and
called to them to go further.

And there was another man, I saw, who was carrying
a sponge in his hand, and every now and then he lifted it
up to his nose and smelled it. It had carbolic acid on
it. We saw that often enough afterward. But that was
the first time I had seen it; and I stood and stared at
him.

I stood staring at him; and all at once it came to me.
"Lord," I said to myself, "these folks are scared to
death."

And right after that I was scared myself — some; and
began to have that feeling that got growing on me afterward.

The trouble was nobody knew about the thing — where
it was, or who had it, or how you got it. Every step you
took you might be blundering into it. You had that old
scary feeling, of a man waiting to be struck from behind
in the dark. It seemed like something dangerous was
standing there behind your shoulder — something you
couldn't see. All that you knew was that somewhere,
somehow, under that clear, cloudless pale green summer
sky, death lay hidden, waiting — all set and ready to
pounce down upon the next one, like a cat upon a sparrow.
And the next one might be you.

So I didn't stay there very long, nor talk to very many.
I did hear that they said the Fever seemed to be checked,
or headed East — like it was in '73, and in that case they
might hold it so it wouldn't get down to us at all. That
was something, anyhow. And after that I started home
right away.

I got on a little old bobtailed mule car and rode down Main Street, sitting up straight on the hard, carpeted seat, for fear of whoever might have been sitting there before me.   And there, on the corner, as I got out, stood John McCallan, the policeman, in the thin shade of an old mulberry tree, holding his old felt hat in one hand and mopping off his red-hot face with the other.

" Well, sor, it's come," he said.

" Yes, John; it has, sure enough," I answered.

" God hilp us," said John, and cleared his throat. " They say they're burnin' the clothes and beddin' of the poor woman on the street," he said, " and they got it all roped off to the alley.   And chimicals and stuff all over the ground."

" Yes," I said.   " I saw it down the street."

" By this time, she'll be buried," he said.

" Yes."

'· God hilp us," said John McCallan.   " They have to bury 'em quick, don't they?   They have to get 'em away under ground right off.

" Yes," he said, looking off.   " There's many a poor feller alive and workin' to-day that'll be lyin' there and the flies'll be eatin' this day week."

" The flies ! " I said.

" God, wait'll you see it," he said, looking straight ahead.   " I saw it, when it was here in '73."

" The flies," I said again.   I never heard of that before.

" We used to find them so — mornings.   Them big green flies on the window."

He stood fanning himself with his big floppy hat.

" And the naygurs," he went along, " don't have it! Plenty o' good white men'll die.   And those naygurs won't any of them have it."   He was always cursing at the niggers. "They'll stay here stealin' from us and makin' trouble."

And by this time the mule car had been down and turned around at the end of the run, and was tinkling back again.

"Well, good evenin'," said John McCallan, treading the step behind the door in the rear; and the little car teetered under his great body as he climbed in. And I turned around and started going up the hill to our street.

That certainly was a hard and unnatural summer for heat, that Yellow Fever year, so hot and dry, they said, the big old trees died in the woods — their roots just dried up in the ground.

Lord, how hot it was going up that old hill! I can feel it now. Dry as a kiln. Not a cloud in the sky; nothing but the white sun — no bigger, it looked like, than a ten-cent piece. Just a glimmering point of white hot light baking the earth up in one solid brick. And the shadows everywhere sharp as if cut off with a knife. "Yellow Fever Weather," they got to calling it afterwards; we had it all that summer.

The great house of my Uncle stood there ahead of me as I dragged along, set up from the street; with its two little magnolia trees, on either side of it, stiff as pompons, their leaves glistening and shining like burnished metal. A locust droned and rattled in one of them — fast and furious, like something gone mad from heat. My head was hot from the white sun overhead. My feet were hot from the hot bricks underneath. My tongue was hot in my mouth, and my soul was hot in my body; and when I opened the side door, and passed into the great dark house, it seemed cool as a cave.

I opened the door and slipped in softly. Vance might be taking her sleep upstairs, and now certainly she could

not get too much. I started going into the sitting room
to throw myself into a chair and cool off, when I saw, in
the study, to the right, Arabella, the negro woman, staring motionless out the window.

She turned her great eyes toward me for a moment,
thinking, maybe, it might be my Uncle; then turned them
back again, and stood there looking down the street —
still as something watching on a path in the jungle. She
had been watching out a lot that way lately; all the niggers had been watching, it seemed somehow to me, since
they said first the Fever was started up from New Orleans.

" Well, Arabella," I said, " it's come! The Fever's
here! "

" Yassah," she said, all unexcited.

" There was a woman died of it this morning."

" Yassah," she said. " Yassah."

And though her voice didn't change one little tone, all
at once her smooth round face broke into a sudden peaceful smile.

" Yassah," she said. " Yassah. The signs all say
so." And she turned her face out the window again, and
her eyes went hunting down the street over the brow of
the little hill toward the city.

" What is she looking for to come up over that hill? "
I said to myself. " What is that old smile about? "

I had heard they said there was something going on in
the heads of those sanctified niggers that summer — of
that special lot that she belonged to. We heard them
howling Sunday evenings, longer than ever before — all
night long, and week nights too, more lately — down in
that chapel she belonged to. " The Hollering Saints,"
they used to call them, then.

There was something on their minds, some crazy new
idea. But who knew it? I didn't; and I believe there

was no one else, no white folks who did, exactly. All they
knew was what they generally know about niggers — that
bowing and scraping; those brown masks — those faces
with all their muscles trained since the sin of Ham in the
Old Bible; since they went out in slavery and subjection
— to lie still and show nothing. And those big old brown
eyes, watching, watching. And sometimes, very rarely
when you surprised it, that glimpse of the real thing behind, when it breaks into hysterics at those nigger meetings; or gleams out in something like that consecrated
nigger's smile that Arabella gave me when I told her of
the Fever.

"Miss Vance upstairs?" I asked her.

"Yassah, she's upstairs a-restin'," said Arabella and
kept on looking.

I went upstairs myself then to my own room, and started
reading at my law. I was behind that last day or two.
But mighty little reading I did that afternoon. My
thoughts went right back to the Fever; to the dead woman,
and the chemicals, and the scared folks on the street.
And my eyes went traveling out the window.

Already folks were going out of town. Already the
sound of wheels sounded on the streets — the sound of the
stampede of those next few days. The folks just north
of us, the Ventresses, I saw, were closing up their house
already, and getting fixed to leave to-morrow

I know I sat there on the window, and thought it over.
I didn't fool myself; I didn't once expect that my Uncle
or I would go. But it struck me, with some satisfaction,
I remember, that now Vance was certainly going to be sent
out into the hill country, like they had been planning once
before in that hot weather.

"There's that much to be said for the Fever," I said to
myself, "it will get her out of here."

For I had worried about her being there all that summer.

And while I sat there wondering and worrying, and caught up like everybody else, with my own affairs, I heard somewhere out the window, the " Whistling Doctor " as we all called him, coming up from visiting some patient down the street.

Dr. Greathouse, his real name was. He was our doctor; a highly educated man, and I expect the leading doctor in Memphis; but so big and careless and full of fun and courage, that most everybody knew him, not by his own name, but for that odd trick he had; for whistling, everywhere he walked, that one old tune he knew — " The Arkansas Traveler." You heard him whistling it all the time on the street — so everybody got to call him the " Whistling Doctor."

I looked down the side street in front of us, and saw him from my window. There was an old lady down below he came to see once every so often. And he was coming out of there now. A big, tall, fleshy, rolling man — with a kind of rolling walk, and a great hearty voice.

Old Uncle Mungo sat waiting for him in his buggy — the old Virginia darky that had always been in his family, and always drove him. I never seem to think of that old nigger outside that old buggy that he kept so sleek and clean. He was just as much a part of it, the doctor used to say, as the upper stories of one of those old Greek Centaurs. For the doctor, as I told you, was a highly educated man — a graduate of the University of Virginia — and he was just full of things like that.

The whistling stopped when the doctor reached the street, and climbed in his buggy. But there had been one cheerful noise on the street, anyhow, I said to myself, and one cheerful face, in all this crowd I'd seen this day, that

wasn't scared. There were plenty of poor sick folks I
knew who listened all day long just to hear that old
whistle of his — broken and off the key, half the time, go
by. And now, with that Fever there, and half the town
half scared to death, it was better than a band of music
going up the street. He saw me where I had got up and
stood looking at him out the window, and waved his hand
at me as he went by — big and rough and careless and
slouched down in the corner of that bran span clean
buggy; and the little old Virginia darkey, brushed and
combed, and cleaned till he shone, tucked up in the other
corner, driving. And so they went on down out of sight.

Time crawled along mighty slowly after that; and by
and by I went downstairs, thinking Vance might have got
down without my hearing her. I stopped by the side of
her door and listened, as I came by, and I didn't hear a
thing.

But when I got down there, she wasn't down there yet.
Only Arabella, staring out the window down the hill, from
the sitting room this time.

"What are you in here for, Arabella," I said to her —
"all this afternoon?" For I knew and she knew too, she
had no business in there that way. She knew that she
was breaking all my Uncle's orders about the house — his
general rules that when she got done in front the house,
she had to leave at once.

She turned slowly toward me, pretending not to understand.

"I'm just alookin' and watchin'," she said, and set her
great brown eyes on me. "I'm examinin' and watchin'
what's goin' on yere.

"Look yondah," she said, in an old secret voice.

I looked out. She was pointing to the Ventresses, the
neighbors just above us. They were sending out their

trunks now to the depot, to be on time that next morning.

"They all a-goin'," she said. "They all a-goin' out."

And I saw the folks across the street from us were getting ready too.

"They's all a-goin'. Eve'ybody's a-goin'," said Arabella, standing motionless.

"You better go!" she said to them, under her breath; "you better go," and nodded to herself.

"Why — what for?" I asked her, trying her, to see what she would say. I liked to hear them talk. I encouraged them all I could always. I wanted to hear what they would say.

"Why!" she said, looking with her big round eyes at me. "Why? 'Cause they're goin' to die. All them in this city's goin' to die," she said in a deep, old graveyard voice.

It seemed silly, but it gave me a kind of start — the way she said it — that, and all I had been seeing that day — the fear of the folks on the street.

"Damn the thing," I said, and shook my shoulders.

I thought to say it to myself, but I saw that I must have talked out loud. For the negress who had started going, looked around and watched me with a steady look. "What thing?" she said, like an old owl. "What you mean! What thing?"

"The Fever," I told her.

"They's more terrible things acomin'," she said, waiting a minute. "They's more monstrous things than that Fever acomin' down upon this city — more monstrouser and terribler for all the folks yere."

And right away when she was saying it, her great smooth, oily face broke out again in that wide, peaceful smile.

She stood a minute, while it died away, and took one

more long look out the window; and then turned around and stalked back to her kitchen.

I stood there wondering what it was that she saw coming up over that hill toward the city. Death, in some form, I expected, like the rest of us. But in what form, and for what purpose? For nothing strange happens in a nigger's mind, except for some old deep mysterious purpose of God — or of the Devil. What was it she saw coming? And why on earth when she thought of it, should she smile?

Then, in just a few minutes more, I heard Vance's light feet upon the stairs, and saw her in the big brown doorway.

" It's come," I said. " The Fever! "

She didn't seem surprised, either, not a bit. She walked across the room and stood there at the window, where Arabella had just stood, and where afterward we all stood so often, looking down the little hill, across the little valley, toward the city.

" Dad was right then," she said.

And I asked her what she meant.

" He expected it last night," said Vance.

" How did you know that? " I asked astonished. For I had especially kept from speaking to her of it. And I knew he hadn't either.

" I don't know," she said, turning. " It was perfectly plain, wasn't it? "

" It wouldn't have been to me," I said, " not unless he told me."

" Oh, I don't know," she said a little absently. " I think it was."

I stood watching her. She seemed nervous and wrought up still, as she stood there looking out the window.

" What is it? " I asked her.

" What's what? " she said.

" What is it you're looking for so strong down the street? "

" Dad," she said. " Have you seen him? "

" It's too early yet," I said.

" Yes, I expect it is," said Vance — and started turning away. But she turned right back again afterwards.

" I don't want him down there," she said. " I wish that he'd come home."

I told her there would be no danger. He would not go near where the fever was. But she didn't answer me. And I thought I saw again that little shiver that she gave the night before.

" They're all leaving; they're all going," she said, speaking to cover it up. " Everybody's going, aren't they? "

" The streets are full of them," I said and waited. But she didn't speak.

" They say the trunks are piled up to the second story at the depot," I went on.

Then we were both silent for a while.

" Are we going? " I said at last.

" No," she said, as if only just half hearing me. " No, we won't go."

" *You* will," I said.

She stood and looked at me a moment. " No," she said. " No, I'll not."

" Yes, you will," I said, confident — for I was certain of it. And then I changed the subject.

" You've seen it," I said, " before — the Fever; when it was bad — that time before! "

For she'd told me that she had.

" Yes, I've seen it, very bad," she said.

" But you never told me much about it," I went on.

She had never talked much about it before. I imagined somehow that she didn't care to. But she talked freely enough that evening of it.

"It's the air," she said. "It's poisoned. That's what I remember most."

"Is that right," I said. "Is that true?"

"Yes, certainly," said Vance. "That's what all the great doctors say. This poison in the air — this miasma!"

I asked her then just what she remembered of that time she had seen it so near before — not there in Memphis; in a little town further west that they lived in before they came there.

"It was the year after my mother died," she said — "the year we lived in Texas. Ursa, old black Ursa took care of me."

She talked low and broken — and stopped.

"I remember mostly," she said again, "the black air — the black poison air!"

"Not really so!" I said. "Not black!"

She had that way with her of telling any story as if she believed it through and through — the most unlikely things. She told them like a child — a nervous, serious child that makes you see a thing almost, because it believes it so. Half like a child; half like a great actress, I sometimes thought, who knows exactly what she is doing — but yet believes it, too, with her feelings.

"No, not really," she said. "I only thought so. I thought at night it formed in the houses where the Fever was — for the Fever always comes by night, you know," she said.

"Always?" I asked.

"Always," Vance answered. "So mornings," she said, "I used to think that I could see that black air coming out through the tops of the windows and the open doors."

" How silly," I said.

" Ursa said so," said Vance.   " I was only seven years old."

She told me then what she had really seen — about the folks, the poor sick folks down in the cabin by the bayou, who had it down underneath their windows ; how the doctor came, how the coffins came, bright new pine coffins standing waiting by the door in the sunshine ; how you heard folks crying in the night.

You heard them when she told you, plain as day — when she told it in that still low voice of hers, hushed a little and breathless ; wide-eyed, secret and still — like children telling their old ghost stories — those old ghost stories that the niggers teach them — to one another in the twilight.

" I used to get up in the mornings," she said, " early mornings, to see that old black air that Ursa used to talk about, coming out the tops of the doors and windows. Like smoke, like old black smoke, I thought it was."

" You crazy thing," I said.

" No," said Vance.   " No.   It's worse than that, the way it is.   It's really worse, I believe."

" How so ? "

" Why, it's there just the same, isn't it ? " said Vance. " It's there ; only it's invisible.   And that's worse, I think. That's worse, isn't it ? "

Her low voice stopped, as she turned back again to the window.   We were still again.

" They died there, you say, in that old cabin ? " I asked her finally.

" Six of them ! —" she said, absent-minded again.

" Oh, I wish he'd come ! " she said.   And when I looked at her I saw her eyes were full of tears.

" What is it, Vance? " I asked her, standing up beside her.

" Oh, I don't know," she said, turning quickly, so she hid her eyes from me.

" Are you thinking of that same foolishness again? " I asked her quickly.

I suspected, naturally, right away. She hadn't got rid of that thing yet — that dream of hers.

" What foolishness? " she asked.

" That dream — that old dream you said you had about your father."

She nodded. " A little," she admitted.

" You ought to be taken out and whipped within an inch of your life," I said.

" I expect I had," said Vance, and tried to laugh.

" What was it? What was it that you dreamed? " I asked her.

But she said, like she had before, " I won't tell you."

" Look here," I said — for I thought then I could understand; with all that Fever around and everything. " What was it? Did you dream he died? "

She shuddered then again — like she had the night before. She didn't answer. But I knew then that that was what she'd dreamed.

" You little fool," I said. " Haven't you got any sense at all? Ain't you ever going to grow up and be like other folks? "

She turned away from me, looking out the window.

" You can't help such things coming to you, can you? " she said, trying to excuse herself.

" But you don't have to believe them," I told her.

" I don't believe them," she said. " I don't! It's just the way it's left me. The way it made me feel."

" You've had the same feeling after dreaming, I believe — if you tell the truth," she said to me.

She had me there. For all of us have had that feeling, I expect — after some dream we had — after one or two at any rate. And I saw too, in a way, how the whole thing must have come to her — worrying about her father — the way she had that summer. It is perfectly plain and simple.

But all I wanted to do was to get her quit of it — of this worry and apprehension, whatever it was.

And so, I went on scolding and laughing at her, and she looking out the window.

" Oh, why won't he come! " she said, impatient.

And then right away again, " Oh, there he is! " said Vance. And we saw him coming up the street.

We looked down the empty street and down over the hill — with the dusty shadows of that parched old summer afternoon lengthening on its east side — on the houses and the fences and the yards. And there came my Uncle Hagar, in his high, old dingy buggy; and his old brown hand bag between his feet, driving poor old Dolly, loose reined, as if there was never a fever nor a danger in the world.

CHAPTER V

"WELL," I said to my Uncle Athiel, as I took the reins of the horse, and started unharnessing. "It's come, like you said it would."

" Yep," said my Uncle.

And when I looked around him, I saw he was a different man than he was the night before — more like he was naturally. His face was set; his eyes were sharp and beady, like they were when he felt sure of himself. And his old bluish mouth was shut straight across his face, and served notice, when you looked at it, that you get no more words out of it than necessary.

" Many new cases? " I tried again.

" Ten," said my Uncle; and turned and hitched off toward the house again, carrying his old brown satchel. I didn't know what he'd been doing with that down town all day. Not collecting rents — not on Tuesdays. Maybe he'd been having small change turned into bills.

He was just as silent during most of the meal time — only answering questions; and then only when he had to.

The Fever bad? Bad enough. Did he go near it? No. Where was it now? It seemed to be going East; staying up North and East like it did in '73. But you could never tell one thing about it.

Crowds in the street. Yes — the fools! He saw a lot of them at the bank — he said then, getting started —

taking out money. Putting it in too, some of them —
the fools. They'd lose every dollar they'd put in. Those
banks were busted — if you know the truth of it. Those
damn scoundrels would get every dollar there was left
there by those fools.

Fools; everybody was fools that night. For a minute
or two he got started talking and calling everybody fools
— especially the folks who were running away and leaving
their places empty.

The fools, he said; when they moved out, the niggers
and the thieves just moved in. The town was full of them.
And there never were so many niggers standing around the
streets, looking, in this world.

"You take that place yonder," he said, nodding out
the window, to that Ventress place, just north across our
yard. What were they thinking of, the crazy fools, running off like that; and leaving their property empty, just
inviting fire and thieves? They might destroy us. They
might set us all afire. They would, too, if that house
once got agoin'.

And when Vance said the servants would stay and take
care of it:

"Niggers," my Uncle Hagar told her. "Niggers.
How long do you reckon they'll stay there? One day!"

Half the houses in the town would be full of niggers
and thieves in two weeks. They'd go in and out. They'd
live in them, if they wanted to. For half the police and
half the firemen, he claimed, had skipped already.

"There won't be anybody left in a week or two," he
said, "to protect the property here."

And after that he closed up again and wouldn't talk a
bit more than he had to.

"You won't have to go down town again," Vance said
to him.

"No," he said, "not much. I got all my business settled up. Only one or two more things to-morrow.
May be."

Vance sighed. She knew, and I knew too, he would go
and come just when he liked. It was no good talking to
him.

"But after that," said Vance, "you won't have to go
down there again."

"After that," said my Uncle Athiel, "I'll be right
here looking after my own property."

"Then you aren't going away," I said quickly.
"You're not going to get out of town."

"Going, no!" said my Uncle Hagar, resting his black
eyes on me. "What do you take me for?"

So we sat there again in the high black walnut lined
room without talking. It was lighter than the night before. The sky was clearer.

"Most sun down, ain't it?" said my Uncle, suddenly,
and got up.

"Yes," said Vance.

"It's time to shut the windows," said my Uncle.

"Good Lord!" I said under my breath.

"Only to-night —" he said, "we're going to shut them
all — the upstairs, too."

"Upstairs!" I said.

"Upstairs and down!"

"We can't stand it," I said, rising up.

My Uncle stood and stared at me — his eyes sharper
than gimlets.

"It's moonshine, anyway," I said. "Isn't it bad
enough with just the downstairs closed?"

"Are you a fool?" said my Uncle Athiel.

"No," I said. "Are you?"

You know how quick and irritated you get in that

weather. And with all the rest to add to the excitement
— the fever and all that, and my quick temper anyway —
I was ready for murder, I expect, that night.

" Beavis," said Vance to me.

" We can't be shut up here — not altogether," I said,
minding her, and talking lower and apologizing with my
voice.

" It's better, I expect you'll find," said my Uncle Athiel,
" than being shut up altogether in a pine box."

" What is this anyhow? " I said, raising up my voice
again.

" You do it now," said my Uncle Athiel. " And talk
about it when you come down."

So Vance took me upstairs to close the windows, while
he saw they were all shut up below.

" What is this anyhow? " I asked Vance again, going
up.

" The Fever," she explained to me. " Shutting out
the Fever — like we used to do. Shutting out the night
air."

Lord, how hot it was in that house — hotter than the
night before — hotter when you went upstairs! Hotter
— a lot hotter in the second story than in the first. You
felt it going up. You smelled that old dry dusty smell
of furniture and carpets — the dyes in them, I expect it
is — that you smell inside the house those hottest summer nights.

I went back to close my room, while Vance was taking
care of hers. I started and slammed down the back
window of the two in my room, and started over to the
second. And then I stood there watching. For, far up
the street, I could see that first old Fever fire burning in
the road-way — before the Snack house where the woman
died. There were fewer buildings then, on our side; you

could see way up the street. And, tho' it wasn't very
dark yet, I could see that fire plain enough. They had
fed that Fever fire they set going in the day, and kept it
going still, after they had burned the clothes the woman
died in, the things the woman touched as she was dying.
There was tar in the fire; and some other chemicals, I
believe. And I could just catch a faint touch of red,
and see, much plainer, over it, the black and greasy smoke,
that swung heavily down the street.

I stood for a minute watching it, with that old feeling
of loneliness, that comes over you anyhow, looking out
into the twilight, with a big black unlighted house at
your back; and I jumped a little when Vance called for
me, at my doorway, to go downstairs.

My Uncle Athiel was there, waiting in the sitting room,
when we two came back.

" Now, sit down! " he said to me. " Sit down and hold
your horses! And I'll tell you something about this
Fever, if you think you want to listen. Sit down! " he
said.

I sat down, without answering back. Vance had been
talking to me when we were coming down from upstairs.

" You ever seen it? " he said to me.

" No," I said —" no, sir."

" I have," he said, eying me. " All my life."

I didn't say anything in answer.

" And when you know about it," he said; " you know
like I do, there ain't any more danger in it than a kitten.
I'm not afraid of it — not a particle."

" Why not, aren't you? " I said.

" Are you afraid of sun-stroke? " he said. " Do you
ever worry about it? "

" No," I said. " You don't have to get sun-stroke,

you don't have to go out where it is.   You don't have to go out and stand out in the sunshine."

"Just precisely.   And it's just the same precisely, with this Fever," said my Uncle Athiel.   "Only one comes by day and one comes by night!

"Now lemme tell you somethin'," my Uncle Hagar said —"and it will be worth your while rememberin': You won't get the sun-stroke, never, not if you keep in out of the sun.   And just the same, you won't get the Yellow Fever — never — if you keep out of this night air.

"I've seen it, and I've seen it working for more than thirty years; and I ain't no more afraid of it; nor half so much — as a good hard cold.   For you know exactly what to do with it.   You know that all you have to do is one simple thing:

"Keep down your windows after dark!   Keep 'em down till morning comes — and shut out that old poison night air!" said my Uncle Hagar.   "That's all.   You do that, and you're just as safe as you would be in Alaska.   Provided that one thing.   Provided you just shut up all your windows nights," he said and stopped talking.

I moved and shifted my chair.   And all at once Vance got up and went and stood at the window.   I saw what it was right off.   She'd caught sight of the Fever fire.   It was getting darker and you could see it plainer now.

"Simple, ain't it?" said my Uncle Hagar.

I didn't say one word to dispute him.   I'd promised Vance I wouldn't.

"It sounds so," I told him.   But I didn't believe it just the same.

So then my Uncle Hagar went on talking and explaining more about the Yellow Fever.

"I know," he said.   "I've watched it everywhere

around this country. You can touch it," he said, " and breathe it; you can bury 'em, and handle 'em and be with 'em all day long. And you'll never catch it. They all know that; it's well known. Any doctor'll tell you.

" But nights," he said, " look out! This Fever's a night disease. It comes at night. It always strikes 'em first just after midnight — always just between the hours of twelve and one. And they're lowest then, after they've got it. And when you ask the doctors why, they don't know why.

" It's a night disease, that's all," said my Uncle Athiel. " That's all they know. It's a night thing. The Yellow Fever's just as much a part of the night as the moon.

" It travels," he said; " it goes traveling on in this old poison night air."

Vance stood there looking; and I sat still. I could look down past her shoulder, down the street and see the old Fever fire brightening as the daylight grew more dim. The gas lights were few and feeble in those days; and the fire light, a dull old red, shone plainer and plainer in the deepening dark. It was growing pretty dusky now; the time the last shine of sunset shows white in the eastern window panes.

" You'll do that," said my Uncle Athiel to me. " Will you? "

" Do what? " I asked, looking over toward where Vance was.

" Keep 'em closed; keep all your windows closed."

" Yes, sir, I will," I said. For I had told Vance that I'd agree to anything.

" For if it once gets in a house," he said, " if it once gets in — that's different. You're a goner — every-body," said my Uncle. " A goner, when it once gets into the house with you."

He looked at Vance then, to see if she was going to answer him — to promise him about keeping down her windows too. For she only stood there watching, with her face at the window.

And then, as it happened, when he was watching, that old Fever fire in the street flared up. Somebody'd thrown more stuff on, I expect, to keep it going. It flared and threw an orange light, down the darkened street.

" What's that! " said my Uncle, jumping to his feet; and hurrying over and standing there back of Vance at the window. And then saw himself what it was.

" Fools," he said.

We stood there for a few minutes — all of us. I was thinking of the poor woman who was dead, and in the graveyard, and her poor little old clothes and furniture and belongings burned and gone, and traveled out across the town in smoke.

" The fools! " said my Uncle suddenly again. " The fools. Judas Iscariot! They might set a fire that way and destroy half the property in this town! "

I looked at him, as he stood there staring — rigid.

Property, property — always property! All the town half crazy with nerves and fright; death and fear of death stamped on the faces of all other folks. And all the time this one little yellow man, with his eye just set on that same old man's fear — for property.

He said good-night then, and Vance and I listened while he poked upstairs again and locked himself in his Purple Room.

" You believe that? " I said right off to Vance.

" What? " she asked.

" That thing about the Fever."

" Certainly I do! " said Vance.

" Well, I don't," I said.

"Certainly, it's true," said Vance. "Any doctor'll tell you so. All these highest educated doctors have studied it all out and they know. They'll tell you it's the night air brings the Yellow Fever."

"Even if it was," I said, "you couldn't shut it out by putting down a window."

"Yes, you could," said Vance. "You ask any doctor — any doctor in Memphis, and see what he says."

"I will," I said; "I'm going to the first chance I get. And I won't believe it till they say so."

But she was sure and positive, like she always was when she took sides. "They'll tell you," she said, "and they know too. We've got as highly educated doctors here in Memphis as anywhere in this country."

"How can you shut out the night air?" I asked her.

"Hundreds of people have, yes, thousands," said Vance. "I know lots of folks myself."

That old Fever fire shone down the street plainer and plainer now. Its light was quite far away; but darkness, as it came along, seemed to bring it always nearer to us. I could see the orange light of it now — very faint on Vance's face. For we hadn't lit the gaslight yet. We were too busy talking.

"Do you mean to say," I asked her again, "that you believe all that?"

"It's just as safe, I believe," said Vance, "as it is in Alaska — if you do what he said to do."

"That wasn't the way you talked this afternoon," I told her.

"When?" she asked me in an arguing voice.

"When you were talking of that old Fever you saw before. When you were worrying about your father."

We stood side by side at the window, so her shoulder touched my arm; and when I spoke again about her father, all at once I felt her tremble like she had done that afternoon — a little shudder pass across her slender body.

And then, right away, it was all that I could do to hold myself from gathering her in my arms. It was the danger of the thing — thinking of the danger from that Fever — somehow. It seemed somehow I must protect her and fend it off from her — and get her away from it. And still I was mad and irritated at her, too, all at the same time.

" You lied to me. You know you lied," I cried. " You do fear it! " We were like two children together, when we thought a thing, out it came.

" No," she said. " I did not. I did not lie."

" Do you mean to say," I went along, looking down at her, " you think you're going to stay here? "

" Yes," she said, defying me.

" Well, you're not."

" I am," she cried again.

" Don't fool yourself. You certainly are not," I said.

I could see the faint yellow shine of that Fever fire on her smooth, thin cheek. I was scared and mad both at the same time.

" I am," she said. " You'll see; so don't let's argue — don't let's —"

And all of a sudden her voice had left her — like it did sometimes that summer; left her entirely and she was whispering.

It scared me always, almost out of my wits.

" God! " I said in an ugly voice.

" You're certainly in fine shape to stay here," I said.

And she — not able to talk back, just made a face at me.

" It's time you went to bed," I said.

And now, when she held back and objected and refused, I just made her.

"Up you go!" I said.

"I don't want to," said Vance.

"Come on, Vance, be decent!" I said to her, and finally she went up and left me there.

I turned and stared out at the old Fever fire, and tried to think.

I tried to think the Fever wasn't going to be much; of how little it was started yet. And how they might be able to hold it down there, as they did in '73, or it might go East as it is headed now. And all I saw was Vance and the faint, faint orange glow of that Fever fire on her face; and her dark wide eyes watching it; and her frailness, and her voice that failed so often that summer since it had come so fierce and hot. And what would happen if the Fever should keep coming on, and coming on to where we were — where she was.

I started to think what would come to me if anything should happen to Vance — if she should stay there and get that Fever. And I couldn't; I wouldn't; I couldn't look it in the face!

So, all nervous, I jumped up and went upstairs. And I tried to read law some, and I couldn't. And I lay down on the bed, all dressed, and tried to think about my law; for it was so hot in there that I didn't believe that I could sleep. But I couldn't think either.

I must have got to sleep finally though — for all at once I woke up with a big start. It seemed to me I heard the tinkle of a bell, of one of our door bells. That it had waked me up.

I sat up and listened; but I didn't hear anything again. And I thought if there was anybody there they'd ring again; or certainly Vance would hear it — she slept so lightly. So finally I thought that I was just dreaming.

I just thought that I was dreaming and got up and undressed myself in that baking room.

"There's one thing, though," I said to myself. "I'd never gone to sleep like that with those windows open, for mosquitoes. They'd have eaten me alive.

"Vance was right," I said to myself, "about that. And I don't know how much cooler it would be either, sleeping under that mosquito bar — with the windows up — than it is now in this great high room, without it."

And after that one night I tried sleeping there without the mosquito bar over the bed. I went around and cleared the room of any mosquitoes that might be in there. And there wasn't but very few. And it was not nearly so bad with that room closed up, as I had at first expected.

It was hot, though, that night and I slept pretty light.

I didn't hear that bell again that night. I heard the usual noises — my Uncle moving late in his big bedroom; a song or call or two in the streets, and the faint tinkle of a street car.

The dogs — the old alley dogs — were hollering across the town again, of course. There was a late moon. I always did hate to hear them — those days; even now I do —"talking death," the niggers call it; on moonlight nights.

But more than anything besides, that night — I remember it even better than that first ring of that little bell — was the sound of wheels upon the street.

CHAPTER VI

ALL night long that sound of wheels never stopped once on the road. I heard them faint and far off, from the hollow paving blocks below on Main Street; and now and then, more occasionally, the rattle and grating of those that went along up our own street; coming slowly up at first, then a little faster, then over the hill, the horses trotting, down the little valley towards the city. They were moving north, most of them — to the depot of the railroads to the north; and from the time of daybreak when I awoke and stayed awake, and lay there listening, that sound of hurrying and restlessness and fear grew and grew to the panic and stampede of that afternoon — when the folks all jammed together at the depots — all trying to get out of town at once.

I saw at breakfast time that my Uncle was no better for any sleep that he had that night. He sat silent through the meal; his hand was unsteady as he drank his coffee, and his right eyelid twitched like it did sometimes after he'd passed a sleepless night. And the brown welts which bad nights raise under the eyes of old folks, showed plainly under his.

We two sat there alone at breakfast, for Vance thought she would rest that morning. And Arabella came in and went out waiting on us.

And about the only time my Uncle spoke at all, was when he looked up and said to Arabella:

" Who was it out there last night bothering the dogs? "

" I dunno, sah; I dunno," said Arabella, all unin-terested.

I looked up at them, reminded for the minute of what I thought I'd heard that night before — of somebody at the door bell.

" Somebody was outside there," my Uncle Athiel said, " and has been there for two or three nights now."

" Yassah, I expect they was. They is quite often — some nigger watchin' and prowlin' in that alley, lookin' over yere," said Arabella.

" You ain't seen him, have you? " said my Uncle Athiel.

" No sah, I ain't seen him," said Arabella. " I ain't seen nobody." And her face kept just smooth and still, like it always was.

My Uncle looked up at her to see if she was lying.

" No, sah," said Arabella, in a kind of meaning way. " I ain't a watchin' or waitin' for sech things no longer. I ain't been watchin' for no thieves — nor money. No sech thing — not now! "

And then, as if she couldn't help herself, that calm, peaceful, sanctified smile of hers opened wide from side to side of that smooth brown face.

" They ain't half so human as a good dog," said my Uncle, staring at her, leaving.

" Some nigger was around. I heard him botherin' the dogs," my Uncle explained to me then.

" I expect so," I said.

They are around, always, nights — like the cats — es-pecially when there's a moon. And then, of course, there was that house of ours that always was attracting them.

That's all we said. My Uncle didn't mention any ring-ing of the bell, and I didn't either. For I was more certain now than ever that it was just a dream — or an impression I had, waking. Maybe I just heard the street car tinkling in the distance. You can't tell what you'll think when you're half asleep.

Then after that we got up, and my Uncle called me out in the yard to harness up again.

" I got to go down town again, after all," he said. " I've got something I've got to clean up. But this is the last day."

We stood out on the old side porch a minute; my Uncle stood there leaning on his cane and watched the people going and called them fools again.

" Fools," he said. " They run out and the thieves and niggers move right in. In two weeks' time there won't be nothing here but nigger thieves."

They were all getting out, all around us — the folks across the street — those folks — the Ventresses — across our yard on the north side. And up the street went that funny old procession of niggers' teams, going hauling trunks to the stations.

" All stirred up; all stirred up," said my Uncle Athiel, " and the scum all coming to the top.

" Come on along," he said. And we started out for the barn and I harnessed up for him. " Lemme tell you somethin'," he said to me, " you're to stay right here today — all day — you understand! "

" Yes, sir," I said.

" Stay right here and keep your eye peeled! You don't know; you can't tell who'll be around here from now on! You don't know who's watching now."

So I said I would. Naturally I had no idea of doing anything else.

That morning I stayed right there. I did my work — what there was to do; read some in my law book; and I looked a whole lot out of my window, and watched the moving on the street.

The procession kept moving and moving all the morning — every old thing that went on wheels was out; all out, carrying the white folks' baggage to the depot. Every rusty old rake of a hack in the place went dashing back and forth, trying to be in two spots at once; and all the niggers, with their little starving rats of horses, perishing with blindness or hip disease, went rambling and rattling with as many trunks as they could stagger to. Everything with wheels was out — wheelbarrows and hand-carts; and I remember one little darkey, traveling down the middle of the street, dragging a great trunk after him with a rope — just drawing it on its casters.

By dinner time, when my Uncle got back, the whole thing was going its wildest, and people were starting for the trains themselves. And there were some folks already — but not so much as later — coming out in our direction from the town, leading dogs and carrying bird-cages in their hands — and some of them bedding; going out from where the Fever was, to find some place out in the suburbs where they could sleep. Like people running from a great fire. They said the sidewalks before the depots were solid full of trunks; and they said when the trains went out they locked the doors of the cars when they were full, and men just broke the windows open and climbed in. And some sat on the engine, and some up on the roofs of the cars — and went out North so.

My Uncle had seen some of it and he was talking more than ever about fools.

" The whole town's upside down; all the crazy fools — the lame and halt and blind, and weak-minded, are up and crawling out of the holes and alleys. And all the niggers in the town standing on the corners looking! "

After dinner, he went back again to town himself; but this time, so he said, it surely would be his last trip there.

"You mind what I tell you," he said, driving out. "You stay right here."

And I said, of course, I would.

I stood watching him, and afterward I went out in front, and watched there.

There certainly were enough queer folks going by. Fear, like my Uncle said, was driving strange things out of the holes and alleys; and everywhere, if you kept your eye out, you saw the niggers watching — standing, watching.

I stood there, looking down the street, from the front of the yard, under one of the little magnolia trees, watching. And right after that, I made my bad mistake, without the slightest purpose and meaning to make it.

I was standing there, only just a little while when I heard the whistle of the doctor, the old cracked Arkansas Traveler tune, coming up the street. And right away I said to myself:

"There's the man. There's the man can tell me about the Fever — about this business of shutting out the Fever nights. Yes, and what we're going to do about Vance."

For I was thinking about her, naturally, all the morning. Especially when I saw she didn't feel like coming down to breakfast again.

The whistling stopped, and I knew the doctor had got into his buggy; and I saw him coming down by us, going down to visit that old lady — that patient of his down the side street.

So I stepped down on the walk and waited for him.

"I want to talk to you," I said. "I've got to talk to you."

"Well, I tell you what you do," he said finally. "I'm going down here a minute. I'll walk the rest of the way, and you get in with Mungo, and he'll drive you down to my house. And by that time, I'll be through here, and he'll come back and get me. How's that?"

I told him that'd be all right. Just like me. I just didn't think — not one thing about leaving the house open. Only one thought in my mind always. I was just thinking about Vance and the Fever. What I was going to do about getting her out.

So, like a fool, I got right in, and drove off with Uncle Mungo, without even telling Vance.

"Yessah, yessah," he said, cramping the wheel to let me in.

"Lots o' travelin' to-day — lots o' travelin'," said Uncle Mungo, making conversation. He was the nicest old darkey that ever lived.

The teams were still going by us up the street.

"Mr. Willy's mighty busy these days," said Uncle Mungo. He called the doctor that always — Mr. Willy. They do that — those old family niggers — call their folks by their old baby names until they die. I expect the doctor was sixty then, if he was a day.

"I expect he is," I said — not thinking much about what he was talking of.

"Does you think we's goin' to have a right smart of this Fever?" he asked me, and I looked up, kind of quick.

"I'm afraid *so*," I said.

"Yessah," said Uncle Mungo, in a kind of dismal voice. "I'm afraid so too. I agree with you. I'm afraid so too."

He was always agreeing with you — the politest nigger you ever saw. An old Virginia house nigger — entirely different kind from the cornfield niggers, and especially those ones around us, down the river in Mississippi and Arkansas. They talked a different kind of language even.

"Mr. Willy'll be powerful busy, I do expect," he said, and sighed. "He'll go right into it. He'll go right where it's the worst."

And after that he sat quiet in his corner of the buggy and didn't say much. But I naturally saw what he was thinking of — about his Mr. Willy. Then he let me out at the house. And I didn't wait very long, though it seemed so. For right away he was back again, and the doctor came bustling into the big old rambling parlor where I was sitting — in that low, old fashioned parlor, with the oil portraits of the Greathouses on the walls — and wanted to know what he could do for me.

I hadn't sat down; I was standing and walking around. I'd got thinking about Vance again.

"Hello. Sit down," he said, spatting me between my shoulders with his great hand.

But I didn't; I simply stood up. "I want to ask you straight," I said, going right at him. "Is it any good for the Fever, to shut down the windows?"

"What windows?" said the doctor.

"Why the windows of the house, naturally," I said.

"Sit down," said the doctor. "Sit down. Stop wearing out my carpet. Sit down, and let's try to find out what you're talking about."

So I sat down and told him about our windows.

"Is it any good?" I said. "Will it do any good?"

"I don't know," he said.

"Don't know!" I said, jumping up. "What are you a doctor for?"

"It might," he said. "Sit down. Sit still. Let me feast my eyes on you in peace."

" Then it *is* the air," I said, and I told him how my
Uncle talked about the poisoned night air.

" That's right," he said. " That's all right. There's
something that carries it in the night air."

" You sure? " I asked.

" Sure, there's nothing surer."

" At midnight? " I asked. " It always comes at midnight? "

" Yes. Nine cases out of ten."

" Just by night? "

" Yes."

" What is it? " I said, looking sharply.

" I don't know," he answered me.

" What are doctors for? " I said. I was pretty bump-
tious then when I got excited.

" I don't know," he said. " You don't expect them to
know much, do you? "

And I looked to see him laugh again and smile, but he
didn't — either.

" Don't they call you an authority on the Yellow
Fever? " I said.

" I don't know," he said. " Do they? You tell me.
All that I know is that I'm not one."

But still I didn't see the faintest fraction of a smile on
him.

" Nor anybody else," he said.

Then he got up on his feet, and started out to walk
himself.

" Lord," he said suddenly. " I wish that I did know.
I wish to God that I could tell you, son! "

He went walking up and down, walking up and down.

I was astonished. I never saw him act so wrought up
before.

" Right there," he said. " Right there! " And

stopped and reached out with his hand. " Right there, just at your finger tips, just always there.

" And when you think you'll reach it, when you're going to close your hand on it," he said; and grabbed with his great hand a handful of empty air, " it slips away. It's gone! You haven't got it. No. It's always out — just out beyond your reach.

" And some day," he said — and stopped in front of me, explaining: " some day there's somebody's going to find it out — blunder on it, get it somehow. That thing, that thing there in the air that none of us can ever reach.

" Good God," he said, letting his great arm drop again. " I'd rather be that man "— he stopped and looked at me again, and I could see the wrinkles come gathering back in the corners of his eyes once more.

" Than George Washington," he said —" or Julius Cæsar — or maybe Cleopatra or Bob Ingersoll! "

And so he passed it off at last, like he did everything else, with a joke.

" This Fever — is it going to be bad this time? " I said, going on after a while, then, " Are you we going to have it very bad? "

" It don't look too good to me," he said, " all running and scattering the way they are — running and stirring it in all through the town — like stirring baking powder in a cake."

. " Well then," I said, back pounding to where I started from; " what do you say about this thing? What do you say about this shutting up of windows nights? Is it any good? "

" It might be," said Dr. Greathouse. He was sitting down again. " And sleeping up in the third story too. There's a lot of the old timers around here will tell you both things.

"It might be," he said, while I was still looking at him, keeping my old quick tongue between my teeth. "It might be, if you could keep 'em shut all the time — every night and all night long — like you could a glass jar. This night air carries it — not a doubt of that. But can you do it? Can you always keep them closed?"

"We could try," I said.

"Yes," said the doctor, and for the minute we stopped.

"Much obliged for telling me," I said. "Thank you! But look here," said I, "what I'm waiting to find out about is this, right here now about ourselves: Is it going to be safe for us to stay that way or is it not? Tell me that."

"Why don't you go?" said Dr. Greathouse, watching me.

"Ask *him*," I said.

"Ask who?"

"Why don't you ask my Uncle Athiel?"

The doctor stopped and thought a second or two.

"I reckon I don't have to," he said — and whistled underneath his breath.

And finally he asked of me: "What does he say about it? How does he act?"

So I told him; and I told him all of it — for I was frank and open with him always; he had been a good friend to me. I told him all about it — the thieves and fire; and the windows and Vance — and all. And all that talk of "Property." And he listened, looking down, drumming with his fingers.

"What has he got there — do you expect?" asked Dr. Greathouse, looking up.

"That Grummit's Bank they talk about," he said prompting me, when I didn't catch him first.

" Oh, I don't know. I never knew. I never thought it was my business to."

" Something," he said, his lips upon his joined first fingers. " There isn't all this talk for nothing."

And then we both sat still; and he was next to speak again.

" No, he won't go," he said, as if the thing was certain in his mind.

" They never do. You never saw one of those old misers," he went along. He always called a spade a spade; and if you didn't like him you could get another doctor. " You never saw one of them you could drive out of the house he's got settled down and fastened in. And the more that the Fever comes, the worse it gets here —"

" The more he will stay right there," I broke in, for I had figured that out myself. " Fire and thieves! " I said.

" Yes," said the doctor. " Fire and thieves. The more the rest go out, the more he'll stay there watching out for fire and thieves. That's reasonable to expect."

" Look here," I said. " He's got to go, if it's going to be as bad as you say it is. He's got to go; and somebody's got to make him. You, for instance. You might do it."

" No," said Dr. Greathouse.

" Yes," I said.

" No," the doctor said, " this thing has got him."

" What thing? " I said.

" Something stronger than you or I," he said —" or he is."

And I told him that I didn't see exactly what he meant.

" You can call it what you want to," said Dr. Greathouse. " A Succubus, maybe — that's what they'd call it once, I reckon."

"A what!" I said. I wasn't very well read then, at twenty-one. I've done the reading that I have done mostly since.

"A Succubus," said Dr. Greathouse, laughing. "A thing that comes and sits down on you, and rides you, and holds you till you die! And kills you finally — sucks out your life from you."

"Another nigger idea," I said, looking.

"No," said the doctor, laughing in his old good na-tured laugh —"some other savages — ourselves, a few generations back."

And I was ashamed of myself, when he said it, I remem-ber, for not knowing. I was afraid of him, anyhow, a little, when he got talking that way. He was a very highly educated man, and I knew it. And I was a good deal of an ignoramus myself. And I knew that too. So I didn't say much then — just sat still.

"But they're real enough," the doctor went along. "I've seen 'em by the hundred. We most all of us get one as we grow older — that holds us down, and feeds on us, and kills us finally."

"You're getting in too deep for me," I said.

"That gets you, and holds you," said the doctor, "Like your Uncle held here, for example. You don't see anything that's holding him here, do you? Noth-ing you can touch with your bare hand?"

"No," I told him.

"And yet, wild horses couldn't drive him out of there," he said —"when everybody knows he ought to go!"

"No," I said —"not if you mean it in that way."

"I do," said Dr. Greathouse. "I certainly do. I mean a Succubus. I scarcely ever go into a house, where I don't see one feeding."

"Ah-hah!" I said. "I don't take much stock myself,

in these invisible things you can't take up and handle in your hands."

He got up then, all of a sudden, from his chair — so quick that he startled me.　He was that way sometimes — very unexpected.

"You're right," he said.　"You're right, son.　Here I'm going around traveling in my mind again.　And you just waiting naturally to find out what to do!"

"That's it," I said.

"I'm tired, I expect — worn out and useless," the doctor said, apologizing.　"Old and tired and useless.

"But that'll do; that'll be all!" he said — sweeping his hand across his eyes.　"From now on let's talk sense, like real men do.

"He'll stay!" said Dr. Greathouse, briskly then. "Your Uncle won't get away.　We can count on that much anyhow."

"Yes," I said.

"I expect we'll count on that," he said again.　"And you?" he turned and asked me.　"Will you be going?"

"Well — I don't love him very much," I said.

"No, I expect you don't," the doctor said.

"But nobody is ever going to say about me," I said, "that I quit him.　No.　I'd stay, I expect, if the devil himself were staying there — if he was as old and feeble as he is now — in that great house alone.　I won't have folks saying about me —"

"No," said the doctor, and grinned.　"No, I don't expect you would," the doctor said at last — and grinned.

"What are you grinning at?" I asked him.

"Nothing," he said, "I was just wondering what holds *you* here.　Nothing you can see or touch with your bare hand."

"Damn *me*," I said, thinking all the time of Vance.

"But the little girl," he said, talking to himself, "maybe we could get her out."

"We've got to, that's certain," I said.

"We will," the doctor said. "We'll do it — if there's nothing ties her here too."

He made me nervous, harping on that thing — that idea of his, about being tied there.

"I'll come to-morrow," he said then, "and see what I can do to get her out."

"She oughtn't be here," I said, "had she?"

"Nothing could be worse," he said.

"I'll go and see your Uncle about her," said the doctor. "I'll find some excuse. I'll tell him I'm advising all my patients to get out. I am too," he said.

So I shook his hand half off, and I came away — not thinking then how long I'd been there.

"You keep your fingers off, you young hot-head," said the doctor, "till I see the old man. Till I can see him anyway."

So I hurried back — remembering, all at once, when I got headed home! I knew then, when I thought, that I oughtn't to have come there in the first place. But I was bound to go anyhow, I expect; bound to know what that doctor had to tell me.

I ran up the steps in the yard from the street; and up into the side door. And there in the hall — just coming down from upstairs, was my Uncle Athiel.

There was my Uncle Athiel coming toward me. And he was panting, and his collar was just melted and run down his neck; and his eyes down to no bigger than a pencil point — shining like a snake's eyes underneath his yellow lids.

"By the great right handed Son of God," he said loud and strong — and stopped to look at me.

" You certainly are a good and faithful servant! " he went on, in a little mincing, sneering voice.

And turned his back on me and walked away as if I wasn't fit to look at.

What had happened? I didn't know. I could only guess and fear it. And I followed him around afterward, trying to find out.

" What have I done? " I asked. " If I've done anything that I can change, it's your duty to let me know."

But he wouldn't say a word about it.

I wasn't sure that anything had happened.

All I saw that night was that we were being held there, by this thing that was holding him, day after day, while that Yellow Fever came crawling up to us from the city.

BOOK III

THE SECRET ROOMS

CHAPTER VII

IF anybody'd come to me that night and said:
"What's this thing like you're so afraid of?" I expect I couldn't quite told him. It lay over there —
that Fever — over there, in the city, out of sight. I'd
never seen it in all my life. All that I'd ever seen were
those fires at night, and the hurrying and the faces of
the folks who were running away. All I felt, I expect,
was the fear of the fear I saw in other faces. But that
next morning I had a different idea.

They tried to tell us still that they had the Fever
checked; that it was going east, if anywhere — and then
only very slowly; and that there was nothing for us to be
afraid of at all. But I never believed them after that
third day; I never had the slightest comfort or confidence.
For it was that next morning that the Dead Wagon went
by us for the first time.

It was another clear, hot morning — yellow and green
— the yellow early sun, and green shadows beneath the
trees, and that old brown, soft-coal smoke from the
kitchen chimneys floating in the air between them. I was
up a little early. And so I stepped out on the porch to
get a mouthful of cool, morning moisture, before that
old hot sun had drunk it all away.

And there, ahead of me, was Arabella, upon the side
porch, making little dabs with her broom, looking

93

down the street. I heard the clack of an axle, I looked down and I saw the Dead Wagon come crawling up over the hill.

It was nothing much to look at. Nothing but a common old furniture wagon, drawn by two mules, two fine, fat, sleepy mules; sleek and lazy, and all fixed up with those old cow-tails those old-time niggers used to put on their harnesses.

They dragged up slowly, their ears wagging back and forth to their walking. And on the seat above them sat that nigger we heard so much of afterwards — that " Make-Haste Mose " that hurried so with the dead.

There were only two coffins on that first morning — two yellow pine coffins side by side in the furniture wagon. Two paupers, going down to the Potter's Field, way out south of town.

Arabella and I stood watching them come by. The negro Mose sat up there, lounging in his seat, eating a piece of cold bacon and corn bread, it looked like, for breakfast.

It was all common looking enough. They went by like any old furniture wagon; and the coffins were pretty well out of sight in the wagon. But I stood and stared like a man in a trance. But it was for that reason, I believe, that I noticed that first time those little black spots — those little black shiny spots, that spattered on the pavement of the roadway underneath the wagon.

The wind was away from me, thank God. There was only one single puff of that monstrous odor.

But then I looked again, and saw, shining in the sun — the first time that I ever saw them — that little golden trail of flies. The sun was quite low still; and there was still some moisture in the air; and the yellow sunlight touched their wings. You saw, when it came back of them, this little golden swarm, that danced, and played, and shifted places as it followed in behind the wagon.

"God," I said, when I caught the meaning of it. "Those flies."

I thought that I was talking to myself. But I couldn't have been. I must have spoken it out loud, for:

"Yassah," said Arabella right away.

My eyes turned toward her, like they would to any human creature in a time like that — I believe — for company.

She stood there, looking — studying.

"Yassah," she said, in her soft, peaceful voice. "Them's green flies!"

I looked toward them, and back into her smooth, brown face. She stood there, looking off then; looking off, like she saw something you couldn't see off there.

"Them's green flies — old green flies. Just the same's He sent down on them ol' 'Gyptians — for signs and warnings."

I watched into those big brown eyes of hers — and something, all of a sudden, seemed to take hold of her. She smiled, like she had done before; but, more — more kind of radiant and rapturous, like something had been suddenly lighted up inside of her.

"Signs and mysteries," she said, looking out behind me. "Signs and mysteries!" she said again, in an old shaky voice.

And I didn't say a word — watching where it would carry her.

"Watch out!" she said —"watch out. Ev'ybody. Watch out! Signs and myst'ries, comin' now! Comin' — like they come down on them ol' 'Gyptians!"

Then all at once she raised her eyes, and the smile stopped where it was; and she shut up. I looked back behind her, and there was Vance — there on the threshold back of me, looking toward the street. The old Dead Wagon was just disappearing around the house. I hoped she didn't see it. I'd given anything rather than have her to.

"Arabella," said Vance. "You better be getting breakfast on the table."

"Yas'am," said Arabella, and went along in.

"You can't get any work out of her these days," said Vance.

"I reckon not," I said, smiling.

"She just stands looking. What was she looking at just now?" asked Vance. "What was she talking about?"

And I told her finally.

"What is it she's continually staring and looking out the window for?" I asked her.

"It's that woman — that negro woman from Arkansas who was prophesying the destruction of Memphis here last winter," Vance explained.

I hadn't heard of it — not to understand it.

"Oh, yes," said Vance, "didn't you hear about that woman from up over there in Arkansas, who was foretelling that this year was the year Memphis was going to be destroyed and swallowed up in the ground?"

I hadn't heard it, but I understood. Once in so often one of these religious niggers — a woman generally — gets started out prophesying that the earth or the city is going to be destroyed. They go around on street corners, and on the church steps, and sometimes in the churches themselves — some of them.

And most generally it starts up a great to-do and excitement among the niggers — or in a part of them anyhow. You can say what you want to, about the niggers, but they're a mighty religious race. The only thing is that what they believe — the ordinary run of them — is so mighty strange and different from other folks. They won't ever tell about it much, if they can help it — only fool you. But sometimes, when you get one right, you can get him to tell you some things they really do believe, way down under.

They believe, every one of them, they're God's people, just like the old Jews. And they believe, in a kind of way, that the Old Bible is talking about them when it talks about the Jews. And King Solomon was a black man. They'll show you that right there in the Bible. And some of them, I know for certain, say Christ was black; and I believe — yes, I know — there's plenty of them think that God is black — a big black God, watching specially after His black people, and punishing their enemies and oppressors.

And every now and then, there's one of them, like I say, gets up and prophesies — a woman generally. And a big cloud's coming up, and the winds will blow and the trumpets. And the black angels will rise out of the ground, and the sinful city will be destroyed; or the old sinful world will come to an end — and the great black God will sort out the wicked and righteous forever. For Heaven's right there, they think, right over your head — a lot nearer than Texas is on the railroad train. And any time that black hand's liable to reach out of a thunder cloud — up over you — and close up heaven and earth together, like a fan.

" But why should she smile about it, Vance? " I asked.

" Why, don't you see? " she said. " They aren't going to suffer — those ones like Arabella. They aren't going to die. They're sanctified. They're just going to be translated right up to Heaven. Drawn up by white horses — this last woman says. They're going to be saved forever.

"And St. Michael," said Vance, "will stand upon the custom house, and Gabriel on the levee and blow their horns. And the city of Memphis will sink into the ground and will be swallowed up and destroyed."

"Is that true?" I asked. "Did she say that?"

"Yes, perfectly," said Vance. "That's what she said."

And so at last, that third day of the Fever I got to understand what it was the negress stood and watched to see coming up over our hillside from the city. Death for us, but not for her. For her, white garments, and sitting at the Right Hand forevermore.

And so after that, we went into breakfast and sat down with my Uncle Hagar.

I looked to see my Uncle ugly, after what I had done — whatever I had done that day before. He was that. But he was more than that. Generally he would not have spoken to me until he got good and ready, but when he did speak, he would be straight and ugly and downright. Now he seemed to me, that very first morning, to be different — to have changed. That day, and those days afterward, he went around with his head down. There wasn't a word out of him — to me, at any rate. He wouldn't look up or speak to me unless he had to, for something he had got to have done. He just seemed to avoid me entirely.

He didn't go off of the premises any more — none of us did that now; and only very little out of doors. From that time on he was in the house, principally; and nearly always in the Purple Room — shut up in that great Purple Room where he slept, and in the little anteroom to it, which he had made into a kind of office where he could keep his accounts.

After breakfast that morning, right away he disappeared there; and it was only after knocking several times that I got him down to see Dr. Greathouse, when he came to call on him, like he told me he would. And finally my Uncle did poke his head out of the door, and ask what it was. And I got him finally to go downstairs.

Just what the doctor said to him, I don't know. For they went in together to Mr. Bozro's old study, at the back of the side hall, and shut the door. I expect he told him, like he told me that he would, the day before — just before I left him — that he was going around telling all his patients they would better get out of town if they were able to; and that Vance ought to go anyhow, Fever or no Fever. And certainly, now, that the Fever had come.

They came out of there after a while, and my Uncle had agreed then that Vance should go. I could tell, both by the way they talked, and by what the doctor was saying to him coming out.

" You'd better all go. You'd better go yourself," he said.

" Go," said my Uncle. " Go! That's easy said."

" I want to tell you something," he said, moving near him, in a kind of secret way. " I've got to stay here. I've got to save what little property I've got left. I'm ruined near enough the way it is."

" Better ruined than buried," the doctor said.

" I don't know about that," said my Uncle, looking him in the face. " I don't know. It ain't so different."

He watched after the doctor, as he rolled away out of the yard, whistling again, of course — but kind of softly — and got into his buggy beside of old Mungo.

And then my Uncle went upstairs again, and I didn't see him out of his room all morning.

All the afternoon it was the same; he kept out of sight in his own room. Vance was in her room resting. And I was up in mine, trying to read my law, and not succeeding. Lord, how hot those long summer afternoons were that we had then! Long enough any time in that country — with the old white sun on the streets; and the river glittering under it, white as the shine of a new tin pan; and those old locusts groaning and rasping in the magnolias; and even the birds in the trees gaping from the heat. You can't work, you can't read, and you can't rest. You just sit there. And that time, when we sat there waiting and watching for the Fever, strange ideas got simmering in your head. They were no good to you; only harm. You knew that. But on they went, just the same; you couldn't stop them.

I got thinking about that old Dead Wagon, and its wake of golden flies; of this invisible poison, that filled the air every night around us — and wondering how far it had got now. And of Vance, and of how tired she looked, and when my Uncle was going to send her away, and whether she would go when he told her to.

That afternoon he didn't speak, nor at supper time; and it was evening again, and the windows closed; and Vance and I in the sitting room — before he walked in and told us she had got to go.

She was standing by the window again — looking out — like we did all those evenings after that, toward the city. She just laughed at him when he told her.

" I want you to go," he said. " And the doctor does. He says you've got to go."

But his voice wasn't very determined talking to her.

" What do I care what the doctor says," said Vance, and I looked at her sharp and mad.

" I believe you ought to," said my Uncle, but kind of indifferent, like he was repeating something he had been told to.

" You aren't going, are you? " Vance asked him.

" No," he said. " I can't go."

" And you haven't changed your mind, either, have you? You think you're safe still if you stay here and close up the windows nights? "

" I know I am," said my Uncle Hagar, talking up louder and more positive, like he did naturally.

" Then why should I go? I'll stay and see you keep your windows shut," said Vance, and laughed a little, and turned, looking down again.

That night there were two or three fever fires again, whose reflections we could see from the window. And one of them, which came up while we stood there — especially bright. It was down underneath, lower than we were. We couldn't see the fire itself, only the reflection of it on the face and cornice of a brick block opposite it. An orange flame, that rose and fell, and shifted the black shadows on the rosy brick. It was newly lighted — just lighted bright and fresh.

" What's that! " said my Uncle Athiel — in a bigger voice — going over close beside Vance.

He stood watching it.

" That's nearer! " he said, sharply. " That's nearer! "

He was right. It was nearer — nearest of any yet. The light, upon their faces and the window, shone quite distinctly now — the light from that reflection, when two nights before, from up the street, it was just barely noticeable on Vance's cheek.

The Fever, I saw it, with a jump at my heart, was no longer going east. It was turning south now, toward us.

" See that ! " my Uncle cried out, watching. " See that ! The fools — they'll have the town afire yet. They'll burn up all the property in it."

And right away he turned and started straight up stairs, the idea of getting Vance to go clean gone out of his mind.

We two stood there, and saw that orange light rise and fall on the face of the old block — fading dimmer now, than when it was just set. And you could see in your mind's eye, down in the street which was hidden out of real eyesight — the dead person whose clothes were burning — there in his house; and the fresh coffin at the door; and the nurse maybe, leaving the empty house, where the other folks had all gone away. And Make-Haste Mose hurrying up in there to take charge.

" And now," I said to myself, " it certainly is turning down this way."

I shivered. I couldn't help it; and especially when I could see plain almost as the shine of the moon that orange light before me on a cross frame of the window; and across Vance's thin cheek again.

" What is this foolishness? " I said. " You're goin', like the doctor said you would." My voice sounded high and sharp, even to myself.

" No, I'm not," said Vance.

" The doctor said so ! " I said again.

" What do I care about the doctor," said she. " What does he know about it any more than anybody else? "

" What do you mean? " I asked, astonished. I never did understand women anyhow. And I don't believe I ever shall.

"What do you mean?   Only two days ago you said the doctors knew all there was about it — especially these doctors here in Memphis, and now you say —"

"I believe my father knows," said Vance.   "I believe he wouldn't say that about closing up the house, staying here, unless he was sure that it was safe."

"What does he know about it?" I said.

"Don't let's talk about it any more," said Vance.   And her voice began to sound tired again.

I looked at her — that slender thing; that frail creature.   You could take her in your hands, and break her into pieces.   You could, but you wouldn't.   That's the thing that drives me mad — with women.   She could stand and defy you forever — indefinitely — laugh at you.   Not because she was strong — but just because she was weak.   Her weakness was the weapon that she beat you with.   I looked at her and listened to her foolishness — and I was so mad I almost cried.   Just helpless mad.

"I'll carry you away if I have to," I said.   "I'll take you away by force."

"Don't be silly," said Vance, laughing in my face.   "What could you do?   I could come right back."

"You'd come right back," I said.   "You'd — Oh, you drive me crazy.   Haven't you any sense?"

"Just as much as you have," said Vance.   "And just as good a reason why I should stay."

And I said, naturally, I didn't see it.

"Do you think I'd go before my father went?" she said.   "Do you think I could?"

"All right, then," I replied, talking wild like a boy does.   "He's got to go; then he's got to go too!   I'll see to that myself.   I'll make him go."

"Beavis," said Vance, "why have you always got to tear the house down?   Why don't you have some reason

about you? Don't you know we never can get him away,
if you start at him like that? Don't you know you'll
spoil everything? " Her voice rose while she was talking, and her big eyes looked me through — sharp like her
father's.

"Spoil everything! " I said, confused again. "Spoil
everything! But you don't want to go," I said to her.

"Who said I didn't? " said Vance.

"You did," I said, " just now. You said you wouldn't.
It was perfectly safe here."

"No, I never said anything of the kind, never," said
Vance. And I stood staring at her.

"If you didn't just say that," I said, " I'll —"

"Oh, don't let's argue. It just tires me," said Vance.
" That's all."

I saw she was right. I saw her voice was getting
huskier and tireder. I knew I had to stop. There was
nothing else for me to do but to stop — beaten by her
weakness.

Just stop standing there, four times stronger than she
was, helpless. So mad that I could have just jumped up
and down!

There was this, though, in what she said. It would be
the worst kind of foolishness for me to try and get my
Uncle Hagar to do anything — the way he felt and acted
toward me that day. It would just hinder what I wanted,
instead of helping it.

And we stayed there, saying nothing, standing by the
window.

And as we did, we both of us turned suddenly, listening,
for we heard my Uncle unlocking and opening his door to
the Purple Room again; and coming out into the hall.
We stood and listened. And he unlocked another door.
We heard his feet upon the staircase.

"He's going up into the third floor," said Vance —
and still we heard him going — and still another door being opened, and his feet on other stairs.

"He's gone up into the tower," said Vance, excitedly.

"Did you ever know him to go there before?" I asked,
listening.

"Never, I believe. Never. Not till yesterday," said
Vance. "Not till yesterday — just before you came in."

"You know those stories?"

"Yes, I know them," said Vance, her eyes shifting off
from mine, so I saw she didn't want to talk of it.

"I want to ask you something," she asked me, after
waiting. "Did he seem to you to act different to-day?"

"How did he seem to you?" I asked her back.

"Suspicious, kind of. Always keeping off and avoid-
ing me."

"Did he act that way to you, too?" I said, surprised.

For I'd thought that it was only toward me that he
acted so.

"Yes," said Vance, "I can't do a thing with him —
not now. He won't even look at me."

CHAPTER VIII

THE TOWER

I NEVER see one of those old vacant towers on top of a private house, but I start thinking of my Uncle Athiel in that tower of his during the Yellow Fever time.

What do they build them for — those towers, do you know? Nobody ever uses them. They just stand there, always empty, always useless — a kind of summer house for spiders; spiders and dust, and now and then a crazy fly upon the windows. In all my life I never knew of one used so much, or to so much purpose as my Uncle Athiel used that one of his during those next few days.

I could hear him moving, faintly, there above me — for he seemed to have left the doors open after him — till late that night; until I went to sleep. And I lay there for a long time wondering.

The first thing that flashed into my mind, naturally, from the time I first heard his steps on the stairs, was Grummit's Tower — that old foolish story that the niggers and children had told each other for so long; that there in that old tower my Uncle kept his money. I had never taken any stock in that story. It always seemed ridiculous to me on the face of it. I had never known the man to go there once before in my whole time with him.

And yet it was strange, I had to say myself, that

now, the very first thing, at the first shock of panic, he should right away bolt up there. I was puzzled; more than puzzled, disturbed and worried. My mind clung to the thing like a drowning sailor to a board — trying to understand it. But I was mighty sleepy that night, too. I would go so far, clutching at it, then drowse; then lose it; then, snap! I'd go, jumping nervously awake, and my mind would start circling round again.

Vance had never heard him there either, I said to myself, trying to let it go — almost sleeping.

And then, I'd hear, almost as plain as if they stood over me, the voices of those little ragamuffins standing on the walk in front of the house, and saying, like I'd heard them say that time, " There's where he counts it! There's where he counts it! "

" How silly," I said to myself, " children's and niggers' talk." But, of course, he might have had it there all the time — Of course —

Snap! I twitched awake again. I drowsed and woke, and drowsed again until finally, as it always does in the longest night, sleep got me — I passed into a stiff and uneasy sleep. I heard the faint voices from outside — the dogs barking, those old howling alley dogs across the town. But they were a long, long way off — calls in the distance, echoing, echoing, out across the town; and then I got asleep.

Vance told me that next day that my Uncle Hagar stayed up there in that tower until almost morning.

" Is there any light up there? " I asked her — for I had been thinking about that.

" No," she said.

" He was just sitting up there in the dark? "

" There was a moon," said Vance, " part of the time."

" Wasn't he sleeping there, maybe? "

" No, he was moving around all night."

" Then what, what —" I started saying.

" I don't know," said Vance.   " Maybe he won't do it again."

I looked at her.   But I got no information from her face.

" The thing is now," she said; " he must have sleep. For nights now he has been without it."

I saw that too.   He couldn't have slept more than three or four hours since that first night the Fever came.   He had been up all hours of the night.

And I saw too from her face how worried and anxious Vance was over it.

" Keep away from him," said Vance, " and I'll see if I can get him to take a nap."

There was sense in that.   She was the only one who had any little influence over him, and he certainly needed it.   His face was dry and old and worn for sleep.   He must have felt the need of it himself badly.   For after a while Vance went up to the Purple Room — where he still kept himself, and knocked, and got him to promise to lie down.   He did too; and slept right through dinner-time, and Vance let him sleep.

" I did sleep," he said to Vance, when he woke up in the afternoon, " I did sleep —" as if the fact surprised him.

But that evening, as the dark came on, and the windows of the house went down again, he was shut up in the tower once more — just the same.

" There he goes," I said to Vance, listening to him go.

" Yes," said Vance.

" What is he there for?   Have you any more idea? "

" Not the slightest."

" Why don't you ask him? "

" I did," said Vance. And when I asked her what he had to say:

" He just looked at me," said Vance, " looked at me and walked away." And we both of us sat silent for a while after that.

" I don't like it. I don't like the way he acts," said Vance. " He acts like he is suspicious and afraid of everybody."

" Yes," I said.

" If I could only get him to pay attention to me," she said. " To look at me like he usually does. But he won't. He won't even look at me."

" No," I said — but my mind was going in a different direction.

" Is there something there," I said. " Do you think there is anything there — in that tower? "

For I knew that she must be thinking some, anyway, of about what I was — that thing that everybody thought about — that gave the house we lived in its name.

" No, I don't think so."

" Why not? " I said.

" I never did think there was anything *there*," she said, hesitating. And I thought then I could hear plainly the emphasis on that last word.

But I did not press her about it then. I didn't want to, if she didn't want to talk about it. And so, after a while, it was bedtime, and Vance went upstairs and left me there in the sitting room thinking.

There was another day gone, and no change for us. The reports from the Fever had not been bad; they said there were not so many new cases that day; and if it was coming south in our direction, there were no signs of it — except that one man who had died where that fire was that we saw the night before. But they didn't fool me one particle — I knew better.   I knew they were making everything as small and easy as they could, and that you couldn't believe a word they said.   The Fever was coming, and we were held there by my Uncle, and he was held tighter than ever by that house of his, and whatever he had in it.

And up to that time, I hadn't known much about my Uncle's money affairs, I hadn't considered it any of my business.   I knew that they were queer.   I knew that everybody talked about him as a great old miser.   But now I thought I had to know and understand, especially if I was going to get Vance away like I intended to — just what it was that was holding him; and whether, as Vance seemed to think, we could ever hope to get him away.

I didn't think we could, for I did believe to some extent that he was just what they said he was, a miser. And I knew then, just as well as I do now, that nobody ever gets one of those old misers out of the house they got used to making their hidings in — not till you drag their souls from their bodies; and it makes no difference how much they have got there — whether it's much or little, they get fastened to their house like an oyster to its shell.   Or at least that's been my experience, and I have seen a number of them.

And so I sat thinking it all over — about what I had seen since I'd been there — all those queer and unusual actions of my Uncle about his house.   His rule against niggers on the place, all but that sanctified Arabella; his orders that she should be kept out from upstairs and the front of the house all that was possible; his closing up and locking up the Purple Room, all but that short time that Vance took charge of it in the morning.   And now, this summer especially, since the Fever came, his jumpy fear of thieves and fire; and his closing of the whole house; and, last of all, these queer visits to that tower.

And when I got thinking over that all, the words of Vance came back to me, and I thought again, that, though she said she did not believe there was anything in that tower, she had almost said that she did know that there was, somewhere in the house, a store of money, large or small, which my Uncle Athiel was keeping guard over.

" If anybody could know," I said to myself, " besides him, she would."

And then I went up to bed. And I knew that then and long after, my Uncle Hagar was in his tower. And he stayed there, I learned from Vance next day, practically all that night again.

It was Saturday that next day, and just as hot as ever. There was nothing much unusual in the morning — except that Dead Wagon going by again. There was something wrong, as usual, with the paving down on Main Street. And from that on, that wagon came around by us over that hill. The coffins were growing more on it, I saw. That morning there were four.

Then, that afternoon, right after dinner, my Uncle was in the tower again — in the daytime, in the middle of the day!

You have no idea how hot it was in that place summers. The white hot sun beat down upon that gray slate on the roof; and streamed in those little bullseye windows until the pitch in the floor boards sweat right out. But into that old oven my Uncle went and closed the door after him. Maybe he had the windows open. I expect he did, but mighty little good that did.

Vance heard him going without a word. Fifteen minutes passed, half an hour, and still I heard that he didn't come down again. And finally Vance came out of the sitting room where she had been reading and listening, and started upstairs without a word, clenching and unclenching her hands. I started after her to the second story, and saw her go up from there to the third, and stand by the door to the stairs to the tower. I saw her try the door, and it was locked.

Then she called to him:

" Dad, Dad," she said to him, " what are you doing there? "

There was no answer whatever — not a word.

And then she beat upon the door and called again.

And again for quite a while he didn't answer. Then there was something — I didn't hear.

" Come down," she called again. " You'll die up there! "

" What are you doing —" the voice of my Uncle came through the door. " What are you doing following me around! "

" It will kill you," she said; " you can't stand it."

But she knew, I believe, she couldn't move him.

" Go away! " he answered. " Go away — I'll come down when I'm through."

" Through what? " I said to myself.

" Was he mad at you? " I asked her, when she came down to where I was, breathless, for the third story was almost as hot as the tower.

" Yes," she said.

" His voice sounded so," I said.

" What will we do? " said Vance sharply. " He can't stay there."

" Let's wait a little while," said I, and very soon afterwards he did come down into his room upstairs on the second floor, and stayed there the rest of the afternoon.

And now it seemed to me the time had come to talk with Vance about what she knew; about these ties which bound my Uncle Hagar, and with him us two as well, to the house; and what, if anything, it had to do with these queer actions of his in the tower.

"Through what?" I said to Vance. "What is there for him to be through with up there?"

"I don't know, I can't imagine," she said.

"He isn't crazy?" I said. "His mind isn't touched?"

For in spite of what the doctor said that idea had got going in my mind.

"No," said Vance promptly. "He's up there for some purpose."

"What is it?"

"I thought at first," she said, "he might be up there watching those fires. You know that first night there was that Fever fire."

"But you don't think so now?"

"No," she said slowly. "You know before that — that evening you were out, he was up there too — the first time!"

"Yes."

"There weren't any fires then — there wasn't anything to remind him of fires then."

"Well, then," I said, when she stopped, "what?"

"I don't know," she said.

"Is it his money, like they say?" I blurted out.

"No, I don't think so," said Vance, kind of faintly.

"There might be," I said, "some reason back of all those stories about the tower."

"I don't think so; I don't think there is any money *there*."

And again she seemed to tell me that there might be money somewhere else.

"Is there any money anywhere?" I asked straight out of her.

"Yes," said Vance slowly. "Yes."

"Is there a lot?" I went ahead and asked.

"Yes," she said slowly, "I think there is a great lot."

"I never asked you before," I said, excusing myself.

"I know —" said Vance.

"I wouldn't now," I said, "if —"

"I understand," Vance said. "But it isn't there in that tower."

"Where is it?" I asked.

"In the Purple Room," she said, "somewhere in that room he sleeps in, I believe."

"How do you know?" I said.

"I saw it once," said Vance. "I saw him with it one night. The door blew open."

"Paper money?" I asked.

"Greenbacks," said Vance.

"That's all the time you ever saw it?" I asked.

"That's all," she said.

"And yet," I said, "he might have taken it up there to that tower just lately — since the Fever."

"It isn't locked," said Vance. "It wasn't till to-day — the door was open after him."

I remembered that she was right. I had noticed that too. That seemed to settle the idea that he had money there.

"Then what —" I asked her.

"I wish I knew," said Vance, "for it is something on his mind eating him up."

And again, for the first time in a day or two, I saw that almost invisible shudder pass over her, that I had noticed that first day or two that she spoke to me about that dream she had; that came to her when she spoke about her father.

What was it that took him to the tower? — I didn't

know. It must be something, even if his mind was going, like I sometimes thought. It would be something, some idea that would take him there. What that might be I did not know yet, but I did know now that, what they had all thought and said about him was true; that he really was a miser. Somewhere in that house, in that old Purple Room, my Uncle Athiel sat and watched his hoard of money, large or small, whichever it might be.

I had never been in the Purple Room — only seen it, passing, through its open door; but I knew in general how it looked and lay — with its high ceiling and glass chandelier, and the fringed purple hangings at the windows, the fringed purple canopy over the bed, bearing the letter "B" in gold, surrounded by laurel leaves, in gold too, like some bedroom in France, some bedroom that Napoleon built, they said. And a long purple bell rope, with deep fringes, beside it. And the gilt bands on the dark furniture.

And in all that showy expensiveness that little old yellow man, common as an old shoe, lay like an emperor. And always at the head of his bed, under where that purple bell-rope hung down, stood his smooth, old yellow hickory cane; and under his pillow was that funny little Derringer that years ago he had shot a man with — in those first years when he first came, a boy, into that Mississippi River country.

I went over the thing backwards and forwards; and after I had done that about a hundred times I made up my mind to what I was going to do. He and I were going to stay there, that looked certain; and if Vance was going, it was time she went.

And I figured then, knowing now for certain what was on his mind, in general, that I'd play for all I could on what would excite him and interest him the most — that need of watching and guarding over his " Property " he was always telling about. It would be an even swap. If he would save Vance for me, and send her away, I would save his old " Property " for him, or do the best I knew how.

I was afraid I wouldn't get hold of him that day. I had nothing but sullen side looks out of him since that row of ours two days before. He kept out of my way. But finally, at the end of the evening, when I had given up, by luck I caught him.

Vance had gone upstairs a little early; the weather was still tiring her. I sat alone in the sitting room for a while, when I heard my Uncle coming down the stairs. He went into the Crystal Room across the hall first, and I knew he was looking for a second time, to see that the house was all locked up. Then finally he came into the sitting room where I was.

He started by me with his head down, walking toward the windows.

I got up.

" You and I ain't been getting on very well lately," I said to him.

He didn't say anything.

" It was my fault," I said. " If you want me to say so — I apologize."

And still he said nothing at all, and started to go along to the windows again.

" I want to talk to you," I said, my voice rising.

" I don't want to talk to you," he said, giving me a crooked look.

" I don't care whether you do or not," I said, my voice rising some more — and then dropping — when I thought. " You're going to; and you'll want to, when you hear me."

He raised up his head then, and stood and looked at me, and I looked at him.

" I want to make you an offer," I said.

" What is it? " he said at last.

" The police are mostly gone out of this town now," I said, " and the firemen. About all they've got now is those nigger militia companies."

I saw from his eye that I had reached him.

" And the time may come," I said, " you will need some help here. You might need me — even."

" You can go any time you want to " said my Uncle Athiel in a dead voice.

I took hold of myself and held myself back.

" All right," I said, " but I'll make you my offer first."

He didn't say anything.

" This town is full of thieves," I said, using his own words. And I could see him move a little in spite of himself.

" Well," he said finally, " what of it? What have you got to say to me? "

" Just this — that's all," I said. " You send Vance away, like the doctor says to. Don't ask her; make her go."

He stood looking out the window. " Ah ha," he said — " Well? "

" Well! " I said. " And when you do that, you can keep me and use me for your nigger, and no questions asked. And there'll nobody get at your old ' Property,' not while I'm alive."

He kept looking out the window.

" Let me tell you something," I said, aiming at that old fear of his —" when this town is all closed out and nothing but niggers loose here, and thieves — you may need another man."

" You're a good man," said my Uncle Athiel, sneering. " What do you think you could do? "

" Try me! " I said.

He grunted.

" You try me! " I said a second time.

" What could you do? " he asked again.   But he was looking at me now, not out the window.

" Do! " I said — I was afraid I would lose him.   " I'll show you! "

" What would you do if I sent Vance away? " he said.

" Do —" I said, getting red in the face and choking a little.

He stood there, waiting — looking up at me.

" Do —" I said, " I'd swim Hell for you — if you asked me to!   Provided —" I said, " you send Vance away right now."

And he turned then, and gave me another look — with a quick, little black twinkle in his eyes, and it was the one friendly look I had had from him in two or three days.

" She'll go," he said, right away.   And so we stopped talking.

" You keeping your windows closed down tight always? " he asked me finally.

" When I promise to do a thing, I generally do it," I said.

And we said very little more before we went upstairs.

I went upstairs and started walking back and forth, in that bedroom of mine — that big old Red Room, with the windows closed.   I was a little excited.   It was hot, fearful.   But we were getting used to it now.

I threw myself down on the bed finally, and went to sleep.

I fell asleep, and then I woke up all of a sudden; I didn't know for a minute what waked me.

It seemed as if there were a lot of strange noises that night. There were too, some of those first nights of the Fever.

I could hear my Uncle moving in his room — come down from the tower apparently. I got up stiffly and finished my undressing and got in the bed again.

Then I thought I heard some one fire a gun once. And by and by, as my mind cleared up from sleep, I understood that. It was probably some one firing a gun in the cellar to kill the Fever. They did that the first part of the time — some. There were some folks who thought it killed the Fever poison that formed in that old cellar air — where they had cellars — nights.

And then, of course, the dogs outside got started barking — then, and several other times that night. I got out once and watched out the window, but I couldn't see a thing.

After that, over north of us the Ventress's cow was mooing and calling to be milked. Their niggers had gone away and left it, again, that night.

I was back in bed again — my sleepy feeling pretty well gone now.

And then, all at once, I started and sat up listening, for I heard again, real distinctly this time, the tinkle of that little bell I heard before. It was in the house, it still seemed to me. It must have been.

And it certainly sounded like one of the door bells, to the front or side door — one of those little bells jingling on their wires in the cellar way.

And I said to myself again: "Is it possible that somebody is out there fumbling around those doors?"

The side door was almost right under my window.

There was nobody there — I could have seen them, but there might be somebody in front.

I opened my door softly, and crawled out into the front hall, and I sneaked up, and stood by the window in the front of it. My Uncle wouldn't hear me — he was too deaf. I stood there a while.

There was a porch over the door, but I could certainly see anybody, if they went away, or certainly hear them on the porch flooring. But so far as I could see or hear, there wasn't anybody there, and I came back to my room at last certain of it. There was nobody there!

My Uncle was still up — there was a light still going under the crack of his door. But he seemed to be going to bed now. I looked at my watch when I got into the room and it was almost three o'clock.

Then I looked out of my window for the last time. There was no sign of life anywhere. The only thing I saw at all was a yellow light — a kerosene lamp down in the second story of the little corner grocery store at the foot of the hill. Somebody was up there, probably getting ready for another day's work, I thought first, for they got up very early.

And then I said to myself — I don't know why — unless it was on my mind all the time, and I was all waked up and nervous the way you are, by those different sounds and noises around the house. I caught my breath and I said to myself —

" I wonder if they've got the fever down there! It would be just the place they'd catch it! "

And just only the thought of it drove out of my mind all the rest I'd been thinking of: my Uncle and his trips to the tower; and the noises out doors, and even the sound of that little bell that had just been worrying me so.

CHAPTER IX

THE LITTLE BELL

IT was the first thing that I thought of in the morning too. When I came downstairs, I asked Arabella if she'd heard anything of the Fever being any nearer to us.

"They's sayin' somebody's got it down there somewhere," she answered, nodding toward the cross street down below us.

They always know what happens — the niggers, it would astonish you how quick. It's like these new wireless telegraphs they've got to-day. Let anything happen, and it's known by all the niggers from one end of the town to the other as fast as a man can walk. It travels down the alleys like wildfire, just by one stopping and telling it to the other.

But that was all that Arabella knew — that story; and all we learned that morning. I had no real reason at all but nervousness to think the fever was there — nothing but a light burning at night the way they do when people are sick. And all the first part of that morning there was nothing to be seen there except that empty street.

That was Sunday — the first Sunday after the Fever. I can recollect it especially because it was that day the city began to have that deserted look it got to have afterwards. The rush to leave was over now, around us any-

121

way. The sound of wheels was stopped. And now the place was entirely changed.

The streets were vacant, the churches were closed; there was no sound of bells; and the houses, around us, anyway, already stood with their doors locked and their blinds closed — with that kind of a human look of an occupied house all gone; just facing out upon the motionless street, their fronts expressionless as the faces of dead men.

They stood there empty, with their sharp black shadows on the sidewalks, and the hot white sunlight out in the road — all still and motionless. And for half an hour at a time not a moving thing went by — not the shadow of a dog or man moved down the vacant street.

And after you watched it a while, like I did that morning, it was like a picture more than something real — like a dream, or something you'd read a long time ago. It wasn't real at all, somehow. It made me think then, quite often, and still more afterwards, of that old dead city in the Arabian Nights they used to read to us about when we were children — where the people were all gone — turned into fishes, out of sight; and just one man sat in the center of it, half turned to a black stone. And a number of times I got to thinking then, when I was alone, especially — for you get queer ideas going in your head at such times as that — that I was like that man. Everything was unreal somehow. Even that common dirty little brick block where they said the Fever was — more especially when you thought it might be right there.

The next word we got that the story might be true was from old John McCallan, the policeman. I saw him going by later in the morning and hailed him.

"Good mornin'," said John, saluting with his billy at his hat.

" I heard it," he said. " I heard they said one of Jakie Otterman's young ones had it."

And he stood and pointed down to the little German's grocery store down at the corner of the street below, the place where I had seen the light upstairs on the second floor, where the family lived.

" But I don't believe it," said John. " They was telling me they wasn't sure. They be'd sure all right if they had it this time. It's the worst it ever was," said John. " I never seen it so bad anywhere.

" It ain't there yet, I don't believe," said John. " It ain't around here yet. But you'll get it. It's comin' all right, down here everywhere.

" Why don't you get out? " he asked me secretly. " What's the matter with the old man? " asked John, lowering his voice and looking behind him.

I didn't have time to answer him. For my Uncle was coming down the side-walk — coming toward us, holding something in his hand.

" John says maybe they've got the Fever down there," I told him.

" Down where? " questioned my Uncle Athiel.

" Down there, over Otterman's store," I said.

" Look," said John, " there's the poor feller out there now."

We saw the little groceryman come up the other side of the street, a little ways from his place, and stand there wavering — a fat little man in shirt sleeves. He looked peculiar to me. I had never seen him before without his apron on. And it didn't seem natural. It always seemed to me like that apron must have been on him when he was born. But now the store was closed, and he had no use for it, of course.

He stood there, kind of wavering, and teetering back

and forth — across the street there, on the edge of the gutter.

"Hi!" called my Uncle Athiel, "has anybody got the Fever down at your house?"

I thought for a minute he was going to answer him. But then he looked at us and shook his head — to himself, it looked like, not to us. And went right back without speaking. And you could see now that he was pretty shaky.

"Poor fool!" said my Uncle Athiel, "he's drunk."

"They get drinking when they're scared," said John McCallan.

"Poor fools," said my Uncle Athiel. "There's nothing to be afraid of. I ain't any more scared of it than I am of sunstroke. All you got to do is to keep your windows shut at night, and keep out of that poison night air."

"Yes, I heard that too," said John, polite enough, but with a way about him of a man who'd heard of all kinds of schemes, like policemen naturally would do at times like that.

We all stood and watched the shaky little figure of the groceryman going in his door.

But it was hardly shut behind him when: "Say," said my Uncle Athiel to the policeman, "I got something I want to ask you about."

I looked at him, and, what he had in his hand, I saw now, was a piece torn out from a newspaper.

"Is this right?" said my Uncle. "This piece in the newspaper, where it says the city marshal tells folks to shoot anybody they catch on their premises after ten o'clock at night?"

"Yes, sor," said John, "that's just the way it is."

"All right," said my Uncle Athiel. "So that's O. K."

"Yes," said John.

My Uncle seemed to me brisker that morning; quite a lot different from those two days before. He was talking sharp and straight to the point, like he usually did.

"I just wanted to know that," he said.

"Yes, sor," said John, "this town is full of thieves."

I looked up at him quick, for he had taken that expression my Uncle was always saying, right out of his mouth. And then I looked toward my Uncle, and I saw, when John said it, that he was breathing deeper.

"And if you catch 'em loiterin' or hangin' around your place at night," said John, "you got a right to shoot 'em."

"And that's good sense," said my Uncle Athiel, "a man's got the right always to defend his Property."

"Yes, sor," said John, "yes, sor," shifting his weight on to the other foot and thinking.

"It's naygurs," said John, "thieving naygurs. All the rest of the thieves have left the town for fear of the Fever, but the naygurs don't have it — the naygur thieves.

"And they're all over," he said, "all over. They're thicker'n grass in a sod."

"They got a new scheme, I notice in the papers," said my Uncle, "they're setting fire to people's sheds and robbing their houses when they come running to put it out."

"Yes, and them nurses too," said John, "they're takin' and robbin' the dead people when they die — some white ones, but mostly naygurs. Oh, they got all kinds of schemes," said John, "them naygurs.

"And they're gettin' into people's houses where they're gone and robbin' them; and just stayin' and livin' there. What's to hinder?" said John. "Half the police are sick or gone, and more, too, I'm sorry to tell you, Mr. Hagar."

" Yes," said my Uncle Athiel, " and half the firemen."

" All they got left," said John, " to guard the town, is these naygur militia — can you imagine it, sor? " he asked —" naygurs guarding a town?

" Naygurs," and John, riding his favorite horse to death. " If I was the President, I'd shoot the half of them ; and the other half I'd send back to Africy where they belong. If there's any divilmint in this town it's them that's back of it.

" Well, sor," said John, " I'll have to be going," and started off like he hated to.

" Oh," he said, and stopped.

" If you see a half-naygur," he said, turning back, " ahangin' round here — a big half-naygur with a scar from a knife across his face, you call me — will you? "

" Yes," I said, looking at my Uncle.

" I wish you would. It'll help me on the force. You can get word to me at the station house," said John. " They say there's one hangin' round here that answers to the description of a naygur they want for killin' a white man down the river — a Jew peddler."

I looked at my Uncle again to see if he was going to say anything about that half-nigger he had kept talking about those weeks before, but he didn't move a muscle.

" He killed the poor Jew for his pack," said John. " He cut him to death, with one of them big knives them river naygurs have on them."

" I expect it wasn't all his fault — the naygur," said John, explaining. " I expect the Jew started hollering, and scared the naygur."

" They're hard customers — those half niggers," said my Uncle Athiel —" hard tickets when they get started."

" The worst they is," said John, " they got the worst of both sides in them."

" They ain't half so human, any of 'em, as a good dog," said my Uncle Athiel.

And so, after talking a while longer, about the Fever, and how bad it was, and how he didn't think sometimes it was just only Yellow Fever, but something else — some old plague or other — the old policeman finally went along. He seemed to hate to go, somehow. He was a great fellow to stand around on a corner and talk to folks, very sociable. And I expect he got lonely on those empty streets, and kind of hungry for somebody to talk to. He reminded me of a child that hangs around, hating to go into the dark at bedtime. He talked around and around, and up and down everything, before he left.

" Lord," said my Uncle Athiel, when he tramped away from us, " it's lucky nobody ever told him about Christopher Columbus — he'd never stop till he brought him down to date."

It seemed to me like my Uncle was a good lot smarter and brisker than he was the day before — that time he acted so suspicious of everybody. In comparison he acted almost pleased about something; and he certainly was a whole lot different, in his actions toward me.

Well, we didn't hear any more about the Fever down below us all that day. Once I thought I heard the Whistling Doctor somewhere — down in that direction somewhere — and that was a bad sign, for he was working on the Yellow Fever now, all over the town. But I couldn't see him anywhere. Then I asked our Howard visitor when he came, if he'd heard anything. But that street was out of his district, and he didn't know. They were going around every day now — that Howard Society — to every house in town, to find out about who had the Fever, and help them. A wonderful fine work it was; and something to be proud of, but a good many of the poor fellows died of the Fever.

So that afternoon and evening passed without anything but a suspicion in our minds whether the Fever was really down there under that hill, or not. I sat upstairs in my room, like the others did, and tried to live through that afternoon. The weather was just the same — only worse — that clear old Yellow Fever weather, with that pale greenish sky, and the white sunshine and black shadows on the streets, and the birds parching and gaping for breath in the trees. And afternoons, just after dinner, it seemed to be the hottest.

If the other afternoons were long, they were nothing to that one. In spite of its being Sunday and all that, I got out my Law Book, Blackstone, it was, on the Rights of Things — on Property. And I sat and stared and tried to read, just waiting for that afternoon to pass, till I thought I would die of old age, just sitting there and crossing and recrossing, and shifting my legs around, and sweating, and trying to read Blackstone, before that afternoon was over.

Sometimes you get drowsy days like that, and can get to sleep. But there was nothing like that for me that day. I was on edge too much — wondering if the Fever was really right down there in that old block ahead of my windows; and wondering when my Uncle Athiel was going to do what he told me he would — and send Vance away.

Toward the end of the afternoon I did hear him come out, I thought, and go into her room, and I said to myself:

" That's better; now he's doing it."

It was evening, though, before I got to learn anything about it. We went into the Crystal Room after supper, and Vance sat down at the big black piano for a while —

like she generally did Sunday nights; and sang some Gospel Hymns. They were mighty popular then, and my Uncle liked them. They were about the only music he did like, and about the only way we celebrated Sunday. We used to sit there Sunday evenings in the dusk, the three of us, under those big mirrors, and those two great paintings of Indians, and listen to Vance play the piano and sing Gospel Hymns, and it was about the only time my Uncle came in and sat down in the Crystal Room at all.

But after a little while, when the dark came on at night, he got restless again, and went upstairs; and left Vance and me there, alone again in the big room — under the eyes of Pocahontas, and De Soto discovering the Mississippi; and the faint figures of ourselves sitting there in the great mirrors.

" He saw you this afternoon? " I said right away to her, " didn't he? "

" Who? What? " said Vance.

" Your father — about going away? "

" Yes."

" And you're going! "

" No," said Vance. " No."

" He'll make you," I said.

" He can't," she said. " Nor you can't — nor anybody. I won't go. Even if you should take me and carry me away on your back, it wouldn't do you any good — I can come right back again."

I sat still — ugly, refusing to speak.

" I'm going," said Vance, " when you go. I'm going to stay as long as you do, and there's no reason why I shouldn't."

" Except," I blurted out, " if you take the Fever, it is sure to kill you."

" No," said Vance shortly.

I didn't talk — I sulked again.

" Don't you see, Beavis," she said, and reached out where she was sitting and put her hand on my sleeve — " Can't you see? "

" What? " I said.

" If I stay, maybe I can get him to go! "

" No," I said.

" Maybe — if I can get him out of this way he is now; get him like he usually is.   Get him to look at me," she said, talking faster.

" No," I said.

" I can try, anyhow," she said.   " I can try —" and her voice started breaking a little.

I looked at her, and I thought that once again I saw that little shudder.

" What is it? " I said, but she didn't answer.

" What is it? " I said.

" Oh, I'm afraid!   I'm afraid for him! " she answered, breaking her silence with a rush.

" Your father! " I said, and she nodded.

" That dream — still? "

She nodded, choking.

" Oh, I can't forget it!   I can't forget it! " she said, and stretched out one hand before her.

" Vance," I said sharply.   " Are you a perfect fool? "

I knew I had to do something to stop it; to break her of the foolishness.

I had at the same time, all the time, that impulse that I always had at times like that, to take her in my arms and protect her.   I knew that sometime, I'd break over — and make a fool of myself; break over and do just that. And I jumped up on my feet and stood in front of her.

" You've got to go, Vance," I said for the hundredth time.

She didn't answer me.

" You've got to go," I said louder.

" Don't," said Vance, " please don't; I can't stand it; first father and then you. Don't — you only tire me — without the slightest use. I'll go when you do and he does. I told him so this afternoon. So don't argue; don't. It only tires me —"

And then that voice of hers went again, and she stopped — whispering the rest.

And, as usual, I stood there, so mad I could cry, almost. Stopped and blamed myself for hurting her. It was enough to drive you jabbering crazy. The Fever right down there under the hill, maybe; coming toward us anyway, and she sitting there and defying us — both of us — to send her away. And both of us unable to send her. For the weakness that we feared for, continually defeated us.

I got up on my feet, I remember, and went stamping up and down the room — over the roses in that deep soft carpet; pink roses they were, as big as cabbages. I remember watching them as I walked.

" Stop," said Vance, finding her voice at last. " Stop tearing around like that. I want to talk to you; and I can't when you're going that way; sit down, you make me dizzy."

" What do you want? " I asked crossly.

" Sit down, first," she said.

So I did.

" What was it you saw last night? " she said.

" When? " I answered, looking at her.

" When you heard that little bell, and got up and watched out the hall window."

" Nothing," I said surprised.

" I didn't either," she said.

" So you heard it? " I said.

" Twice now," said Vance. " Yes, and once or twice several weeks ago."

" What is it? " I asked.

" I don't know," said Vance. " I thought first it was one of the door bells."

" Let's go and see," I said, getting up.

So Vance got a candle and we went out through the kitchen to the cellar stairs; to the back of the back stairs where the bell hung.

There were four of them, I remembered when I got there — up above your head, in a row. Two for the two front doors and two others. You could see them when Vance held up her candle — four little bells on their coiled springs. You remember them, maybe — those old-fashioned door bells, fastened on at the end of the coiled wire, and you pulled the knob at the door, and it pulled a lever, and a wire. And another lever jerked at the other end and shook the coiled wire, and set the little bell dancing and jingling at the end of it.

" One to the front door, and one to the side," I said.

" What are the other two? "

I had never paid any attention to those.

" One to Dad's room," said Vance, " and one to mine."

And then I did remember, I had heard about it. Mr. Bozro, in building his great house, had put in the bells for calling servants from upstairs, like he had seen in those great houses he had visited in his travels abroad. One for the Purple Room, where he slept; and one for the room of Mrs. Bozro, the Ivory Room that Vance had now. And the bell-ropes, big flat kind of tapes, with fringes at the end, hung down exactly as they did in those great houses in France or England — only I expect — in fact I know — they did not work exactly the same. Only as near as he could make them, in Memphis then.

" But those two were both disconnected," said Vance. " They have been ever since we first came here."

We stood there underneath them, looking up by the light of the candle in Vance's hand. The bells and coils were fastened back of the stairs on the rough boards, with dust and cobwebs all around them; all rough work, as the back of things are apt to be in our country — and the South generally, where so much of the work is left to niggers. Just all splintery boards behind them, and above them and under them two little cleats they were fastened to some way. But the two bells to the bedrooms were disconnected like Vance said. You could see the old rusty wires where they hung down. Some nigger's job, I expect — shiftless; anybody else wouldn't have left them swinging there like that.

" Do you suppose," said Vance, looking up, " that a mouse or some little thing like that could crawl up there and get on one of those little cleats and run over those springs — or touch them some way? "

" How could he get up there? " I said.

" I don't see," said Vance.

" I don't," I said. " No."

" I still believe," said Vance, " that somebody is out there, outside. I believe that that is what Dad is doing up there in that tower," said Vance.

" What? " I said.

" Watching," said Vance.

" Oh, moonshine," I said. And I stood and stared and puzzled over those four bells, set up there in a row above us.

" Listen," said Vance, all at once. " What was that? "

It was that man down the street, firing off his shot gun again in his cellar to kill the poison Fever air that he believed formed there. I hadn't thought much about that before, so far as we were concerned. It was like a lot of other strange things they did. But there we stood, at the head of those dark stairs, and I could smell that old damp cellar air under us. And all at once it scared me — all that talk of poison air everywhere was getting on my nerves a little; more and more, as the Fever came crawling over toward us. And it might be that the Fever bred down there, I said to myself. Who knew?

" Come," I said to Vance, " let's get out of here. Out from this old cellar air; come! " And I took her by her wrist.

And all at once, without the slightest idea in the world I was going to do it, I had her in my arms pleading with her, begging her to go and get away where she would be safe. I just gathered her up in my arms like you would a child — to protect her, with some crazy idea in my head that I could shut her out from the danger that was around her — from that poison air and the Fever.

" Beavis," said Vance, struggling. Some of that hot wax from the candle came down on my hand, I remember. I remember that old cellar dampness in my nostrils, and I remember too, always, the warm fragrance of her hair against my face.

She still struggled silently to get away from me. But I paid no attention; I just held her away from me and looked into her eyes.

" Please, Vance," I said. " Oh, please, for God's sake, won't you go? "

Now that I had gone that far, I didn't care; I was beside myself. She was so frail, so slight; the danger was so great for her; she was so much to me. I could never doubt that now, never. And the thought blazed over me like a flash of lightning. If she should die of this thing; if she should not be here forever, what would the rest of my life be worth anyhow? You know how it is when you're twenty-one, life stretches out before you forever, and the thought of it without her burned and stung me and threw me into a great foolish panic.

" No," said Vance, " no.— Please! " she said faintly, and dropped the candle.

And the light went out, leaving us in the darkness.

I was ashamed of myself — yes, and scared.

" Vance," I said, in the darkness, " I am ashamed of myself. I apologize."

She didn't answer me.

" Will you forgive me? " I asked, and still she didn't answer.

" Will you? Will you? " I kept asking her.

" Yes," she said, after awhile. " Yes, but don't, don't ever ask me to go again — not until my father goes, my father goes — and you! "

Then we lighted the candle again, and went back in the front hall without talking.

It was Sunday night. The niggers were having their meeting somewhere, those sanctified niggers. I could hear them when I went upstairs. All night long they were going: Clap! Clap! Clap! Stamping and dancing and marching around, and singing those marches, and those old mournful " long metre " hymns — that slide up and down like dogs howling at the full moon. Doing just like they used to do, I expect, round the fires at night in Africa. They were getting more and more excited, those last few days, by death and the Fever, and those old nigger prophecies about the end of the world that were circulating round again.

There were one or two Fever fires on the streets in the city that I could see, and down under us, looking out the window, I could still see the yellow light over that old grocery store like I had the night before. Then I went to bed finally.

But the last thing I remembered was the niggers clapping and singing somewhere down south back of the hill.

CHAPTER X

HAGAR'S HOARD

ALL night, when I woke in my restless sleep, I heard the sanctified niggers clapping and singing and marching around; and then, toward daybreak, screeching and hollering, and getting saved and sanctified — a strange noise, more like something barking than a man, especially when you listened to it at night. They're afraid, afraid, and screaming for fear of Hell, and yelling with wild, scared joy for escaping it. And in that Fever time they were getting all excited around us, anyhow. They had to stop them afterwards.

It must have been almost daybreak that morning before they finished. But when we came downstairs to breakfast, there was Arabella, up and waiting, with that same calm, contented, cat-look on her face, stronger and more peaceful than it ever was.

"Yassah," she said, when I asked her that question — we all wanted first to know —"Yassah, it's come, they got it."

There wasn't a change in her old smooth face or a flicker of excitement on her face. Only it seemed somehow to shine from the inside, with peace and contentment, more and more every day.

"Down there?" I asked, pointing, and I jumped up and ran to the window.

"Yassah," said Arabella. "Down to that little groceryman's. They've got them chimicals all over the street

— you kin see it plain.   And yondah at the front of the yard you kin hear that poor woman acrying for her child; and the poor child going ' Um-um-um,'— that regular ole Fevah cry out the window."

" Come back here and sit down to your breakfast," said my Uncle.   For both Vance and I were at the window.

So we went back; there was nothing to be seen from there anyway.

" When you goin'? " questioned Arabella, suddenly to Vance.   " When you goin'? "

" We're not going at all," said Vance.   " You're not going, are you? " she said.   And when Arabella shook her head, " Then why should we? "

Arabella stood staring at her.   " The colored race," she said, " they don't have the Fevah.   No'm — not to speak of.   But the white race — they goin' die.   All that stays here.   They all goin' die.

" You better go," she said, and I noticed her voice was beginning to rise up and grow sharp the way it did the morning before.

" Your father better go.   This ain't no ordinary Fevah.   No'm! " she said, solemnly, and rolled her head.   " This ain't no common Yellow Fevah."

My Uncle didn't say one word.   He only looked at her for a second, and looked down again.   But after that she didn't talk any more through breakfast.

" Oh, look! " said Vance, from the side door, when we went out.

The street in front of the Fever place was white — with lime, I think it was.   I can't explain just how it struck you first.   Like the silent street, and the golden flies following the Dead Wagon — strange and unnatural

and unclean, somehow; strange as snow in summer; unnatural and threatening, like some scary dream of a
child.

"Come back here, Vance!" my Uncle called out.

"Why?"

"I don't want you out there."

He spoke to her that way as often as not, more like she
was twelve than nineteen. I was glad he did. For she
came back.

But he and I went out to the edge of the yard and
looked down there and listened.

There wasn't much to see — only those white chemicals
on the empty street. That old block where the grocery
was looked like it was deserted for all you could see.
Closed below — the old chicken coops standing empty under the wooden awnings; and all the shutters up. And
upstairs where the Fever was, nothing to be seen besides
those wide open windows.

But then all at once, that old common place changed
for me into something different. For I heard for the
first time through those open windows the Yellow Fever
moaning, that curious noise, half murmur and half moan;
that old "um-um-um" they keep agoing. And once I
did think I heard a woman crying.

And then, right away, that old common place — that
old cheap grocery block, changed into something strange
and fearful and fantastic. You have the same feeling
sometimes, when you run suddenly upon an accident; and
a man's face turned up from the ground all drained white.
I do, I know. And after that, for a while, it was like
something deadly hidden down there in that old brick
block; and I wouldn't have been surprised any minute —
one particle — if I had seen that old black poison air

Vance thought about when she was a child, come drifting out those open windows. It was a strange feeling, I don't forget it.

My Uncle stood by me and looked at it for a while. He had seen it plenty of times before; and if he had any feelings about it at all, he didn't show it in his hard, old, yellow face.

But then he turned and walked back to our house, and I with him. The sun was coming up, clear and hot again. It glistened on the east side of the shiny, rubbery leaves of the magnolia trees; and the locusts in them were drying out their wings and getting going by fits and starts into that old hot weather song of theirs. It was another old Fever day, hotter than ever. The damp was going, and you could smell the heat of the day in your nostrils already; and feel the first dry smart and tingle, when the sun first fell upon your cheek.

Vance was inside, in the side doorway. My Uncle walked straight up to her.

" Get ready," he said. " I want you to get ready right now."

" What for? " said Vance.

" You're going to-day," said my Uncle Athiel.

I was more than glad. " Now," I thought to myself, " the time has come, young lady, when you're going." Her father wasn't like he had been the past three days — moonshiny and absent minded; he was quick and nervous and determined, like he usually was.

" Are you going? " said Vance, to her father, looking at him, with her great dark eyes.

" No," he said.

" Then you can't expect me to," said Vance. " It's no different from yesterday. I'm going when you and Beavis go."

" You're going when I tell you to," and his black eyes were ugly.

" No," said Vance. " I wasn't taught to think that's what Southern women do."

" What? " said my Uncle.

" Run! " answered Vance, " get scared and run! "

" You're going if I tell you to," said my Uncle.

" No," said Vance.

" You'll go if I have to take you by force! " said her father, and caught her by her arm. She shrank the faintest bit; then stood still and passive, looking in his eyes.

" You hurt me," she said, " don't. You just hurt me! " And her voice was very low and even. They stood for a minute and looked at one another. He dropped her arm finally, and went away, muttering to himself, and Vance stood watching him, her hand holding at her arm where he had gripped it. She was breathing hard.

" You've got to go, Vance," I said.

" No, sir," said Vance.

She stood there, her lips parted, still panting for breath.

" Sit down," I said roughly. " Sit down, anyhow."

She looked at me a minute and I saw tears come up into her eyes.

" Go away," she said. " Please leave me alone."

So I went out into the stable and set about my work, muttering to myself.

We got no further with her, not a step. Her father hadn't moved her an inch. Her weakness had won against him, exactly as it had with me. Her weakness was her strength, like it is with women, anyhow. It had beaten him just exactly as it had me.

It was an hour or two before I got back to the house again. And when I came in the side door I heard Vance and her father talking in the big hall. And I thought with a gleam of hope that it was talking about her going away again.

I stopped to listen to what he would say. But it was Vance who was talking.

" Where are you going? " asked Vance, in a sharp high voice, like she was scared.

But he didn't answer.

" You aren't going down there to those tenements? " questioned Vance, and her voice grew sharper still. " The Fever's all around there. You aren't going down there, no, sir! "

I'd come around by that time to where they were standing, facing each other again. My Uncle stood there with his old hand satchel in his hand. And then it came to me right away. It was Monday again, the day for gathering in the niggers' rent. It was a week from that night he had gone home prophesying Fever, the night before the Fever came. It seemed more like a hundred years.

" It's no use, anyhow," said Vance.

He just stood looking at her.

" There's no use," she said. " Nobody's paying any rents any more. It said so in the paper."

" No," said my Uncle, and his voice was rougher than ever. " You don't have to remind me. I know that without going down there. I know that property is worthless like the rest. You don't have to tell me I'm ruined."

She stepped back a little, he talked so loud and ugly.

" I'm not going down there — don't you worry," he said. " I'm going in here," and he tramped on toward Mr. Bozro's study.

When he went in, Arabella was there.

"What are you doing here?" he said to her. "Ain't you through here yet? Well, get through and get out!"

So in a minute or two she came out looking back of her like an old cat when somebody's got her usual chair, and she shut the big brown round-topped door after her.

"Now, what's he doing in there?" Vance asked me, when they were both out of our way.

For my Uncle hated that place, that study, and made all manner of fun of it, with its big black expensive furniture, and its great center table; and the safe that Mr. Bozro had built into the wall — that the key to was lost now, so it could never be used. He never went in there to sit by himself from one year's end to the other.

"First the tower," I said, "and now this!"

"But there's one thing," said Vance, "he acts better now. He isn't so gloomy and down-hearted."

That was right too. He seemed as sharp and smart as I had ever seen him, and I had to admit it; but that didn't explain why he was in there; why he had gone in there with that old hand satchel of his that he carried his money in, and why he stayed there all day.

At first it seemed to me that maybe he might be there because the Fever was down on that side of the house, and he could look out the windows and see what was going on in the street. For his room upstairs was on the wrong side of the house for that. It might be he was going to stay in there in that Study right along now. It was more understandable anyhow, than his trips into the Tower, even if Vance's explanation of his going up there to watch was right.

But what bothered me and made me mad was the way he had forgotten, apparently, everything he had said and promised about sending Vance away. Whatever he was thinking of, now, had wiped that clean off his mind. Naturally I was mad. I didn't care much what he did himself; he could do what he pleased. There was only one question with me now. How were we going to get Vance out of there?

But I did think then too that his actions were strange; and I could see that Vance did.

But the most comical thing of all was Arabella, standing or passing along in the hallway outside, muttering by the closed door, and trying to figure out what he was doing; what all this meant. She had been used to having that room, and those windows to look out of so long that she thought they belonged to her, and now, when the Fever was right there, she had to go outside in the yard to look.

We were all looking down that way naturally now. I sat up in my own bedroom window reading my books for quite a while. And I could see, out there, Arabella go out in the yard, several times, her two dogs following her, and stand in the shade of a tree and stare down, over the block where the Fever was. And come back again, calm and stately as a steamboat on the river.

I was sitting there in the afternoon, when she was coming back, and I saw her do a mighty curious thing. She had got about opposite my Uncle's window, when all of a sudden I saw her stop right still; just stand and stare. Then after a while she went along, looking indifferent again — but she must have been there staring a half a minute or so.

It was after that, about an hour, when I came downstairs to go out in the yard, and I ran across her again, lurking about the back of the main hall, standing at the entrance to the dining room, and I made it my business to go outdoors that way to see what she had coming on her mind now.

I turned my head and looked at her when I came by and right away she started talking and asking questions in a queer kind of ghostly voice. She was excited about something, that was certain.

" You ever think — you ever think what you be doing *then?* " she asked me, very slow and solemn. And the " O-O-Os " in her words came out of her like an old owl in the twilight.

" Then! " I said. " Then what? "

" You ever think," she went right along, " what you be doing when that Day comes around? "

" What Day? "

" That Judgment Day! "

I stood right still and watched her. She had been different, a little, all that day. From the excitement, I reckoned, from the Fever, and after that Meeting she had been to all that night before.

She was always a little different, mornings after those Meetings. But she was talking more anyhow — instead of just standing, looking.

" Where'll you be? Where you goin' to be? " said Arabella, like one of those old exhorters; but talking yet in a kind of whisper. " You ever ask you'se'f?

" Where you goin' to be? " she went along, " when He comes? Playin' cards and gamblin' and swearin'; and cahying on? Or is you goin' to be found aprayin', down on your knees prayin'? " she said, talking louder; and stopped, looking at me and catching her breath.

For she was pretty mighty fat and heavy.

" We better be; we better be! " she said.

" They's some," she said, looking in a meaning way at me — looking at the door into the hall; " they's some will be found a-sittin' and a-countin' their money.

" But that ain't goin' do him no good," said Arabella,

her whisper rising louder, "that ain't goin' do him no good — you mind what I tell you," she said. "Money, just old money, that ain't goin' do you no good, not much longer!"

Then right of a sudden she called me over by the window.

"You see them clouds — you see them clouds," she said, pointing over in the west. "You see them old clouds comin' up?

"Maybe they's the ones! Maybe they's the ones!" she said. "Maybe it will be comin' down yere to-night! You can't tell! You can't never tell! But you know — it ain't long now! It ain't long!

"Signs and myst'ries!" she said, in that old secret voice; "signs and myst'ries eve'ywhere!

"Look out," she said, loud and stopped, for my Uncle moved a little in his room.

"Look out!" she said softer — and rolled her eyes at me, and then turned back suddenly, back to the kitchen.

And I went outdoors smiling to myself — thinking what wild things the niggers were, and what strange thoughts got going in their heads. I didn't have the slightest idea then of what she was driving at.

It was about half an hour after that when I had to come back to the house for something. And for some reason I looked up just as I passed under the Study window and looked in. The window was pretty high; you couldn't see much generally. I looked in, and just as I had seen the negress do, I stiffened up and stopped. I stopped short, then I thought, and went along, for fear he would notice it.

For there, at the great table in the center of the Study I saw my Uncle Hagar sitting, and the table in front of him was all covered up with money! I couldn't doubt that now at last I was looking with my own eyes at that old " Hagar's Hoard " that they talked so much about! I saw it with my own eyes!

He sat there in that high backed chair, one of those high black expensive carved chairs that Mr. Bozro had in his study, dozing, it looked like, half asleep, with his hands out on the arms. Right ahead of him, propped up on the table was a book — a big black book, with a red back, like the book-keepers use. And at the farther end of the table sat that little, old, brown hand satchel of his, wide open.

But, in front of him, where you could see it perfectly plain, were all those piles of green-backs — fifteen or twenty piles I should say, anyway, all fastened up with paper bands around the middle — twenty piles, maybe more.

And there, over them, with the windows free and open, sat my Uncle dozing in that great black chair. I went along, looking neither right nor left, stiff and unnatural as that old steam automaton they said they had in Philadelphia at the Contennial. I went along into the side door, and upstairs — and into my own room. And there I sat down and tried to think.

I certainly couldn't understand it, that was all. For, suppose the man was all right in his mind; and he seemed to me — that last day anyway, as straight as a string — what was he doing there with all that money spread out in the public way in broad daylight?

But suppose the other thing. Suppose all that fear of his — all his losses, and his great house, and his fear of fire and thieves, had come to a head and his mind had worn out under the strain of that Fever time — why then,

why wouldn't it be natural to expect that the worse and
more excited he got, the deeper and deeper into that great
old house he would have hidden that money of his?

I sat there for an hour or two and puzzled my head
over the thing; and I got nowhere, not before supper-
time. Only, the more I thought, the madder I got over it.

There, under my window, was the Fever at our doors.
I could see the chemicals shining white on the street; and
the woman, the mother of the sick child, sitting in the
window; and sometimes if I strained my ears, the moaning
of the child. There was the Fever under our windows,
and certain as to-morrow morning, to come to us. And
there underneath me, sat that damned old fool; thousands
of dollars before him — enough to take us all to Alaska
and keep us there the rest of our natural lives! Sitting
there, bent up in his chair — over those old green-backs
— like a drowsy child over his playthings.

And we all tied, and fastened, and bound here against
our will, by that pile of paper he sat playing with.

BOOK IV

THE HALF NIGGER

CHAPTER XI

THE LIGHTED MATCH

IT was cloudy that night — dark early. There were ragged, tousled thunder heads in the west that smothered the twilight. And down the vacant street the lonely yellow light in the place where they had the Fever was started watching for another night.

" Poor woman," said Vance. " Poor baby! "

She stood beside me at the window again, after supper, watching as we did every evening now, up toward the city, toward where the Fever lay.

" You remember her, that little one with such white hair," said Vance, very softly.

She stood beside me, staring with those deep eyes of hers, lips slightly apart, like a child at the tragedy. Frail, sensitive women are so, I expect sometimes. But I never knew one just like her — she was such a very fine and delicate thing — like one of those harps they set at the windows, played through and thrilled by all the unseen movements of the air.

She stood rigid again, watching the lonely light under our little hill.

" Vance," I said, finding my own voice, with some trouble, " when are you going? "

She looked at me, reproachful for asking her that same old thing again.

" When are we going? " she said.

" He won't go," I said, looking back over my shoulder

to where the high brown door stod closed to the Study.

"Maybe he will," Vance answered slowly.

"I believe," she said after a while, "I believe I could get him to go myself, if he would only look at me. I think," she said, and choked a little, "I think my father thinks a lot of me in his way, but now he won't see me, even.

"And I can't force myself on him. That would be worse than nothing," she said. "You know that."

"Yes," I said.

She waited till her voice grew steadier.

"If it wasn't for this thing always on his mind," she said. "What is it? What do you believe it is? What is he always thinking about?" she said, looking up at me.

"Property," I said, "his Property." I caught myself just in time from saying right out "His money." For that would never do to tell her — that queer business of her father's that I had just seen that afternoon — not if I ever hoped to get her away from there.

"No," said Vance.

"What then?" I asked her.

"Thieves and fire," said she, repeating from her father.

I shook my head. "That's just another way of saying it," I told her.

"But I believe he's watching something in particular, or some one!" she went on. "I've said that all the time — in the tower at night, from his room, and now in there. He's watching there," and she nodded toward him where he was sitting in the Study.

"No, sir," I said, "I know positively that isn't so. I know he isn't watching!"

"How can you know for certain?" she asked. And naturally I could not tell her of the thing that I had seen — that sight of "Hagar's Hoard" through the windows

that proved for certain he could not have feared there
were any thieves about.

"Well," said Vance, contradicting me, "I just know
that it is!"

"Why?" I said — just to hear what was in her mind,
certain all the time she was wrong.

"Because," she said to me, "in the first place I believe
there is some one watching *him*."

"Watching him," I said.

"Always," she said, "for days. What is that bell?"
she asked. "That door bell ringing for?"

"Have you heard it again?" I asked.

"Yes — again last night," she said.

"And why are the dogs so restless, always, after midnight?"

"I don't know," I said. "I expect they always find
something they can bark about."

"They do," said Vance, looking at me —"around this
house."

"It's mighty easy, Vance," I said, "to get too nervous
at a time like this."

"Don't you believe it? Don't you believe I'm right?"
she said. "Isn't it sensible to think so? All those stories
they started; that got the niggers talking. All those
thieves and jail-birds down here along the river. You
know yourself what it's like down there; what happens
to an honest man out there alone after nightfall. How
many of them — gone, and never seen again, excepting
maybe far down the river! And now, just like Dad
says," she went along, "the whole town is full of thieves.
Some of them, I believe; some of them, are certainly watching us."

"So your father says," I said, and smiled at her —
certain she was on the wrong track.

"Isn't that so?" asked Vance. "Aren't there thieves now everywhere? If everybody didn't know it, would they have that?" and pointed.

Up the street from the city, while she was talking, two nigger soldiers — two of those nigger militia in bright blue and red uniforms, that they appointed to keep peace and order in the town — came along by, patrolling the town, as they did, after that, in pairs.

"No," said Vance, looking at them going by, "somebody is certainly watching here!"

"I expect," I said, "you'll say pretty quick you've seen that half nigger that your father talked about this summer."

"That's what I was coming at," said Vance. "I believe maybe I have. There's been one to-day and yesterday, loitering in the alley; a great fawn-colored nigger with a great long scar on his face."

"You saw that!" I said, quickly, for I saw right away that here was John McCallan's man, the nigger wanted on suspicion of the killing of that Jew.

"Yes," said Vance. "And I believe that Dad's been seeing it too. I believe that's all he's been doing — first in that tower, and now here."

"And I know that it isn't," I said, more sharp and certain.

"How do you know?" asked Vance, again.

And again I couldn't tell her.

"I'll tell you sometime," I said, "but not now."

"You're wrong," said Vance, just as certain as I was.

"And another thing," she went on, then; "Another thing I'm going to ask you: Do you believe anybody could be in that Ventress house?"

"Why?" I asked her.

" Well, there are in lots of houses now — all over the city — you know that.   All these vacant houses."

" Yes," I said, " but that doesn't prove anything about this one."

" No," said Vance, " only I got it into my head some-way —"

" Why? " I asked.

" I don't know," she answered — like she didn't care to.

" But why? "

" The shades," she said at last.   " It seems to me the shades in those windows there are different, are changed some way on different days."

" Oh, moonshine! " I said, and laughed.

The servants might have been back in that house again. She might be entirely mistaken about such a little thing as the position of a window shade.   If ever there was a woman's way of seeing and worrying about things, that was it.

" Let's talk of something real, Vance," I said.   " Let's think about the Fever.

" There it is, right here," I said, " right within a stone's throw of us; what are you going to do? "

" What can I do? " asked Vance.

" Are you going to go like we want you to? "

" When you do," she said again.

" But that's no time at all.   He won't go," I said — " your father, he won't go at all."

" He might, perhaps," said Vance.

Then I lost my head a little, as usual, at her arguing and obstinateness.

" There it is," I said, " under your windows, death for certain!   The air alive with this old Fever poison.   Do you expect, now it's got here, you can shut it out?   Do

you think you can shut out that poison by just only closing down your windows in the night time? "

" I believe my father knows," said Vance, faintly.
" After all the times he's seen it. I believe he knows, if
anybody does."

" It will be all around us in three days," I said. " Do
you believe it will pass us by?

" I expect you think," I said, bitterly, when she did not
answer, and seemed not to be listening to me at all — just
looking off. " I expect you think it will go right by our
closed windows, without getting a one of us."

" One of us," said Vance, starting. " Oh! "

" What is it? " I said, moving toward her.

" One of us! " she said again, catching her breath.

" Oh, I see! I didn't understand you first." And then
tried to pass it off, and couldn't.

I saw then what I had blundered into. She was shivering now, noticeably, through all her slender body, worse
than ever before.

" Vance," I said, and put my arm about her shoulders,
steadying her. " Vance, quit it."

For I knew of course it was that dream again — about
her father.

" I will; I will," she said. I could feel the muscles of
her arms tightening with the effort.

I stood there, waiting for her to control herself.

" I must go now," she said, in a husky voice. " I'm
going upstairs."

" I'm sorry, Vance," I said, apologizing.

" No, I'm a little fool, that's all," she said, and left me.
But she turned back as she was going out.

" I had two other dreams like that," she said, " and
both came true. One of them, when my mother died."

She turned, and left, and I watched her — her lithe,

little figure go climbing up the stairs into the dusky upper hall, and I thought what all of us have at different times, I expect, what a strange, different creature a woman is from the rest of us.

I went back thinking about it; puzzling and worrying over the way everything was going, the way we were tied and snarled up in that invisible net that binds up men and women's lives. How I cursed that house in my heart — that black old house, and what there was in it; that " Hagar's Hoard " I had seen that afternoon! And that old miserliness, and fear of my Uncle for his " Property," his money. Yes, and even the loyalty, and nervous dread of his daughter. All the invisible bonds that held us there, strong as the cable of a ship, while outside, hour after hour, death rose up under our windows.

I found myself again by the window, as I worried back and forth over all this trouble. We were there, all the time, at those north windows — drawn in spite of ourselves by the expectation of what we might see — especially at night — when the Fever fires were lighted on the empty street, and there seemed everywhere that feeling of fear and waiting.

I saw the vacant street, the yellow dots of street lights, and up the roadway, in front of the city, now, the lights where the nigger militia had their camp on the bluffs. My eye fell now and then on the Ventress's house next to us — black and high and ugly, just beyond our yard.

I looked and looked, and turned away to watch the rising thunder clouds in the pale west, when my eye went suddenly back to it, that house of the Ventress's.

In the sitting room, through the central window that faced toward us, there shone a little glow of light. Somebody had struck a match there. I could see nothing else there — no one, not a soul. The curtains were three quarters down.

The little light grew slowly — faint and bluish, like those old matches did, and then rose into a yellow glow, and finally died, shaken out.

I stood and watched and watched, after that, but there was nothing more — nothing at all that I could see. But I was sure now. There was some one there. And I had thought the house was empty. Of course, I said to myself, it might have been one of the servants; one of their own negroes come back there. And yet, I didn't think so, exactly.

I stood and watched, bound on seeing what did not come again, when I heard behind me the click of an opening door. My Uncle came out from the Study across the hall. And he came out, I saw, as he turned around, empty handed. The old hand satchel that he had taken with him, that stood upon his table, while he was counting out and examining his greenbacks, he hadn't brought out with him.

" He must have left it all in there," I said to myself, " unguarded, on the ground floor of the house."

There was that safe in there, of course. But he had no key to it. I knew that. It wasn't the slightest use to him.

And I couldn't understand at all. He must certainly be crazy.

My Uncle Hagar came over to where I stood. And when he came, I caught his eye. It was as far as you could think from the eye of a crazy man — or from any old man's dull eye. There was a curious old black twinkle in it. If I had seen it in any man's eye, I would have said for certain, he was laughing. And then, there certainly was, it seemed to me, a kind of crooked smile upon his lips.

He looked at me a second, and that smile went away.

"Where's Vance," he said.

"Gone upstairs," I answered.

Then he stepped up alongside of me at the big high window.

"A cloudy night," said my Uncle Athiel, looking out.

"Yes, sir," I said.

"Looks like we might have a thunder shower," he said.

"Yes, sir, it does," I said. Those great old navy blue clouds had shut off the last lingering white patches of sunset.

"I hope we do," said my Uncle Athiel; "they're good! They wash this old Fever poison out of the air."

That was one of the ideas they had about the Fever then.

"It will make it healthier," said my Uncle Athiel.

"And maybe cooler," I said.

It was hot still; still close and disagreeable in the house; shut up that way at night. But you didn't mind it somehow, after a while. Somehow, after all that talk about the poison in the night air, I had got by that time so I was glad, and more than glad, to keep my windows all shut down as tight as any one. I expect, in a smaller house, it might have been a whole lot harder. That was one thing, like Vance had always said, about that great house of ours. You could stand it being shut up there.

We stood there quite a few minutes, the two of us, looking out. It was a sad looking old blue night, now, very dark — and silent — silent as the grave.

It seemed to me my Uncle loitered a little more than usual. And on his old blue lips I thought that I could see again that faint, curious smile.

"What do you see?" he said to me after a while. "What were you looking at?"

I was watching the Ventress's house, I expect, without realizing it.

I made up my mind, right away then, I'd let him have it.

"You've had a great lot to say about thieves lately," I said; "thieves in houses. Now I'll tell you why I'm looking and watching here. I'll tell you. Maybe I've just seen one. I just saw somebody, anyhow, light a match in there at the Ventress's."

"Just tell me that again," said my Uncle, leaning over; and that faint smile got a little plainer.

So I told him again, louder. "Do you think we ought to go over there?" I asked him.

"No, sir," he said sharply. "No, not in that damned poison night air, with the Fever right down there, not for any man. Not for a thousand Ventresses."

For he never got on very well with that family, anyway.

"It might be only one of their own niggers, after all," I said.

My Uncle kept looking at me without speaking.

"We might tell the police, I expect, to-morrow, anyway," I said.

"Police! Hell!" said my Uncle. "Tell the police!" And he laughed. "What police? There ain't any! Why should we tell them if there was?"

"To save the house," I said, "if somebody is in there robbing it."

"Save it nothing! If anybody's been robbing that house," said my Uncle, "they'd had it robbed and done with long ago."

It made me mad, the way he had that night — all his actions, and the way he acted about that house especially. I can't describe it. His voice was harsh, and kind of ugly and insolent. Yes, and younger — that was just it — younger.

And he seemed to be jeering and flouting at me all the time.

" All right," I said, for he got on the raw with me more and more. " Suit yourself. But now I've got something else to tell you."

" Oh-ho! What else? " said my Uncle. " Out with it! "

He made me madder still, the way he talked. But I liked less than anything else that smile he had on his face — quite plain now when he looked at me.

" If I had money," I said, looking him in the eye —" a lot of money around the house, I don't think I'd be so open about it."

" If you had money," said my Uncle, and his eyes twinkled into mine, before he lowered them again —" ah, ha? "

" Well, then," I said, " I'll tell it all to you like it was. I just saw you, and that old money of yours, spread out before you there this afternoon — right there in plain sight.

" I don't expect you thought when you did it," I said, " but if there are any thieves or bad niggers, or half-niggers, around this place, or the next one," I said, looking at him, " they can't help seeing it as well as I did.

" I'm telling you this so you'll be prepared — so you'll know," I said, and stopped and looked out of the window.

And all at once I turned suddenly round, for my Uncle burst out laughing — stood there, just laughing fit to kill himself. It wasn't the pleasantest laugh I ever heard, but it was a laugh just the same.

" What's the joke? " I said, getting madder yet.

" Well, I'll just show you," said my Uncle, moving toward his study.

" No, I won't! No, I believe I won't to-night. I'll wait till to-morrow morning," he said, stopping himself.

" But meantime," he said, touching me on the arm, " meantime you keep your eye peeled; keep your eye peeled at that house next door! "

I couldn't make out, quite, whether he was laughing or in earnest when he said that, when he gave me those old directions of his to be watching out.

I just stood there, gaping, as he went upstairs.

My mouth opened like a fool. But I was boiling over inside.

He went poking along out, not noticing me. But when he got to the door he stopped and turned around and looked at me. And then again he broke into that ugly laugh once more.

" Judas," he said, looking me over, " you certainly did look sad."

And then he laughed again.

" Sad," I said after him, getting madder.

" You ought to seen yourself."

" Seen myself! " I said, madder and madder.

" Just standing," said my Uncle Athiel, " just standing there with that look on your face," said my Uncle Athiel. " Sadder'n a sick mule in a cemetery! "

And he gave that laugh again while I worked hard to hold on to myself. For just for that minute it seemed to me the man must certainly be crazy. But then, when I thought it over, I wasn't sure — not about that laugh, anyway. It was not a crazy laugh, no, not in the least.

It was just mean and disagreeable. The meanest laugh that I ever heard.

CHAPTER XII

I KNOCKED at the high brown door of his Study very softly. It was about half-past nine. My Uncle had said to come when Vance went upstairs after breakfast.

" Come on in," said my Uncle.

It was kind of darkish in there. The sun was on the other side of the house, and one window shade was down.

" Sit down, over there," said my Uncle. And I went where he pointed, over to the far corner of the room, back from the window.

I could see better now; the high room, with the big black shiny chairs carved with dragons on their backs, and the big table in the center. I sat down, and felt the body of one of those old twisting dragons at my back. Then I sat up again and stared. For there, on the center table, was " Hagar's Hoard," fixed just like it was the day before.

There was the red-backed book-keeper's book, and the old hand-satchel and all the green-backs in their little banded piles, and over it my Uncle Athiel sat in his high chair — only not drowsing now — his eyes as sharp as jet buttons, and on his blue lips that same crooked, disagreeable smile. He was cutting himself off the sliver of tobacco he chewed. He poked it into his mouth on the big blade of his jack-knife.

163

" Well," he said, smart and deep, " how do you like my lay out? "

" Like it," I said, and that was all. My voice was hoarse and dry. I was staring like a fool. But he sat there, watching with that cold grin on his face, until I finally found voice enough to ask him, " What is it? "

" Can't you see? " he asked.

" No," I told him, my voice coming back to me.

" Here, catch! " said my Uncle Athiel.

And, reaching over on the table, he took and tossed over to me one of those fat packages of green-backs.

And in some way, I managed to catch it.

" Take a look! " he said to me. And I did!

It was just nothing but those old Confederate bills — a parcel of that old ghost money of the Confederacy that they gave the children to play with.

I looked up at him, finally, and saw that smile again. And for a minute I sat there, with an awful case of the " dry grins " on my own face, thinking what a fool I had been made of.

" But then," I thought to myself, " this can't be all done just for a sell on me — there must be something else."

So then, " What was it for? " I said to him.

" Count it," said my Uncle, and sat there, chewing a bit of tobacco and watching me.

" Five thousand, ain't it? " he questioned, when I got through.

That's what it was — all in big bills.

" And twenty piles in all," said my Uncle. " That makes a hundred thousand dollars, all together, don't it? "

" Yes," I said, looking up under my eyebrows.

" A hundred thousand dollars," said my Uncle, " it

must be that one hundred thousand dollars the niggers talk about. It must be that old man Hagar's Hoard."

" Must it! " I said. I was getting right tired of this fooling. And just then the smile went out in my Uncle's face, quick as a lamp in the wind.

" It must be — but it ain't," he said, with an oath. " No. It's just one of his gilt-edged investments."

But in a minute or two afterwards his smile came right back to him.

" How do you like 'em? How do they strike you, now you see 'em? " he asked.

" What is this? " I said. " What is this, anyhow? Just a sell on me? "

" No," he said; " not by a jugful! " And he turned and spit through his teeth into that fine expensive fireplace, with its marble trimmings, back of him. And that old smile on his face was changed again. The laugh was all gone out of it; it was plain straight and cruel.

" You thought I was crazy, didn't you? " he said to me. " Well I ain't; you'll find I ain't.

" But you certainly looked funny," he said to me, " goin' by lookin' up under your eyelids."

I had gone about as far as I was going; he was giving me more than I swallowed from any man.

" Look here," I said, " if you think you can sit here and tease me like a sick dog, you're damned mistaken."

Our eyes met then, and there was no smiles in either one of them.

" Now you tell me," I said, " what is this thing? What is this stuff here on the table? "

He looked at me a minute, before answering.

" It's bait," he said — and when he said it, I saw that half smile come sneaking back in spite of him, at the corner of his mouth.

"That'll do," I said, getting up. "That'll do," I said, and started for the door.

But my Uncle was up ahead of me.

"Sit down, you fool," he said. "Stand back away from that window; he'll see you!"

There was nothing crazy, nor foolish, nor joking, about that voice. It was clear and pert, and strong as a young man's.

"He'll see me!" I said, falling back into my chair. "Who?"

"That half nigger in the next house," said my Uncle

"You mean to say," I started.

"You bet, I mean exactly what I said," my Uncle Athiel answered. "He's likely laying there on his belly right now; looking out underneath the window shade into here now."

"You say he's in that house now!" I said.

He kept his little black eyes on me.

"Yes; and he's been there since yesterday morning."

"And I saw him there last night — saw him lighting that match," I said.

"Yes."

"And this?" I said, pointing at the table.

"That's just what I said it was — just exactly."

"Bait?" I asked.

"Bait for niggers," said my Uncle Athiel.

He looked at me, and I at him. And there was real, genuine pleasure and amusement in his eyes. I don't know when I had seen it there before. He was a different person somehow; a new man I'd never seen before, pleased and smiling over something he was going to enjoy. And I moved uneasily, more uncomfortable than those uncomfortable chairs made me — when I sat looking at him. For I didn't care for him, this new man who watched me over the table — nor for that smile he wore upon his face.

"Lemme tell you about it," said my Uncle Athiel, and he went along and told me how he had been watching that half-nigger from the tower first. How he went up and saw him that first day, when I came back from the doctor's.

"You can see half the town from there," he said.

"But now you've got him here," I asked, "what next? How are you going to catch him? The police?"

"Police!" said my Uncle, sneering. "No police! something better than that!"

"What?"

"Ourselves," said my Uncle, and he passed to me a kind of look of understanding.

"You know what you said to me the other day," said my Uncle Athiel.

"I said I'd swim Hell for you if you'd get Vance out of here," I said, remembering, and wanting to remind him, too.

"I liked the way you said that," said my Uncle Athiel, and looked very friendly at me.

"And I'm going to do what you asked me to," he went along; "I ain't forgot; I'm going to get her out; don't you worry."

"When?" I asked.

"To-morrow," said my Uncle, "and then," he said, "then I'm going to show you something; I'm going to show you how we handled those damn niggers in the old days." And he gave me the look of a man who was going to share a treat with you.

"I'll show you something you never saw," he said over again, and he went on talking about the grudge he owed the niggers generally.

" I've had 'em watching and goggling around this house long enough; I've had 'em whispering round the alleys; and talking that tom fool talk of ' Hagar's Hundred Thousand Dollars ' for years enough! What they need is a lesson. You can't never teach 'em anything. They ain't human! What they've got to have is a practical lesson, and, by Judas H. Iscariot that's what they're going to get! That's what we're going to show them with this one — this half-nigger here! "

I had a kind of start when he said this. It was a good lot the way he said it.

What was it, anyhow, I said to myself, that he was proposing — that he and I were going to do to this nigger thief? He hadn't said anything but hints so far.

" Well, how are you going to catch him? " I asked, feeling around. " There, in that house? "

" No, I reckon not," said my Uncle. " We ain't going out in that poison night air, not for any nigger."

" Well, what? " I said.

" He's coming here to us," said my Uncle Athiel. " We'll sit right here and he'll come right up; right up step by step till he takes that bait."

" Will he take it? " said I.

" Will he take it? Take it! " said my Uncle. " Will a garfish grab a minnow? "

" Won't he suspect? " I said. " Won't he get suspicious? "

" Did you? " said my Uncle, laughing at me.

" No," I said, hanging my head a little.

" Well he won't, then. A nigger won't," said my Uncle. " A nigger! I know 'em — I know 'em, through and through; they ain't half so human as a good dog!

" Don't you fret," he went along, " we'll get him; he'll come along — right up to the window here; not long now

— to-morrow night, maybe. He'll come right up here
and then —"

"And then —" I said, after him, "what?"

His blue lips looked pleased; his face was young, just
young with expectation; and his little black eyes just
shone. It struck me all of a sudden: How many times
had those little black eyes, of those round-headed men
from the hills, looked down their gun-barrels at the men
they were hunting, with just that kind of sparkle in
them; just that enjoyment of killing.

"Then," he said, "I'll show you something that you
never saw before."

"You'll kill him, you mean!" I exclaimed, sitting up.

"Kill him!" said my Uncle, acting just disgusted with
me. "Who said I'd kill him?"

But the way he said it, I wasn't sure of anything, only
that he was disgusted with my talking.

His smile came back though, after a while. He was
too much taken up by his plans.

"No, I won't kill him, I expect," he said. "You'll
see; though I've got a perfect right if I want to; you
heard that; I've got a perfect right to shoot anybody on
my premises after dark. The Marshal said so in his
Proclamation. And if I did it would be a good sight
better'n that nigger deserves, and the world would be a
good sight better off."

He went on talking then — more than I ever heard him
talk before. And as he talked I watched him and I
thought I understood; I was listening to Athiel Hagar,
who lived thirty years ago — to young Athiel Hagar,
who jammed his way along in that old pioneer time in the
Mississippi country. And if there was a rougher and
cruder place on God's footstool than that was, it isn't
very well known by anybody yet.

He talked especially about the niggers, about the way they had changed; and about the way they used to keep them down around War times, and just after. He didn't know, so he said, just what he was going to do with this one when he got him. But it was going to be a real lesson, the kind that he'd carry around with him for a while; the kind that would keep the whole kit and boodle of them off folk's property after that when they looked at it.

And so he went along for a while, telling stories of what they used to do to the niggers, when they got too brash and come-uppy in the old days.

" I'm going to get this nigger," he said, " and you're going to see me do it; and you'll just laugh yourself sick to see how easy I get the damned black fool."

He pulled out his old red bandana and wiped his head and lips; and sat for a while thinking with his head down, and the little holes working in his cheeks as he chewed. He sat there, a coarse little common figure, in that high expensive chair, with the shiny black dragons on it twisting and curling over him. And by and by he got to talking of the tricks they used to do with thieving niggers in those old days — the traps they used to lay for them; and the way they handled them generally, those days he was out in Arkansas and Texas. And his face changed and lighted up, and he went back, with the pleasure any man does, going back over the enjoyments and amusements of younger days.

He told me the story about blowing up the nigger — that slick Guinea nigger — with the train of powder, set up to a lot loose in a can. It didn't kill him, of course, as he said, but it must have marked him up something frightful. And all for an old harness.

He laughed when he told it. And I expect I laughed too ; I had to.

Then he told about heading up another nigger for something or other he'd done, something about some cotton, and a mule — heading him up in this old turpentine barrel with just his head sticking out. And taking him up on a little hill, up over a little creek and setting it afire, and then starting him rolling down the hill. He had to roll and save himself in the water.

" Roll, you damn black dog! Roll! " said my Uncle Hagar, jumping up from his chair and back again, and calling out just like he must have called out to that nigger. And then he slapped on his thin old knees, and laughed till he wiped his eyes, with his old red handkerchief, and got weak laughing.

" Didn't it kill him? " I said, catching my breath.

" Kill him? No! " said my Uncle Hagar. " Hell, you can't kill a nigger."

Then he stopped short; he happened to think, I expect, that we were staying too long in there, and he was making too much noise, and Vance might hear it, he said, before he sent her away.

" Now, get along out of here," he said, " we've been here long enough. But you come back here about four o'clock this evening, when she's resting. And I'll show him to you; I'll let you see him."

And when I went out the door he was smiling that new smile of his, sitting there over his false green-backs. It struck me then, just as I was going out, what that smile was like.

It reminded me of those boys you see sometimes in the country — those little boys that sit and poke the eyes out of frogs with a sharp stick, and sit and laugh and laugh.

CHAPTER XIII

T HE middle of that day dragged out as endless as they all did — only with this difference. The Fever was no longer something hidden that folks were running away from, over there out of sight in town. It was right here where we could see and hear and almost touch it, and I knew for certain that if Vance was going to get away, it had got to be soon — in that next twenty-four hours anyhow, it seemed to me.

I saw Vance just at dinner-time. She went upstairs again soon afterwards — where she could be cooler and rest through the afternoon in her own bedrom. She was resting more than ever. I saw her very little in the day-time. All the morning she was caring for that great up-stairs of the house; and all the afternoons she spent in resting. And I knew she was growing tireder and tireder.

I sat a good part of my afternoon, in my own room, making another feeble try at reading at my law — and really waiting and worrying, and looking out of the window.

I saw the Dead Wagons as I sat there, one coming and one going. There were two of them now that went by our place, and more, a good many more, in other parts of the town, I suppose. They passed by us now regularly, like busses to a station — always loaded. One was go-ing out while I sat there, a half dozen coffins piled up like trunks — and the golden flies trailed out behind it, and the old lazy mules and the nigger drowsing on the

172

seat. And the other wagon was coming back to town again, with the mules and the harness, and the niggers' clothes all covered up with that old clay dust of the country roads, fine and dry as bolted corn-meal.

There was no more doubt about it now. The Fever had gone loose from them, and was spreading out east and north and south — fast as a fire that the gunners have started in the woods in the fall. They were having lots of trouble already getting coffins enough for the dead; the niggers were fighting against digging the graves; and the little crooked man who had the contract for burying folks from the town had given up in despair, and got drunk; and for a day or two they couldn't get the dead out from among the sick and living.

And so I knew that it was a matter of hours — just hours — if any of us was going to get to go, as I sat there that long afternoon, and waited for four o'clock to come when my Uncle Hagar was to take me up with him into the Tower and show me that half-nigger. And all the time, I made and remade imaginary speeches that I was going to make to him to keep him to his promise of getting Vance away out of there — if he didn't bring it up again himself.

Five minutes to four came, and I heard him moving in his study underneath me; and before four o'clock he was climbing up the stairs to my room. I met him half way on the stairs.

"I'll go first," he said. "You crawl up afterwards. I believe she's sleeping, but you can't tell."

So five minutes afterwards I crept up after him and stood there beside him in that old roasting tower.

"Here's where you get a good look at things," said my Uncle Athiel, wiping his forehead. "Here's where you can see what's going on and nobody the wiser."

You could, too. You looked over the top of everything. Over east and north, you saw the streets of the
city, empty and white in the white sunshine, with one or
two little doctors' buggies standing hitched on the shady
side, like the little animals before those little old Noah's
Arks the children have. And in the middle of the town,
on a corner, I could see one of the places they piled up
their extra coffins on the sidewalks, high piles now, bright
and new in the sunshine. And there was nobody, hardly,
moving anywhere. And over to the west the old river was
shining, white and flashy, in the low hot afternoon sunshine. And right below you looked straight down over
the fences into the neighbors' yards.

"Right over there," said my Uncle Athiel, pointing
me to the Ventress's back yard. "Keep your eye right
there, and you'll see him."

We stood there and looked — it seemed like an hour to
me — out of one of those little round bulls-eye of windows.
There was a little northwest wind blowing in, that played
like cool water on your face, but your back was running
sweat, and your nostrils were just choked up with the
dry heat of the place.

"You look — you keep looking," said my Uncle.
"Your eyes are better than mine," and stepped back and
sat down on an old black haircloth sofa there was up
there.

But there was nothing there that I could see.

"He'll come," said my Uncle. "Keep looking!"

And then, finally, all at once, I saw our dogs and the
way they were acting. There was a little shed over there
in the Ventress's yard, between us and them. I saw Belle,
the little black and tan, first, going up to it — slow and
cautious, and then jumping back again.

"That's him," said my Uncle Athiel, getting up and

looking. " He's in back there getting acquainted with the dogs. He was last night."

The little dog would step up close to the shed and jerk back again — from something out of sight behind there. And old Gen. Sherman, older and feebler and more ramshackle than ever, stood out further back — and looked with his head down. But Belle, the black and tan, lively and young and full of that woman's curiosity of hers, kept edging in and edging in — and then jumping back again! But she never got quite close enough to be caught.

Till by and by, the figure in there that we couldn't see, came out following her, and I saw that half-nigger for the first time.

He came inching out, reaching out his hand, squatting on his heels the way nobody but a nigger can, teasing and coaxing for the little dog he couldn't quite get hold of.

" That's him," whispered my Uncle Hagar, from in back of me. " Look at him! Ain't he a bad nigger!"

He certainly was, what I could see of him — a great huge brute, a great gorilla-shaped nigger with arms most as long as his legs.

" When you see him close to," said my Uncle, " he's got one of those great scars that those levee niggers have, cut from his eye clear down beneath his chin."

" He's pretty bold," I said. " How does he dare do it? Right out there in plain daylight!"

" There's nobody in those houses, now," my Uncle said —" not any of them, and he's got that shed in between him and us."

I had forgotten that. You couldn't see him from anywhere below us in the house.

He squatted there — we watching him — reaching and coaxing, still and patient as an old fisherman in his skiff on a bayou.

"He's gettin' to 'em gradually," said my Uncle. "He'll get 'em," he said, watching like a man who sees a game.

"What's he planning to do?" I asked.

"Feed 'em something, I expect," said my Uncle, stiff and watchful.

"Kill 'em?" I said.

"Certainly," said my Uncle, speaking low like folks do when they're watching. "What would he do?"

"And we ain't going to try and stop it?"

"Stop him!" said my Uncle, astonished. "Stop him! Why? That's the next thing, ain't it? He can't come near the house with those dogs around — or that black and tan anyhow — she's too noisy.

"A good little watch dog too," he said, considering. "That old fool, that Gen. Sherman mongrel, is no use; you couldn't squeeze a bark out of him, not now."

The nigger reached and reached, and snapped his fingers, but he couldn't quite get that little dog. And all at once, he got up finally — got up and spanked his knees; and the dog stood off and moved away; and he slouched out into the alley, and looked around; and we saw him start out across and down one of those crooked paths along the river bank, to the levee out in the front of the town.

"After something to eat," my Uncle Athiel said.

"He won't get 'em to-night, I expect," he went on, again.

"But he's bitin', he's bitin'!" he said — smiling, and his black eyes snapping out again. "It won't be long now before he's comin' in to call on us."

I thought he'd go down then; we were being roasted there alive. But he looked at me then a second or two, and said the thing I was waiting to hear.

" And now to-night," he said, " I'm going down, and I'm going to get your cousin Vance out of town.

" I ain't been worried yet; I ain't so scared of that Fever," he went along, " as the rest of them are. I know you can keep out of it, if you keep away from that night air. So I ain't been afraid of that for myself or her either, or anybody.

" But now," he said, touching the top buttonhole of my coat, " she's goin'. This ain't any time to have women underfeet," he said. " This ain't any business for women.

" But you and I'll stay right here," he went along, getting up close to me, and talking in my face. " You and I'll stay and take care of this half-nigger. We'll give the niggers a little lesson they'll remember. We'll show 'em to leave folks' property alone."

" When are you going to have her go? " I asked him.

" To-morrow; she's going to-morrow. And look here," he said, standing off and eying me. " You want her to go, don't you? "

" I certainly do," I said.

" Then you keep your hands off," said my Uncle Athiel. " Whatever you see me do. You keep your mouth shut, if you think I talk to her too rough. You've got to talk up to 'em sometimes to handle 'em — this high strung kind like her, and like her mother was."

And I told him I would. I would have done most anything to get her away from there.

" Now we'll go down," said my Uncle. " I'll go first, and you follow, when the coast is clear. You follow — easy, now — easy! "

He went down then, as quiet as his lame leg would permit him.

And I looked out the window, for a last look. There

was nothing over toward the Ventress's any more. Even the dogs were gone now. Then I turned and looked down the street, out of the eastern window.

And I saw two niggers in an old light wagon, bringing down a fresh yellow coffin to the place on the corner, where the Fever was.

I saw it, but then I had to come right down, for at any time, Vance might be out and catch me.

I got down all right and into my room, without her seeing me. And I saw again from there the two men with their coffin. They stopped and went upstairs with it, up over the dingy, empty little grocery store on the corner.

I wasn't the only one watching — as usual. Out in our front yard — the furthest corner — I could see Arabella, standing looking.

Then by and by, after a little while, the two niggers came out with the coffins again, between them, hurrying — and drove off south with it, toward the poor folks' cemetery.

And after that, sometime after — I saw Dr. Greathouse coming out the door. And he whistled once, and old Mungo drove in from around the corner, where he had been standing in the shade, I expect; and they drove up the road, home, by our house.

The old doctor was tired, I could see that, from where I was. He was unshaved, and he was in his shirt sleeves — careless and untidy. He looked bad to me — hot and tired and played out for sleep.

And all the time, in our front yard, Arabella stood staring, taking it all in.

CHAPTER XIV

THE FEVER FIRE

"YASSUM," said Arabella, at supper time. " She's daid. The next to the littlest one — with the whites' hair. Daid — daid and buried by this time. Yassum."

She stopped where she was with a plate of biscuit in her hands. " And old Mek Haste Mose was there, yassum, bringing in his coffin. Just going round like he does ev'ywhere at them Fever houses — going round and saying to 'em:

" ' Mek Haste! Mek Haste! Mek Haste! ' "

She stood there, making up those faces, the way niggers do when they get talking about death — talking and whispering like an old ghost gibbering in a graveyard. Her eyes rolled and her hands went, and her head stuck out forward. And she talked low, and fast, and hoarse, showing how he went round.

That was the most she had been excited, that night. We all got pretty nervous — that night they first set a Fever fire going on our street.

" Yassum," said Arabella, getting all the time more worked up, the way they are when they've got strange news to tell. " And the two others got it now, and the old man. And all the chillun and the old man. All of 'em but the woman — she ain't got it yet.

" Down there, in our front yard," she said, taking

breath, " you kin hear 'em. You kin hear 'em plain.
The sick ones, ev'y now and then going ' *Um-um-um*,' that
old Fever sound — ev'y so often. And that poor woman
aprayin' all the time. Just sittin' there at the window
aprayin' for God to spare 'em."

" Poor woman," Vance whispered.

" But He won't spare 'em. He ain't agoin' spare nobody, not now, not any more!" said Arabella, louder.
" It's gettin' too late now; it's gettin' too late!"

" That's all," said Vance. " Put them down and go."

For the negress stood still there, with the plate of bis-
cuits in her hands, talking hoarse, and rolling the whites
of her eyes.

She went along then, looking back.

" When you goin'? " she said, half-way out. " When
you goin'? "

" Never mind," said Vance.

" I heard that woman hollerin' myself," said my Uncle,
looking up from his eating. " Those Dutchmen, they
take things mighty hard when it strikes them. They
holler easy. They's a lot of 'em up around St. Louis
there — I used to see 'em up there."

" These folks have a right to take it hard," said Vance,
quickly —" with the Fever there! "

" Yes," said my Uncle Hagar, in that dull voice of his,
" they have. You're right. I've seen whole families go
that way when the Fever once gets inside the door."

And he went on eating, and we didn't any of us talk
much more.

I thought maybe he would say something to Vance right
then, when he had started talking. But he didn't, and
when the meal was done, back he went into the Study
again — and his play-acting — with his false money, I
expect. And Vance and I were in the sitting room alone

when they started up that first Fever fire, right there, under our windows, on our own street.

We both got up and stood looking at it. It was twilight yet, and we hadn't lighted the gas, and it shone bright and clear, when they touched it off at first — all that light cotton stuff, and the straw mattress, and the child's clothing. It was a clear bright fire, when they first started it. And standing back a little, and looking down I watched it over Vance's shoulder, and saw its light, like I had seen that first one the week before — upon the window-frames, and across her hair and cheek. Only that first fire had been so faint and far away I could scarcely see it. And now this fell, as plain as yellow paint, upon her thin cheek, and the frame-work of the window-panes.

The fire dulled after that. There was something white in the flame at first, some chemical or other they put in. And then, after that, they put on the tar, and smothered it down. And the first flame changed to an old smudge of greasy smoke, with a red fire at its heart. I shivered a little, and started talking. But just then Vance turned away from looking, and spoke to me, and asked me a question I didn't expect.

"What were you doing in that tower to-day?" she asked, looking at me curiously.

"Nothing," I said, making up my mind in a second. "I wasn't in the tower."

"With Dad?" she kept right on, keeping her eyes on me.

"I wasn't there, I tell you," I said. "Why — what —"

"How long since you started lying to me?" asked Vance. And after a while she said, "You can't do it, Beavis; you can't lie to me. You just don't know how."

I certainly did look foolish, I expect. But I kept on lying. I didn't raise my eyes, but I kept right on. And all the time I knew she never took her eyes away from me. I got red and ashamed, but I held right to what I said. And then, finally both of us stopped, for my Uncle Athiel came out of his study.

He came out and stood behind us, and I moved out back to let him get nearer to the window.

" That's wrong," he said, " all wrong. They scatter it, I believe. They scatter the Fever poison around in that smoke more than they kill it.

" See that! See that! " For somebody added something to the fire. I could see the lights start up on their faces and the window-frame.

" Look yere! " he said, turning quick and savage towards Vance. " Didn't I tell you to get out of here three days ago! "

" Yes, sir," said Vance.

" Well, when are you goin' to pay attention to me? "

And she went back and lighted up the gas.

He left the window then, and followed her.

" I wonder, sometimes," said my Uncle Hagar, looking at her in a funny disagreeable way, " what God A'mighty made 'em for."

" Who? " said Vance.

" Women! " said her father. And he started off, cursing and swearing at the uselessness of women. Lord, what didn't he say? I've forgotten three-quarters of it. There was this to be said about a nigger — you could drive him to work like a mule; you could get something out of him. But a woman, God A'mighty, a woman with notions in her head. " Uppity-uppity; pee-wee-wee-wee! " He stood and mocked and made queer crazy sounds of women giggling and snickering. What did God make 'em for; he couldn't see.

"He must have had something special against me," said my Uncle Hagar, with an oath, "from what He sent me! First your mother, and then you."

Vance, staring at him, winced and stepped away, when he spoke her mother's name. And I stepped forward and opened up my mouth — and then closed it. For I caught his eye, and remembered what he said to me about keeping out of this if I wanted Vance to get away.

"Two high strung nervous women," he said. "Always under foot.

"Always doing what you don't want 'em to."

Vance started toward him first, like she was going to answer him. Then she looked at him and stopped. And when he kept on going, she shrank back — got back against the window sill — and put her fingers in her ears. He stepped right up to her, and pulled them down again.

"What's that for?" he said. "This ain't no time for that. I ain't got time now to giggle and squirm and talk sweet-pretty the way a man generally has to talk to women folks. We're going to talk now like ordinary humans. What do you think you're staying here for, anyhow?"

She didn't answer right away.

"Come on," he said, "there's got to be some reason."

But she didn't, or she wouldn't answer him.

"What is it you want? Do you want to kill us?"

"I'm going to stay," said Vance, "as long as you do."

"Now I want to tell you something," said her father. "I don't expect you'll understand it. But you've got to hear it — for it's God's truth, and you can like it or lump it, just as you like. If you stay here two more days you've got about three chances out of four of killing the whole lot of us."

" Why? " said Vance, her big eyes watching him.

He took her by the arm.

" Why? " he said. " Look yere! " And he held her there before the big gilt mirror on the side wall. " Look yere, that's why! "

She stood looking there, into that big dark pool of a looking glass — the dim light of the gas-jet in the chandelier behind her, surprised, scared a little, I expect, and mad, too. Her lips parted, her great coil of black hair, and her deep eyes — full of apprehension and wonder, staring from her white face. She had that look she often had, when she got a little bit excited — intense and wondering, and a little scared — that made me think sometimes of a young prophetess in the Old Bible, and she certainly looked pale and delicate.

" Do you see now — if Fever was around — who'd have it? " said my Uncle. " Tell me that! Do you see? "

" But you said," Vance answered, " you said — if you kept out of the night air — You said so! And I've always —"

" I said, ' generally,' for the usual run of folks. I wasn't talkin' of anythin' like that," he said, pointing to the mirror. " Anythin' just achin' and ripe and certain to get it — if it came within gunshot. You can see that yourself. You ain't a fool."

" I won't go," said Vance. " You can't scare me that way."

" And if you get it. If it gets inside once, inside this house —" and his voice grew uglier yet. " Why, then — we'll all take our turns. You'll have the satisfaction of not only havin' it yourself — but givin' it to all the rest of us."

"I won't go," said Vance. "I can't. I can stay and help."

"Yes," said my Uncle, in a disagreeable, sneering voice, "help kill us!"

"Do you believe that, Beavis?" said Vance, turning round to me.

"I certainly do," I told her. "I certainly don't want you around," I said, for I was getting desperate. And it seemed to me already that he had failed. That he wasn't going to get her to go after all.

He thought so, too, I expect for he started off again on the foolishness of women, worse than ever.

Our nerves were all going, I expect, under the strain. He made me so mad I couldn't stand it.

"That'll do!" I said, "she'll go, I believe."

"But I won't go," said Vance. "You know I won't. Why, I can't —" she said, and looked over at her father. "You know. I couldn't —"

And I recognized at once what she was talking about — that same silly idea — that presentiment she had that her father, and nobody else, was going to die — to be sick and die out of that house of ours. And when that struck me again, I was just more ugly and desperate than ever. Between the two of them — he with his "Property"— with his money, whatever it was that he had there; and she with that worry and anxiety over him, that had gone now right up to the edge of superstition and craziness — I was desperate.

And then, just then, I looked out and my eye fell again on that old Fever fire smoldering on the street, and something took me; I could feel myself going — the blood rushing up back of my ears into my head. I gave up. I didn't care any more what I said or did.

"Let her alone," I said, talking hoarse. "Let her

stay if she wants to. But she knows now for certain how we feel. She knows that she's a burden and danger to us. And now she knows it — let her stay if she wants to — let her stay!"

"Beavis!" said Vance.

I didn't look at her. But I knew she stepped back, and away from me. I could hear her drawing in her breath, surprised.

"You never talked like that to me before," she said, afterwards, in a low voice.

But I didn't look at her. I kept my eyes away from hers — the way you always do when you're mad.

"It's settled," I said, not answering her, going right ahead with the meanest talk I could think of. "It's settled — you'll stay; we'll all stay. And you can get the Fever and give it to us. And we'll all die together. Then you'll be satisfied."

"Beavis," said Vance, standing before me. "Can't you help me? Won't you help me when I'm trying to do what I think is right?"

"You're not doing right," I said. "You're doing all wrong, and you know it," I told her, and wouldn't look at her.

She stood looking at me a little longer; and then turned away toward her father.

"Good-night, Dad," she said.

But he didn't move a muscle toward her, or speak.

And finally she turned, we standing there, and stood there in the doorway, looking back a minute at her father. She didn't even glance at me.

"I'm going to stay," she said. "I'm going to stay. You can't scare me that way."

It seemed to me as she stood there looking at him, that I saw that little nervous shudder come over her again.

Lord, how I would liked to have helped her! How I wanted to go over and take her in my arms and comfort her! But of course, I didn't. I just stood there, like you do when you're mad;— looked away, still as a log, just disregarding her.

And she went out alone, and we heard her in silence, as she climbed upstairs to her bedroom.

I turned and faced my Uncle then.

" How does she look to you? " he said, looking sharp at me.

" Bad," I said, " as bad as she can. Just all tired out."

" Yes," he said, and stood looking out the window, thinking. " Yes."

" She won't last a week after the Fever's here," I said.

" She'll come around," said my Uncle Athiel, after a while, like he was telling himself so. " She'll come around."

And then he went on, talking to me.

" You did just right," he said, " I was afraid one time you wouldn't; but you did just right."

And when I didn't answer him, or pay any attention, he went on again.

" Just right," he said, " just right. That's the way to handle women."

" How? What do you mean? " I said, looking at him.

" Hurt their feelings. Make 'em think they're wrong. Set 'em thinkin' they're harmin' you — then go off and leave 'em — let 'em think! Let 'em worry! "

I stood and listened to him, while he went along, talking to himself.

" Keep away from her after that. Let her think about it. They'll come around. They'll come around sometimes. They can't stand it, especially those high strung and nervous ones.

"It's the only way to handle 'em sometimes. Especially those high strung ones like her and her mother. Hurt their feelings — blame 'em! And then leave 'em alone and leave 'em think."

I held my tongue to keep from talking. But he went along too far for me.

"You'll see," he said. "You'll see how it acts with her. She'll be round, all ready to go, to-morrow."

"Hell!" I said, breaking loose. "A million devils!" For it made me sick to hear him talk. "She won't go, nor any of the rest of us. We'll be here — you, she and I, and all of us, staying — watching your ' Property '!" I said. "We'll stay here and when we move at all, we'll move under ground!"

My Uncle looked at me — more quiet.

"That's the only way I know," he said. "That's the only way I know to get her out. Do you know any better?"

"No," I had to say. "No, I don't."

"Then keep away from her. You keep away from her. And let me try and see how it works."

"All right," I said. "I certainly will. I'll try anything now.

"And now," I said, while he stood watching me. "Let's talk and settle how we'll save that ' Property ' of yours — your house here and whatever else it is you've got there," I said, looking at him. "Let's find out how we'll kill that half-nigger!"

They say that fear strikes different folks in different ways, at different times. It made me, at that time, I know, like a wild savage beast. I just wanted to hurt somebody — like I was being hurt.

" I mean it! " I said to my Uncle Hagar, who stood looking at me. " I mean it! I'd kill anything, by God! For six bits, I'd kill you! "

He stood still looking at me in the eye, reading me. " That's the talk! " said my Uncle Athiel. " You'll do."

And his face came out again into that mean old crooked smile.

After that we planned together for a little while — for watching out for that half-nigger that night — and for getting him. But not very long, either. I left the planning of it mostly to him. And pretty quick I went along upstairs, still mad and savage.

But when I got upstairs, up alone in my room — I don't deny it — I just stood there, and turned my face to the wall — put my head up against my arm and cried. For it seemed to me likely now, we'd all go, now — all die. But Vance for certain.

CHAPTER XV

THE TRAP

IT was my share to watch the last part of that night
till daylight. My Uncle was to stay there in the
study until two or three o'clock; and if anything
happened, which we didn't expect that night, he would tap
on the ceiling just under my bed with his cane. And if
there was nothing, he would come up and scratch at my
door when he wanted me, and I would stay there in my
own room and watch — for I was just exactly as well
placed there to see, as I would be down below.

So, at half past two, I heard him scratching at my
door, and I got up and rattled the knob, and my Uncle
Hagar went along to bed and left me watching.

I sat and watched out the window, and I saw just nothing at all. Too mighty little in fact. It was too quiet.
There wasn't one thing that showed alive but that yellow
lamp upstairs where the Fever was down under the hill.
And at three o'clock, the lamp-lighter putting out the
gas lights. But not one sound, I noticed, from the dogs.
I did notice that. I didn't see our dogs once. And the
other dogs weren't so noisy now. They had killed a great
lot of them off since the Fever came — poisoned them.

But I didn't think about the dogs or anything, so much
as I should have, I expect. My mind was too full of
what I had seen and understood, and been scared about
during that long day I'd just gone through.

The night, there by the window, was just as long and
190

longer. And I had plenty of time to go over all that day again — one thing after another — the Fever, and the chances of getting away from it now; and all those crazy, unbreakable, invisible chains which bound us there, while death climbed up on us, up the street.

I thought about my Uncle and his " Property," of that " Hagar's Hoard," or whatever it was he really stayed for; and of that half-nigger he was watching now, like a wild Indian in ambush, with no mind left for anything else. And Vance — most of all, Vance — with her obstinacy and her great danger, and that foolish presentiment of hers about her father.

Vane! I saw her fine, delicate, drawn face ahead of me in the dark all that night. Her pale face set off with its crown of thick black hair. Her parted sensitive lips, and her deep eyes — deeper now for that crazy fear and apprehension that had caught her since the Fever came. Vance, with that fear in her eyes, half like a young prophetess out of the Old Bible — half like a sensitive child afraid of the dark. I sat and saw her, and her danger, staying there; saw it the clear way you do sometimes, at night, and I saw more and more all the time, what it would mean to me, if anything should happen to her — if she should stay there and die.

I sat there and looked out into the dark — a frightened boy, in love — just staring eternity in the face! And shivering at it, and ·scared. And when my mind traveled back again, over it all; and I realized the thing that held her there — just the shadow of a dream — I writhed in my old armchair, and got up on my feet and walked the room.

It was crazy, if you looked at it so, absolutely crazy. And yet, since that time and during it, I haven't ever undertaken to say just who was sane, or what was, in such a time as that was. They say in shipwrecks, folks get that way — and rant and stamp and have strange ideas, and show plain just all the thoughts and wishes and anxieties that really have control and government of their mind. And even at that time, when I was going through it, I understood partly the strain that folks were going under, in that Fever summer — their fear of death, their flight, their funny crazy ideas for cleansing and burning and shooting that Fever poison out of the air. And the superstition of the negress, and the strained actions of all kinds that went on around us. And I could see, too, partly, how that impression had fixed itself on Vance's mind. First the worry for the Fever generally; then for her father in particular. And then that dream came out of it and brought that sharp sense of fear that everybody has had sometime or other after some bad dream, I believe. Only hers was multiplied and kept alive continually by everything that was going on around her.

About her father, whether he was crazy or sane, or not, I never did pretend to say — not to this day. What is being crazy, anyway? You tell me. I can't say. We all have our ideas that just won't balance right — if we will only stop and watch them. And all I know or think about, when I remember now how my Uncle acted then, is that old common fear which grips and rules the mind of all of us sometimes — and especially when we get old — that fear for property — of losing what we've got. In all the actions I remember most of him, as I tell them to you now, I see that old specter of fear grabbing him and taking him along with it, out from our eyes into eternity — just as real and actual a thing as anything in this world.

At breakfast time, I know, he and I sat alone again. Vance was not feeling well, and sent down word she would have to be excused. And so, though I had planned and planned what I would say and do when she came down, I didn't even see her. She just stayed away from us.

Arabella moved around, taking care of us at breakfast time. Another one of the German children in the house below was mighty low, she told me. And she said the Fever was moving on, now — was gone into two other houses on that street below there.

" You ain't seen my little dog this morning? " she asked us, when she got through talking —" You ain't seen my Belle anywhere? "

We hadn't, either of us.

" She ain't been around all mornin'. Gen. Sherman, old fool, he's been in, but I ain't seen nothin' at all of Belle since way along early last evening."

And my Uncle winked at me — one of those deep, slow winks that old-fashioned people give you — plain and clear as drawing down a curtain.

" He's got her! He's got her! " he said, after Arabella left the room, and smiled.

He hadn't slept much, it looked like. His face showed that. But he was cheerful — almost happy acting — that morning, and quick and full of snap almost as a young boy.

" She'll be round at noon," he said about Vance. " She'll come around and go before the twenty-four hours are up." And he said he was glad that she wasn't down that morning, so we could have it for ourselves to talk. Then he took me, right away, into that study, and showed me more about that old trap that he was laying for the half-nigger.

" I don't expect too much. All we got to expect is he'll come, and take a look. All he'll do to-night, I expect," he said, " will be to come alookin'.

"He'd have to look; he'd just have to look anyway," he went along, "or he wouldn't be a nigger.

"But," said he, "if we get him on the premises —! That's all we want!"

I shrank back a little bit; I expect I showed it. For I thought naturally of what the Marshal had said about shooting down on sight anybody that you found loitering around your premises. And by that time I'd got over that first flash of wanting to hurt and kill something that I had the night before. And I did think, whatever he said, that he meant to kill that half-nigger or hurt him monstrously, anyhow, when he got him there.

"Don't fret; don't get excited," said my Uncle. "I ain't agoing to kill him. I ain't made up my mind yet just what I am going to do; I'll get him somewheres, but I won't kill him right outright."

Then he showed me more about his trap — how he'd worked it out — sitting there counting and working on his books, and how at night he put away his Confederate money behind some books and left it there, and how sure he was that some of the time, anyhow, the half-nigger had been over there at the Ventress's watching.

"I don't mean I expect him to get in here," said my Uncle Athiel, "right away. All we got to look for is to get him up here — up to those windows there."

There were two of them, French windows, that opened out on two little balconies, two of those stiff looking little balconies, with heavy wooden railings around them and thick short posts like dumb-bells — where nobody ever goes out to sit.

"If you can get him in there on one of those," said my Uncle Athiel, "we've got him.

"Now then," he said, "let's me and you go out and

take a turn around the yard. Maybe we might find out
something about that dog — that little dog of hers."

So we did; we went out; and around the servants' room
and the big empty barn, and the stable — the shed we
used for the old horse — out beside the alley. Finally,
all at once, my Uncle stooped down, and dragged out
something stiff from underneath the corner of the shed.

"Look yere!" he said.

It was Belle, the little dog, flat and stiff as a board.
Her back was hunched and her front legs drawn up underneath her.

"Strychnine," said my Uncle Athiel, kicking it back
under with his foot. He talked pretty low and soft.
Then right away he talked up a lot louder.

"Who did that? I'd like to know who did that? I'd
like to catch him at it," he said loudly, and winked at
me when he said it.

"You can't tell where he might be watching," said my
Uncle, when we had got back again in the house.

"That looks good," he said, "that looks like a good
sign. He's comin' on; he's comin' faster'n I thought.

"Now, you get along out of here," he said. "I'll see
you later," and he closed himself in behind the big brown
doors again. And went on, I suppose, with his play-acting — and tolling in that nigger, with his old Confederate
money. And I went along and tried to kill off the time
in another day.

Most of all I wanted to see Vance — just how she
looked, if nothing else. And yet, I didn't want to see her,
either — not so she would have a chance to talk to me.
I couldn't talk to her — not after that last night.

So after all I tried to persuade myself that it was better for me and for her that I didn't see her; that maybe

by keeping away and just leaving her to herself both of us, like my Uncle said to do — she would finally come around herself, come to her senses and get out.

But whatever I thought I was, or wasn't going to do if I saw her made no difference, for I did not see Vance that day, not alone. She stayed in her room late that morning, till I worried for fear she was taken sick. But later on she was out around the upper story at her morning's work, and at noon she was at the dinner table. But silent, talking not at all to either her father or to me.

Not one of us were talking, not even of the Fever, nor how it was running out now to other houses from that Fever house there on the corner. And right away again after dinner, Vance went back again upstairs.

"Let her alone," her father said. "She'll come round and go."

That afternoon, it was, the second child of the grocer, Otterman, died, in that house below. The niggers came with another coffin, and I heard the mother screaming as they took it out again — much worse than the first time. She was getting in hysterics now — alone in the house with all those sick folks, and only a nigger nurse they sent her in to help her. She got quiet after a while. But it made you crawl whenever she got started — hearing her and thinking what it meant. And what it might mean to you and all the rest. And all the time I knew, of course, Vance sat up there alone, listening to it.

That monstrous day passed finally. Time for supper came and went, and Vance came down and went right back again, and shut herself up in her own room — still silent.

There was no fire in the street, before the Fever house, that night. When there were a number sick in a place like that, they got careless about their fires. There wasn't bedding enough to go round, most likely. I know

I saw that afternoon, the mother, the little German woman, crying and hanging out the bedclothes to dry in the back yard.

But as far as I could see, my Uncle Athiel paid no attention to all of this. He might have been in Russia for all the thought he gave the Yellow Fever. He had his mind on just one thing, that game that he was playing; that tolling in of that half-nigger.

And after supper a while, he came and called me.

" It's comin' on better'n I expected," he said. And I made up my mind he had seen the nigger moving about the Ventress's place. Once or twice, I knew, he had gone up in the tower that afternoon — alone. For he did everything himself, that day; he was spry and active as a boy. And if he wanted anything of me, he said, he would call and let me know.

" The dogs won't bother him any now," said my Uncle. " That big one won't do anything but sleep — now that black and tan is gone. He knew that, he figured on it — that's why he didn't get him too.

" He may come, I wouldn't be surprised — he may come lookin' to-night — you can't tell. Things are movin' on pretty good."

And then he told me what he wanted me to do. He had planned it further while he was sitting there that afternoon.

He was going to leave one side of both those French windows out upon the balcony without locking it.

" If he once gets up there — on a balcony — like I think he will; just a touch, just a touch — and it will swing open and he's inside. And then —" my Uncle said.

" Then —" I said after him.

" Nothin' will keep him — nothin' will just keep a nigger from steppin' in. And when he does —"

"Yes," I said, waiting.

"You let him have it. Let him have it till we get him."

I was to stand between the windows in the dark — back a ways, with that old great hickory cane of his. A club, it was really.

"You want to watch out for him though. You can't be too careful. A nigger's eyesight is different from a white man's. A nigger's a night thing," said my Uncle Athiel, "just as much as an owl. He can see in the dark just like an old owl. That's why they are always out so, all hours of the night.

"Look out for him. You want to look out for him. Be sure and get him the first crack. He's an ugly nigger — a hard customer," said my Uncle. "A hard ticket. And they've always got somewhere around 'em — those levee niggers — one of them big knives they cut and slash each other with."

"I'll get him," I said.

"Yes, I reckon you will," said my Uncle, looking me over. "You're pretty strong and husky.

"But if you don't," he went along, "I can. I'll get him somewhere."

He meant that he would get him with that old Derringer of his.

So it was all fixed up. I was to go up to my own room, upstairs, and by and by my Uncle Athiel was to come up too, and close his door, and lock it up. And all the lights in the house would be out. And then, after a little while we would both crawl down.

"And Vance —" I said.

"That's her lookout," said my Uncle. "If she stays, she'll just have to take what comes along — like the rest of us.

" But she'll come round; she'll come round and go to-morrow," he kept on saying. " You'll see."

It was about ten o'clock before I heard him coming up. I'd got almost crazy waiting — waiting and watching down there where the Fever was.

There was the excitement and the moving around of lamps in that first Fever place below us. And the German woman, those children's mother — screamed again, once. And then, after that, she made less noise and out-cry. I heard her still, but it was different. It seemed to me finally that it sounded more like she was laughing than crying. But the windows were all down, and I couldn't hear her, or anything, very clear.

I got downstairs ahead of my Uncle.

" Nothing yet? " I whispered when he came.

" No, nothin'," he told me.

" But he's there," he was whispering, " he's there! certain! "

We took our places like we planned. I on the inside between the windows with that great club of a cane. He, in the corner, back a little, with his old Derringer. We stood there — waiting. Nothing — not a sound. Only that German woman who had lost her children, over there — only now and then that German woman laughing.

" That last young one's dead, I expect," my Uncle Athiel whispered.

It got on my nerves terribly, after a while, hearing her.

There we sat — waiting and waiting — like hunters in a duck-blind. A half hour, and an hour, nothing! My Uncle sat down finally, back there in the corner.

" Wait," he whispered, once or twice. " Wait, wait! "

The side of the French window, the one between him and me, blew open just a crack. I heard a mosquito in the room, around me. I closed the window with my finger. I heard my Uncle striking softly in the dark at the mosquito. Then he waited.

"Keep back!" said my Uncle. "Listen!"

There was something — after awhile — something along outside the wall of the house.

We stood there, frozen, hardly breathing. There was something light, a great yellow hand, I made out finally, on the dark brown balustrade of that balcony to the window between him and me.

And still I heard nothing — only once the cry — the laughing of that woman again down there below.

Then an arm came up, and a leg; a leg and a bare foot. And softly and slowly the great half-nigger stood on that old balcony between us, waiting!

I could feel the old smooth, hard hickory cane in my hand, and a piece of bark which still stuck out on the handle. It felt like I was holding a feather. And still we stood there holding back.

Still we stood there, a long, long while. Then all at once there was the scratch of a match, and we shrank back, both of us, flat back against the wall. The match-light grew up, shaded in a big saffron colored palm, first blue, then yellow. And I could see, from where I stood, just one piece of the cheek of that great half-nigger, flat against the pane — pressed flat and white against the glass. And a great long scar, with knobs and roughness in it, whiter than the rest, running clear across the smooth yellowish meat of the cheek.

He stood and looked — for a second or two — we still waiting. Then like a flash the great coarse saffron palms just closed on the match and it was out again. He must have thought he heard somebody passing on the street.

For he turned his back; hugged close to the window, and waited — waited till he was sure.

But all at once he moved a little — he must have moved, for the unlocked side of the window gave way — and the great nigger half stumbled, half rolled in onto the floor between us.

"Stomp him! Stomp him!" yelled my Uncle Athiel. "Let him have it!"

But like a cat the half-nigger rolled, and when he rolled, he kicked me with his great bare foot, and in a second, there I was, rolling on the floor myself.

And in another second "Whang!" my Uncle's old Derringer had gone, and the room was full of its blue smoke.

"Missed him, by God! Missed him!" said my Uncle Athiel — in the voice of a man just dying in despair.

The half-nigger was gone; he hadn't hit him; there wasn't a sign of blood or anything.

I didn't wait; I was out after him. Over the balcony, out into the yard, running as if the Devil was after me. Out in the middle of the back yard before I stopped.

What was I running for? Where to?

I stopped and listened. Not a sound or a sign. Not a sign of the half-nigger to be had.

Barefoot, gone — out into the darkness! Not a sound!

Not a sound anywhere. Only, once again, that German woman who had lost her children, laughing.

"Come back in here, you fool!" my Uncle called from the side doorway. "Come in here! Come out of that poison night air!"

I stood for just a second, and I did what he told me to.

I'd heard so much about it — all the time — that poison Fever air. How deadly it was; and how it got you. We had shut it out so carefully. And it seemed somehow, when I stood there, like I could feel it — just feel it — thick and poison, all around me.

I shivered and went hurrying back — and in the door. And it seemed, when I went in, like that woman was down there laughing after me.

"You fool!" said my Uncle Athiel. "You double-damned fool! Now you've exposed us all. You've got us all the Fever, most likely."

Not a word any more about the half-nigger; not a word. But then, on the stairs; behind him — her black hair in long braids below her waist; a long white India shawl, that was her mother's, over her night-dress — Vance was calling in a high sharp voice:

"What is it? Oh, what is it?"

"Nothing, nothing," said my Uncle Athiel. "We were just shooting at a nigger — a nigger sneakin' through the yard. We were taking a shot at a nigger."

He gave very little explanation more than that. Just sent her back to bed, scared and wondering.

BOOK V

VANCE HAGAR

CHAPTER XVI

THE HEADACHE

I HAVE often thought of her, lying there alone that night, in that high old empty Ivory Room, which Mr. Bozro built for his wife's grand boudoir. Alone and wondering, with nothing more human for companionship than those little simpering frescoed cupids looking down on her from the ceiling. Left to herself, not knowing what had really happened, in all that row and shooting down below her. And the Fever mounting up under her windows. And that German woman laughing and crying out there. And all the time that shadow of her strange monstrous presentiment about her father.

I expect, probably, from what she has told me afterwards — though she never speaks of it more than she can help — that she lay awake all that night, growing sicker every minute toward the morning, and yet, though she certainly must have known what the symptoms were most like, never calling out to either one of us — though both of us were lying there awake — without a doubt — in those rooms next to hers.

"Oh, I didn't want to disturb you — I didn't want to. I just didn't want to," she told me, trying to explain it. For she was sure all the time, so she has always said, that she never was in danger — that there was only one of us really who was, her father.

"I can't explain it to you," she said. "I just knew. And I knew it wasn't I."

And so, we all three lay there that night, awake. For I am certain my Uncle Hagar was awake too. We all three just lay there, thinking out our own thoughts, though one of us, I expect, was too sick to think much.

" Now we all of us can go to bed and sleep," my Uncle had said — when he locked up the side door — after I ran in; and Vance had started back again to her room, and there was nothing to be seen outside through the windows.

" He won't be back again to-night," my Uncle said, talking of the half-nigger.

Now it was easy enough to say, " Go to sleep," but it was something different to do.

It was Thursday night — for one thing; and the niggers — those hollering saints — were out again for an all-night meeting in the sanctified chapel down back under the hill. We didn't hear them much, earlier; they were slow in working up the meeting, I expect. But now, when I had got up into my room, we heard the Clap! Clap! Clap! and the Stamp! Stamp! Stamp! of the sanctified niggers perambulating round and getting drunker and drunker on salvation. And after a while they were dancing and screaming and rolling on the floor, getting saved. I never heard them before or since get quite so bad. The Fever had something to do with it, naturally; and those old prophecies of the nigger woman from Arkansas about the end of the world, or Memphis, or whatever it was.

The noise, and all that, was bad for rest and sleeping. But it wasn't all the time. It came in kind of gusts and stopped again. And I was used to it, more or less, and the windows were all down, anyway. And speaking for myself, I know the thing that really kept me from resting that night was just my own thoughts — and the way I felt ashamed of myself.

I was worried and scared at the Fever, and desperate, now, almost, about the chances of ever getting away from those old bonds which held us there while it came around us. That was the thing that scared me. But from that minute, funny enough, what troubled me most was my shame and humiliation for the figure I had cut in all that thing that night. My cheeks burned when I went over it, and I pulled my full strength at my finger knuckles, and turned and twisted in my chair — as I sat there, looking out the window. We feel that way at twenty-one — over any mistake we make. It's worse than any fever — worst of all when it's just a little public.

My whole action in this thing had been so foolish. The half-nigger had gone — slipped away from our fingers. I had bungled that myself — once in losing him; twice in following him out. There was only one thing that, in my heart, I could be thankful for — that my Uncle hadn't killed the nigger right there under my eyes and nose.

"But that wasn't my fault either," I said to my-self.

While I sat there, staring, thinking, the old dog Gen. Sherman started up and barked once or twice in the yard — barked quite sharp and growled. I got up and looked out the window — glad to do something that would take me away and set me free from that old rolling squirrel-cage of my thoughts.

"Hullo!" I said, half out loud to myself —"That old fool is still alive!"

For we said — both my Uncle Hagar and myself — that now that little nervous black and tan was dead, the old dog would just lie and go to sleep nights — never watch at all.

But he barked once or twice, quite loud; and growled, and finally just stopped. I thought first it was Arabella coming home from her meeting. But it was too ugly a bark for that somehow. And after that, too, I could hear the niggers still stamping, and calling and crying, down back under the hill.

"The old fool must be having a bad dream," I said to myself, and finally sat down again.

The dog was barking, it seemed like, out back in the yard — out near the big barn. But there was nothing to be seen and after that there was not another sound, that I heard, all that night.

It couldn't be the half-nigger, I said to myself. He had gone, out of our way; he certainly wouldn't be back again, that night, anyway, like my Uncle said. He had just gone — and the fear and danger from him; he seemed unreal now, like everything else. The folks were gone out of the houses; the ordinary noises from out the streets; even the sound of wheels and of running away! And the only real thing left out of all of it; the only real thing it seemed like in the world, was that old invisible thing we couldn't see, or touch, or understand — the Fever that filled the air — that old poison night air outside that window-glass.

I could hear — in my mind — continually, the woman laugh again, from the open windows of the Fever house. They had got her quiet now. You didn't hear her really. But that laugh of hers kept sounding in my ears. And when my mind came round to that again, I stiffened up, and pulled my knuckles, and sat straight and scared once more. For I heard, for the hundredth time, my Uncle calling out to me!

"You fool! You fool. You've got us all the Fever!"

For if all those theories, that everybody had then were true, about the night air and the poison in it — it might be that, after all I'd feared and worried, it was I myself that, for the first time, had really gone and exposed the whole of us to the chance of dying by that Fever. I didn't know anything about it, of course. Nobody did much, those days. But all I could think of was, that at that time, when the Fever was there, right on us, just my recklessness and general foolishness — might be the thing that was going to give us all that Fever. Just when I ought to have been cool — and kept my head — I'd broke and rushed in, like a wild blundering half-trained young dog in a covey. And I was ashamed and humiliated, and scared, when I remembered it.

The more I thought of it, the jumpier and more nervous I got. There was only one possible escape now for us that I saw — haste.

"Hurry! Hurry!" something kept saying in me. "If we get out at all now, we've got to hurry!"

But how could we get out? We were fastened there.

And so I worried and tossed and twisted in my chair through that monstrous ugly night; and woke up, after a few snatches of late, broken sleep, into an uglier and more dangerous day — and to the sudden shock of that morning.

My Uncle came in after me to breakfast, and sat down — very shaky, and I looking at him cornerwise. I never saw one night change any man like that did. His right eyelid twitched the way it did when he was tired; his hand was trembly, and his face was yellower, and his lips were bluer than ever. If he had gone back twenty years when the excitement of that hunt of his was on, he'd gone forward twenty more now that it was done. The flash and go was all gone out of him. And he seemed to have shrunk and weazened and waxened all at once into an old man. The flesh had sunk and fallen in between the bones of his face — in his temples and in his cheeks.

I noticed, then, after we sat down, that he kept watching continually toward the door.

" You heard your cousin Vance, this morning? " he finally asked me.

I told him that I hadn't, and he put his eyes back down again on his plate. But every now and then he still looked up toward the door.

" You go up and see what's keeping Miss Vance," he said to Arabella.

And when she went, he kept on eating, without a word to me.

" Miss Vance ain't acomin' down," said Arabella, coming back. She'd grown more important and grand those last few days; that old catlike smile of hers grew all the time on her old smooth face.

" Ain't comin'! Why not? " said my Uncle Hagar, right away.

There was something funny about the way the negress talked.

" A haidache — it seems like she's got, a right bad haidache," said Arabella, and though her face was just as smooth and peaceful as it ever was, her eyes rolled, and her voice was a warning. She knew just as well as anybody did what she was saying.

" A headache! " I said, jumping up.

" Yassah," said Arabella, " a bad haidache, she just kin raise her haid for the pillar."

My Uncle jerked up onto his feet, as fast as his old stiff legs would let him.

" Yassah," said Arabella — for good measure — " yassah, and she's shiv'in' considerable too."

" Shut up, you black fool! " said my Uncle Athiel, and came along where I was standing waiting for him.

"I hope you're satisfied!" I said, staring him in the face.

He didn't answer me. He started round me for the door, but his face was like tallow — dead and lifeless and yellow.

"You and your damned money!" I said.

"You go and get the doctor!" he said to me. In fact, I had started already myself. I had my hat in my hand already. But I couldn't go without blaming him; without saying what was boiling over in me.

"You —" I said, pointing my first finger in his face.

"You — you — damn you!" I said, and that was as far as I could get.

And I whirled around and hurried toward the door.

But when I got there, going out, I whirled again.

"By God!" I said, "if she's got it, you ought to die! If she's taken it I'll just come back and strangle you with my own hands, I believe."

But my Uncle Hagar didn't say a word, nor pay any attention to me. Just went along steadily into the hall and upstairs.

Then I turned and ran towards the doctor's. But before I did, I saw him going up the stairs — tugging at the banisters, lifting his feet slow and heavy — like it was hard work raising them from the floor — an old, old man, with a bloodless, tallow face, dragging his old broken body up the stairs.

And then I said to myself, going out — it came across me in a flash:

"You're blaming him — when it's you that did it. It's your fault more than his. You brought it in to her last night."

And then I was running, running down the street, thinking, "You did that for certain. It was you."

And pretty quick, as I went running, my feet were going to a kind of chant like you make at times like that, sometimes. I was just chanting to myself; and my feet went beating out over and over again to that same thing.

"God Almighty — I did that!

"God Almighty — I did that!"

It couldn't have come to her, of course — not that way — from anything I did. But I didn't know that then.

The doctor was coming out of the gate when I got there, whistling his "Arkansas Traveler" as high and gay and out of tune as usual. And Uncle Mungo sat waiting for him with his buggy out in the front. It was the prettiest time of day. There were roses still, out in the garden; and a mocking bird was singing foolish gladness in a bush somewhere; and that old clear, faint, smiling, pale-green Yellow Fever sky was hung out over the world like the proclamation of a universal holiday.

"What is it?" said the doctor, stopping whistling.

"Vance!" I said, choking.

"You come along after us," he said; and jumped inside of Mungo, and they were gone along up the road before I knew it.

But three minutes after I was there behind them, standing outside the door of the Ivory Room, listening.

The first thing I heard was the doctor's voice, and, let me tell you — I went numb when I first heard it.

"What you been doing to this child?" was the first thing I heard him say, talking to my Uncle.

And my heart gave a great high bound. That couldn't mean the Fever, it seemed like to me.

"Nothin'," said my Uncle Athiel, in his old dead voice.

Then they were both quiet for a minute, and it was my Uncle who spoke next.

" We thought," he said, and caught his breath, " it was the Fever."

" It couldn't be much more like it," said the doctor. " But it isn't."

And the flood of joy and happiness and comfort came back over me this time completely, as I listened there behind the door; all at once my whole soul and body just cried out " Glory, Glory Halleluiah! "

" What is it then? " my Uncle went on asking him.

" Nerves! This girl is on the ragged end of nervous collapse! " said the doctor. And I heard my Uncle sigh.

Vance laughed then, or tried to.

" What did I tell you? " she said. But you could only just hear her.

" There's nothing to laugh at," said the doctor. And her laugh died down. " I don't understand it," said the doctor. " This thing must have been going for days. What I don't see is how she has kept up till now.

" What have you been doing? " he said to her. " What's the matter with you? " And when she tried to laugh him off again —" don't laugh," he said. " How long have you been having these shivering spells? "

" Oh, a few days," Vance whispered, offhand, like she always did, talking about herself.

" Yes," said the doctor, grunting at her. " I see — I see you have.

" Now the first thing you've got to do is to get her out of here," he went along, talking to my Uncle.

" I been tryin' to," my Uncle said, " but she won't go."

" Won't go! " said the doctor.

" No — and I can't make her go," my Uncle said.

" Why? "

" Ask her," said my Uncle Athiel.

"I won't. I can't. You can't make me," Vance whispered.

"You see," said my Uncle's voice again.

"Why not?" the doctor went on asking Vance.

"I'm going to stay. I'm going to stay as long as he does," said Vance's whisper, louder and more excited.

"Oh, I see," the doctor said again. "Well then; all right; you get ready to go," he said, "for he's going. Your father's going."

"And Beavis, too," I heard her say. And her voice seemed stronger immediately, right away.

"Yes, both of them," said the doctor to her. "Lie down! Lie down!" he said again. "You won't go for a day or two yet. And when they all go, depends upon just one thing — on you; on how quick you get fit and ready to be going. You understand?"

I heard her lie back again with a sigh. And right after that the two men came out together.

"I can't go," said my Uncle, when the door was shut.

"You saw her!" said the doctor, looking at him.

"She's got to go without me. Beavis here can take her," my Uncle Athiel answered him.

The doctor only just looked at him.

"Can't you make her go?" my Uncle said.

"You've tried it, haven't you?" the doctor asked him. But my Uncle kept on arguing. "You don't understand it," he kept saying. "I can't go. I can't go and leave my property. I can't do it," said my Uncle.

"You saw her," said the doctor a second time, and stopped.

My Uncle stood there — just stood there, motionless.

"I can't go! I can't go!" he said again after a while. "I'm near enough ruined as it is."

"That's your business," said the doctor in a chilly way. "My business is my patient. Now I'll tell you about that. And it isn't a very long story:

"If she goes away she'll be all right in two weeks. If she stays with this nervous strain that's got her now, she won't be alive ten days from now. I can promise you that. And that's not talking about the Fever, understand! If she gets that, like she probably will, she's dead beforehand!"

"She's crazy," said my Uncle, in a low old voice, "she's crazy — or she'd been gone long ago."

"I don't know anything about that," said Dr. Greathouse. "It's hard telling now, who's crazy and who isn't these days," he said, giving a meaning look at my Uncle.

My Uncle stood, not noticing him, and wet his bluish lips with his tongue.

"I can't! I won't!" he said. "I ain't agoing to go and leave everything I've got just for a school-girl's nonsense.

"No, sir. You don't understand," he said, while he stood there watching him. "I'm ruined now, near enough. I'm bound out to the poor house now," he said, "for sure and certain. But I ain't going till I have to. No, sir! I'm going to stay right here and watch my property — what little I've got left."

And I jumped up then, raging and cursing. That "property" talk was the last straw.

"Property! Property!" I called out to him. "You old devil. Property! You old murderer, if I ever hear you talk of that again, I'll choke you till your tongue hangs out your mouth longer than a blacksnake!"

"Shut up, you young fool," the doctor said to me.

"What'll it be?" he said to my Uncle Athiel. "It's going to be one or the other. Which'll it be — that

' Property ' or that little girl of yours?　And you yourself, in the bargain — probably! "

And when my Uncle Athiel didn't answer him, nothing
but a sort of old low groan, the doctor went along himself, talking low and quiet, but still the way men talk when
they're giving orders.

" Now," he said, looking straight and steady at my
Uncle, " I'll tell you what you're going to do.　You're going to get out of here.　Right away, too.　You're going
to take what you're guarding here, and get out! "

" What I'm guarding here! " said my Uncle, looking
around.

" Yes sir," said the doctor, looking him in the eye.
" We've got no time now for dancing and teetering and
mincing words.　Yes — what you're guarding here —
and sacrificing yourself and everybody else for."

" Guarding," said my Uncle Athiel, talking quicker —
getting excited, " what is there left to guard? "

" I don't know," said the doctor.

" I reckon you don't," said my Uncle.　" I expect you
don't! "

" I don't.　It's none of my business," said the doctor.
But my Uncle didn't hear him, apparently — went right
on with his own thoughts.

" Nothin'," he said with a groan.　" Nothin'! "

" Well, if that's so," said the doctor, " you certainly
have got no excuse for staying here anyway."

My Uncle stood there — staring, just staring at the
wall — at nothing.　Not speaking, looking, his eyes
down, scarcely breathing.

" You're going," said the doctor, " like a white man
should."

And still my Uncle stood staring at the wall, while he
waited.

" I'll go," he said at last, in an old miserable voice, and very low. So low you could hardly hear him.

" I'll go," he said, louder, a second time — like it was torn out of him.

" All right, then," said the doctor, " I'm glad to hear it."

And I thought, looking, I'd never seen a man change so much as my Uncle Athiel had in that one night — and that morning. That flash of youth he'd had, was out ; the fire was down again — lower than ever, almost to its embers. The flesh had sunk and fallen into holes in his face — in his temples and his cheeks, and his eyes were dead and hopeless. He was an old, old man where he stood there looking at the wall.

" I'll go," he said a third time, like he was speaking to himself. " To-morrow ! "

" Not to-morrow," said Dr. Greathouse. " Maybe the day after. But to-morrow she won't be ready to go. She's got to rest a day anyhow."

" All right," my Uncle said, like a man who wants to stop talking. " The day after, then."

" And mind," said the doctor, " I can't promise anything certain."

" She ain't dangerous now ? " my Uncle asked him, and looked up at him.

" No. But to-morrow is a long way off, these days," said the doctor. " And the day after is a good lot further.

" It's all around you now," he said. " Back and front, and everywhere. The Fever's all around you."

They started downstairs together.

" Keep your windows down, nights, still ? " the doctor said — making conversation, it seemed to me, for my Uncle didn't talk. He'd just stop talking.

"Yes," my Uncle answered him — and that was all.

"I would, I believe," the doctor said, "until I went."

I noticed specially when he said it — but my Uncle didn't notice, or look up even.

"And if there's anything I can do," said the doctor again, "to help you about watching this property here after you're gone, I want to."

"I'll see," said my Uncle, but that was all. He didn't look up or thank him even.

"I hope you get away," said the doctor, waiting at the door. "I hope you get away all right."

And it was plain he wanted to talk as kind and friendly as he could now. "It's not only what you've got to do for your little girl, it's what you ought to do for yourself. It won't do you any harm, I expect, to take a little rest yourself."

"Me," said my Uncle, "me! What difference does it make about me? I'll have rest enough before long," he said. "I'm through, I'm done for."

And he spoke in that old, dull, miserable voice, like a man who is really all through, and sees it. Like a man at the end of a game, broken, cleaned out.

Like a man at the end of a game, when the lights are down, and the glasses empty, and the cards scattered on the floor. And one last player going, ruined, done for.

And in spite of myself I couldn't help but feel sorry for him, stumbling, crawling with his old heavy feet up the long dark stairs, without speaking. Up the stairs, and back again to his Purple Room.

I was sorry for him. But I was glad at the same time — too glad to think of him very long. Happy and excited, and full of sudden hopefulness after that monstrous morning.

There, across the hall, upstairs, lay Vance, still free

from the Fever, anyhow. With still a chance of escaping it.

And when I thought of her again, lying there, tired and scared, as determined about staying till the last one as she ever was, I could see as plainly as anything in this world, that if we all got out of there alive without getting that Fever, it was to her, just only to her, that we would owe it — her weakness, that aggravating, obstinate weakness that women have, and use forever, as their weapon; that weakness and obstinacy that win for women in the end.

CHAPTER XVII

THE SONG IN THE STREET

VANCE was asleep in her room, p acefully and quietly sleeping, thank God, ard my Uncle was in his Purple Room, where he h d gone right after the doctor left, and stayed, only coming out for dinner. And I was there all alone, restl ss, worrying, trying to pass the time away, that everlasting time before we could go.

"Hurry, hurry!" something kept call ng in me, now that I knew we were going. And I knew just now how all those folks felt, those first few days, running away out of town, with those frightened stares on their faces. Were we going to get out soon enough, now that we were going? That was the question continua ly before me.

For the Fever was in back of us now, like the doctor had said; back and front and all around us. And it was only reasonable to expect that that old Fever miasma, that poison, whatever it was, was all around us too, in the air.

So I sat and looked and twitched my fingers and waited. For that was all I could do now. Just roamed around like a homeless dog. From downstairs to up, and from upstairs down again — tiptoeing and worrying.

I sat there in the sitting room, finally, looking out north again. They said the whole town was empty ow of white folks; most all that were left were sick; and ow they said they were having trouble to find coffins enough for all that died. And the Dead Wagons went by creaking and groaning. I can hear them now, under those great toppling loads of coffins. And they said that now even the niggers were getting the Fever and dying with it like the white folks. And there just seemed to be no end to it.

I looked there quite a while, before I noticed that there was somebody else in the house besides me who was watching and waiting, and expecting the Fever.

Arabella had come in while I was there, I expect — and stood over there across the hall in the Study, looking out again down over the hill, toward the city — like she had from the first when we were looking for the Fever; staring down the hill from that same old place in Mr. Bozro's Study. My Uncle had gone and left it entirely, and kept himself upstairs again.

And by and by the negress came sidling in to me — asking what the doctor said about Vance.

" She ain't got it after all, didn't he say? " she asked.

And though her face was as smooth as it always was, her voice was warm and friendly. For I knew she thought the world of Vance.

" No," I said, " she hasn't."

" Then she better be goin'," said Arabella. " Better be goin' quick as she can." And there was that same old secrecy and mysteriousness in her voice, and her eyes began lighting up again like a warning.

" Better be goin'," she said, " better be goin'. You better be goin' right off now; they ain't no time to spare."

" We're going," I said. " Day after to-morrow," I told her, when she asked me, " When? "

" Mighty late! " she said, in that old graveyard voice. " Mighty late! "

"Oh no," I answered back, more cheerful than I felt. "We won't get it; we'll all get out of here before we get the Fever."

"Fevah!" said the negress, in a kind of warning voice. "This ain't no Fevah."

"What is it then?" I said, getting curious again. For her mind was running now, I could see plain enough, on that old religion of hers. And her eyes fired up, and her old smooth round face began to light up like a jack o' lantern.

"This ain't no common, ordinary, Yellow Fevah," said Arabella. "You kin see it if you look. Look at 'em! Look how they die! Right off — on the street, without warning. And some of 'em's spotted, when they find 'em — just all spotted like a dog. Yes, the niggers now are having it too — and dyin' just like white folks. No suh, no suh," she said, shaking her old head in a meaning way, "this ain't no Yeller Fevah."

"What is it then?" I went on and asked her.

"Don't you know?" she said, rolling her old eyes at me. "Not yet?"

"No"; I told her that I didn't.

"It's the punishin' of God acomin' down on Memphis," she said to me. "It's the punishment of God afallin' on this old wicked city for its sins. It's the aind; it's the aind!

"But you white folks won't see it!" she went along warning me. "You won't see it 'tall, and eve'y day the signs gettin' thicker'n thicker around you. Signs and mysteries, growing closer and closer eve'y day!" she said, staring out behind me — with eyes looking right on by me.

And her voice grew higher and louder.

"Why, my good Gawd!" she said, her voice still rising.

"It's here! It's right here now. It's *here!* And yet nobody won't see it.

"Look yondah!" she said, jerking out her arm to the window. "In just a day or two and you'll see it — see it coming. It'll be acomin', acomin', acomin', up this road. Just a few days longer, just a few days longer now.

"Just a few days longer, He'll be here," she said — chanting now, sort of singsong. And that old peaceful smile spread out across her great wide face again.

"Just a day and a day; just a few days longer," she said, beaming and showing her white teeth. "Just a few days now, and He'll be acomin' up the street; and the trumpets will be ablowin', and the clouds will be arisin'; and the folks will be acryin', and arunnin' and awringin' they hands, and Memphis will be asinkin' right down, asinkin', sinkin', sinkin' right down into the ground. Memphis will be destroyed. Just all overcome and gone."

She was just gone, changed into a wild savage, while I stood looking at her; a wild African, chanting low and mysterious, like some old savage nigger on the Congo.

"And right yere, acomin' up the streets — acomin' up the streets," she said, pointing, "who'll yuh see? Who'll yuh see acomin'? Right yere before your eyes. Him! Him! Him! He'll be comin'— the Lamb! The Lamb in his white garment — and the chayiot and his great chayiot.

"And them great horses; them great white horses, comin' and acomin' and acomin', adrawin' him up this hill! Acomin' and acomin' and acomin' on — and ahollerin' Victry! Victry! Victry! Ahollerin' it at the top of they voices."

She saw them coming there — right up there over the hill. You could almost see them for yourself. The black angels blowing their trumpets and that black God of

hers, and those great white horses there before him, coming, calling up over the hill.

The sweat stood out on her face, and her body grew
stiff while she was telling it; and her eyes looked down the
street — and way out beyond; far off — somewhere out
back of the world.

" Yassuh," she said, finally, wiping her wet mouth with
the back of her hand. " Yassuh, you goin' see it." Her
voice was hoarse. " Yassuh, yassuh, you goin' see it
right away. Right away if you stay hyah.

" Yassuh, yassuh. Oh, you better go. You better be
goin' and takin' her away," she said, moving out again to
her place back out in the kitchen. And that old smile,
bright and shiny, on her glossy face.

I stood there and watched her go, wondering for a minute at what I'd seen — at what a nigger'll show you when
they lift a corner of the curtain over their strange souls.
And then I turned again, looking out the window —
thinking my own worries, and my own thoughts.

There was nothing much to see that day — some signs
they had the Fever in some houses down below there.
But nothing of the half-nigger; nothing wrong either, in
the Ventress's house across the lawn. One of their own
niggers had been back that day, and went all through it,
looking. And there was nothing there.

I did notice that old dog once or twice, when I was out
in the yard — first when I was doing my work in the
morning — that old dog lying there by the door with the
glass top that went into the harness room in the big old
vacant barn.

" He's got a new place to lie," I said to myself, and
thought no more about it.

I couldn't see Vance at all that day. She wasn't strong
enough to sit up yet, and what she wanted anyhow, was

rest. And for that matter, I didn't plan to see her anyway — not after being out and exposed myself to the
Fever that night before. And so I didn't go near her
door even, though the Lord knows I wanted to see her bad
enough — if only to see how she was looking.

So there wasn't much that day. I slept a little myself,
late that afternoon. I was tired enough to, after that
night before.

Then my Uncle and I ate supper together, talking a
little of Vance, and of the Fever, and of our plans for
going away. He was going to take us up back into the
hills — around our old country, toward the middle of the
state.

But my Uncle Athiel didn't want to talk. His head
was down; and his eyes were down. And he kept that
general listless look and motion of a man who has lost
the game, and doesn't care about anything any more —
all broken.

He didn't even want to talk to me much — not even
about watching the house that night.

" He won't want to come back again, not right away,"
he said. " We scared that nigger too bad ! "

But I wasn't so certain sure as all that — though I
thought likely he was right. But it looked to me as if
I'd better stay up and watch a little.

And so evening went, and night came again; I sat up
there in my old Red Room bed-chamber, looking out, and
wondering whether, after all, we were going to get away
— and worrying and fretting over Vance.

The town was all changed — even the sounds at night;
and that night, with the niggers quiet and so many of the
alley dogs got rid of, there was scarcely any noise anywhere. The bell they used to ring every night, those
days, was still; the wheels were gone from the streets;

you heard no more drunken men go calling home — nothing, only the little mule car, underneath the hill, going tinkling by every half hour, regular as a clock.

I did not feel sleepy any. I was nervous, I expect; and I had slept just about enough that afternoon to take away my appetite for sleep, but I laid down at last with my clothes on, just to rest myself. And then for a minute or so I must have fallen asleep.

It couldn't have been long, though, a few minutes, maybe, for then I was waked up right away by that song on the street.

I sat up listening. I hadn't heard for a number of nights that old sound of a drunken man going singing home in the night.

It was right out there in our own street, I noticed — coming slowly up the hill. It sounded strange and silly and drunk. Then after a while I noticed the tune that he was singing. It was that funny old nursery song they used to sing to the babies — something about the " Fly on the Wall " our words used to be. But really it's a German song, it seems — an old German song. The Germans call it, they tell me, " Du Lieber Augustin "— a simply, silly, wearisome old song, going over and over again.

I listened — and I didn't understand the words at all, hard as I tried. And the reason was, naturally, that he was singing them in German. I could hear the footsteps of the man, unsteady.

It was very still.

Then there were other steps, I noticed — the steps of a heavier man; and all at once there was a kind of scuffle of feet on the walk in front of us — like two men struggling. I got up to the window, and stood listening.

Then suddenly, while I stood there, I heard that door-bell go — Jangle, jangle, jangle, in the cellarway.

There was some one there this time — that was certain! I grabbed the first thing that I had — an old spoke of a cartwheel it was, I'd got in my own room, weeks ago, when my Uncle first was talking of thieves and robbers.

And I started out and crept and crawled downstairs, as fast as I could go, and still keep quiet. There was a dim light in the upper hallway. We were keeping it there while Vance was sick. But not one sound from my Uncle's room. He hadn't heard a thing. He wouldn't; he was too deaf.

I slunk and crept down the black stairway, and hugged the smooth paper on the wall. Lord, it was dark there! Only the light from the street lamp through the ground glass on the front door, and that dim light above.

But this time, I said to myself, this time I'd show them! This time, if there was anybody there!

I listened then by the outside door. I stopped and listened. I turned the key in the lock, the knob of the door — turned it quick as I could turn, and jumped out, saying:

"Now, damn you!"

And it was only old John McCallan, the policeman, standing there on the sidewalk in front of the house, begging my pardon, and holding up another man, rolling and babbling in his arms.

I looked, and it was that little German grocer, down below — that man who had the Fever — half-dressed — in shoes and trousers and his night-shirt; and that old German song still going feebly on his lips.

"You'll excuse me for disturbing you, Mr. Beavis," said John, "but I got to get this poor Dutchman home. He's out here wanderin'— crazy with the Fever."

There it was finally, the Fever come up to our own door.

"I'll help you. Let me help you," I said, like a fool, laying down my old cartwheel spoke and going toward him.

"Stand away from him," said John. "Don't touch him. I don't need you to do that; one's enough!"

"What do you want me to do then?" I asked him.

"The naygur nurse they gave him has gone asleep, I expect," said John. "That's what's happened, and he has run away. And you can run down now, if you want to, and wake the naygur up, and have him come and help me get this poor feller home."

So then I ran along down and hammered on the door, and woke the nigger. And he stuck out his head above me and told me he'd come.

There was a lot of talk about the nigger nurses in that Fever time, I want to say. And a lot of it wrong and mean and ungrateful. They were pretty mighty faithful, a good lot of them. But the great trouble they did have with them, really, was keeping them awake nights to watch the folks that they were nursing.

So after that I ran back again to where old John stood waiting, with the little German, where he had him lying there propped up now against our stone terrace wall.

"Poor feller," said John, looking down at him, and I standing off away. "Poor feller, this will finish him, pretty likely. They get loose every now and then, and run out like this — when they get wrong in their heads. And every time, most, it kills them.

"You've got to lie still," he said, "with this Fever. If you move around too much it kills you. Sometimes they run off, away, like this, and crawl off in some place and die. They found a number of them this last week, down there in the business blocks."

I turned. It seemed to me, while I stood there, I heard some one calling me.

"Poor feller," said John. "And he thought he wouldn't have it. He'd had it once before."

The nigger nurse was coming now, scared, running up the street.

"This ain't no regular Fever," said John. "I've seen the Yellow Fever now, for years. It never acted like this before. The naygurs are all getting it now; and all the folks that had it once before. That's new. And those that had it die right off — a lot of them. I've seen thim — just right off after they get it. I never seen it come like that before. No, sor," said John McCallan, "no, sor; it ain't natural for the Yellow Fever.

"No, sor," said John, shaking his old head. "No, sor; I'm telling you this ain't no ordinary Fever. And those that can," he said, "will be watching to get out now. For it's my opinion, it's my opinion," said John McCallan, "that all of us that stays are goin' to die."

"I don't see you going out," I said.

"I can't," said John. "How could I on my job?"

"There's others have," I said.

"Yes, and I'm sorry to tell you that they have," said John.

The nigger was there now; and I stood for a minute, watching them lift up the silent little bundle of man.

It was all just like me. From first to last I was so excited — first by that bell — and then afterwards doing what I had to do outside — I hadn't thought, or considered or remembered one thing — about that old poison night air we all were standing in.

And just when it first struck me — just when I thought about it, standing there, I certainly thought again I heard my name whispered there behind me.

"Good-night," I said to John. I stepped inside and closed the door. And stood there in that pallid light that came in there through that old ground glass window in the door.

And there — a white figure swaying forward, face against the door-frame, stood Vance.

"Hullo, what's this? Vance?" I called, surprised. "What are you down here for?"

But she didn't answer.

"What is it?" I said, taking her by her shoulder. She had thrown — she had just thrown that white shawl of her mother's, that great long white India shawl, over her night clothes, and come running down.

"You wouldn't come!" she whispered, not answering me. "You wouldn't come! You just stood there, in that poison night air!"

I shrank back from her, right away then, thinking where I had been.

"Come," I said, "you've got to go back to bed. How did you come here anyway?"

"The bell!" she said. "I heard the bell!"

She swayed a little. I could see her plainer now — my eyes accustomed to the dim light. She swayed — I thought that she would faint and fall; and I caught her — though scared to — fearful of God knows what exposure I might have brought to her from outdoors there.

I caught her in my arms, and held her, shuddering. She hadn't fainted though; she was still conscious.

"Oh, how lonely I've been," she whispered, "how lonely." And I thought now she was growing light in her head, light and flighty.

" And you wouldn't come! You wouldn't come, when I called you, Beavis!"

Her arms reached unsteadily to my shoulder, and she kept on talking in a whisper.

And longing and anxiousness and that continual fear that never left me now; the fear that I would lose her after all — swept over me. And I held her closer, when it overtook me.

" You wouldn't come," she said, shuddering slightly, once again, " all day — all day — And now you wouldn't come when I called you. You don't care — you didn't care. You didn't care for me!"

" Care for you!" I said, and choked.

" You didn't come," she repeated — weak and a little feverish, I expect. " You didn't care!"

And when she said it over a second time — I was out of my own control — out of my mind, I expect, too — for happiness and fear, all mixed together; and dread of what, in spite of me, might be about to happen to her; to take her away from me forever.

It was like we were the last two folks, somehow, in all the world. Just standing there in that dim hall; that black house behind us. Like all the rest were dead — and that damned Fever outside there, crawling, crawling, crawling to the door to get her from me — take her out from my arms forever.

" Care!" I said. " Care for you!" I said again. " God Almighty, Vance, I'd tear down the sunset and bring it to you for a gown if you asked me to."

I was only twenty-one, just a boy. And it seemed to me like we just stood there in the dark — defying Death and Time and the universe together.

And when I spoke, I felt her little body soften and relax in my arms, like a tired little child at bedtime.

I took her bodily in my arms then, and started up the stairs, for I saw it would be impossible for her now to climb them. And I thought, too late, what it had meant for her — the strain, the exposure of that trip of hers down after me in the dark.

I took her up in my arms and carried her upstairs, like carrying nothing at all. Her lax, childish body — slender and young and soft in the folds of that soft old India shawl, weighed like nothing in my arms. She lay against me, like a sleepy child; and as I passed up toward the dim gas light in the upper hall, she raised her light hand to my face with an uncertain gesture, and drew it down and her deep dark eyes looked up at me, close into mine. And I went up that old long staircase carrying her, watching her and wondering in my heart if now — now that I had her there, I might lose her, right away — forever, from that Death that lay waiting outside there all around us.

We'd reached the top of the long stairs almost, my face down watching her, when I started and looked up. There above us, waiting, stood my Uncle Athiel, staring down. There was not a word from him, not a question.

"Give her to me," he said in a hoarse old voice and took her from me.

He took her from me — lame, old, scarcely able, he looked like, to hold himself upright — he took her from me into his arms, and some way went on carrying her down the dim hall to the Ivory Room.

"Good-night," I told her, before I gave her up to him, and kissed her.

I'm sure she told him as he was carrying her. I could see her whispering in his ear. I waited. He came back very soon.

"Will she be all right now?" I said, and looked him in the eyes. "Will there be anything we can do?"

" No," he said, " she had scarcely touched the pillow before she was sleeping."

We said no more. He made no talk of blame or comment. But the strength and vigor that had come to him when he took her in his arms and carried her down the hall from me, was gone again.

He looked again like an old, old man.

I must have gotten asleep again finally, sometime — a thin, miserable, restless sleep, for I woke up with a jerk and said to myself: " I must have been dreaming it all over again, or I'm crazy maybe!" For I had the impression I had heard that bell again — one of those bells downstairs in the cellarway jangling.

CHAPTER XVIII

I WOKE up; the sun shone in, a little narrow yellow wedge upon my carpet; I woke up and jumped out of bed, and started out on that last day, the last everlasting day, before we finally were to go. I had overslept; that late dead sleep that comes at the end of a sleepless night had been too much for me.

I looked out the window while I was dressing me, down to the Fever house, where the little German was, over the closed grocery store, and wondered about him — if he was living still. And I noticed then, out my back window, that the old dog was still there, lying there in front of the harness room of the great closed barn.

" This will be the second day," I said to myself, wondering a minute, " that he's been lying around out there." Then right away it passed out of my mind when I went downstairs. For the first thing naturally, was Vance. How was she? When could I get to see her? And I tiptoed by her silent room and on downstairs, hoping and fearing.

My Uncle was down below at the breakfast table, and said that earlier he had looked in and she was sleeping peacefully, breathing soft and regular as a child.

I thought, maybe, he would say something more — after that night before — when we sat down to breakfast there alone together. But not a word came out of him, and

I couldn't speak myself, though I tried to several times. But for that matter my Uncle didn't look like he cared to hear me talk. He sat, downcast, looking at his plate, stiller and bluer and more motionless than I had even seen him, in any of those blue days of his when he talked about the poorhouse. And so I waited and waited, till the doctor came — anxious to know just what he would say when he knew of everything — especially when he heard of that great thing that had been chasing me awake all night — the fear that I certainly must have exposed Vance to the Fever — on that night before.

And meanwhile I went out — late — and fed old Dolly, who was stamping to be attended to. And then again I saw that old dog there in front of the big barn. He still lay there, curled up on the top step of the door into the harness room. He raised his head when I came along and looked at me out of his little blood shot eyes, under his old eyebrows, and laid his head down again on his paws when I went along by.

I didn't stop going, for I was in a hurry to attend to the horse; and coming back I went right by him, for I heard the sound of the doctor coming whistling in the front yard. I saw him right away as soon as he came into the house, and I told him what I'd done that night before — about being out there with that German.

" Ah-ha," said the doctor, " I heard of that. So you were the fellow? "

" How is he? " I asked. For I knew the doctor had him.

" He's dead," said Dr. Greathouse.

Then I stopped for a minute, like you do when anybody says that about somebody you've just seen moving around, and heard talking.

" Dead! " I said. " Then they're all dead? It's got

the entire family?" And I saw them while I was saying
it — all those little white headed youngsters, and the little fat man that used to stand there serving us behind the
counter in his long checked apron.

"All but the mother," said the doctor. "That's not
the only case," he said, "there's plenty of families, poor
folks especially, that are going that way — after the
Fever once gets into the house."

And I caught my breath then, and went on, hurrying,
telling him about what was bothering me all night long —
about Vance, and the danger I had exposed her to — the
Fever, when I first got in the house. I didn't tell him
everything, naturally. I just told him I had found her
there in the hall way when I came in; and helped her up
the stairs.

"I wouldn't worry about that yet," he said. "You
can't give it to anybody, I believe, till you've got it yourself."

That was some encouragement.

"But the real thing is," he said, "to see how she stood
it all herself — the coming downstairs, the excitement.
That's what ails her anyhow — what's on her mind. Her
imagination always was bigger than her body — from the
first day that she talked."

He went upstairs, and into the Ivory Room, and, waiting just a minute or two, I heard him laughing, and I
heard her laughing too, with her voice back again, quite
a little, quite clear and high, but not exactly strong yet.
And after a while he called me.

"You can come in a minute," and in a second or two
more Vance's eyes were shining into mine.

"You can't understand 'em," said the doctor laughing.
"Nobody ever understood a woman. The first thing
they're away down from something you don't know any-

thing about, and the next, they're back, higher than ever, on account of something they won't tell you."

And Vance's eyes turned and looked out the window, and I grinned a little — and stopped when my eyes caught my Uncle's looking up dull and tired into mine — and turning right back again, looking out the window.

" I'm well, *well*," said Vance, in a minute, her eyes shining back at me again. " I'm *well*." And some way, though it wasn't strong yet, I hadn't heard her voice so clear and hopeful, not for weeks.

" And to-morrow we'll be going! " she said, looking toward her father.

" Praise God. Hallelujah! " I said quickly. But my Uncle said nothing, standing where he had gone, over by the window looking out.

" I'm going to get up," said Vance.

" Later, if she sleeps, perhaps," said the doctor, to my Uncle. And he nodded that he understood.

" And now," the doctor said to Vance, " you're going to sleep."

" To-morrow," said Vance, " we're going to-morrow! And this afternoon I'll be up! "

" Maybe," said the doctor. " But now you'll just pull down your shades and rest."

And so he put them down and we went along out.

" It is wonderful how she's changed," said the doctor, " but let her rest all she can." And he went on talking then about our leaving town.

" I've got it all fixed up so you can go," he said. " And you're not getting out of here any too quick.

" There were three deaths down that street below," he said, " two besides the little German grocer. And one in back of us in the alley on the next block, a nigger. And one in the side street.

" It's all around you," said the doctor.

" It's in the air," my Uncle Hagar answered him. " The ai 's all full of Fever."

But he talked dull and listless, even about that — not excited a bit; like a man who doesn't care what happens to him next.

It was all fixed, it seemed, so that the doctor would come around occasionally and keep his eye on the house when we went. And I was to talk to John McCallan and let him have the key to it. There was some of those that stayed on through the Fever — and he was one of them — that had more than a hundred keys given them of stores and houses

And then when he had told me that, my Uncle went upstairs and sta ed there, to be near Vance, he said.

But before he went away he spoke to me for the first time about her and mysel..

" I expect," he said " you'll think, before long, you'll want to marr, her? "

He talked in a dull, dreary kind of voice, and looked at me once, and turned hi eyes down again. But I was glad anyhow, that he didn't fight it.

I didn't know exactly what he would do, for naturally, he knew I didn't have a dollar.

" As soon as I get the money to," I said.

" Money," said my Uncle, like a dead old echo. " That's it.'

And my heart went down in my boots again, when he went upstairs — but not for very long.

It wasn't very long before he called to me to come up there. " Your cousin, Vance," he said, and he hitched a little on the ' cousin,' " wants to see you; she's up and dressed and wants to see you. I expect that you can go in there for a little while."

So I stopped, a breath or two, outside the door of the Ivory Room; and knocked and went in.

It was a big high place — very pale and delicate colored — ivory and palish blue and pink. Mr. Bozro had built it for his wife when they thought they were so rich. A tall, lean woman, they said, with a leathery, coppery skin, and wonderful diamonds.

And all the woodwork of the room was ivory, and all the stuff on the white bureau for her hands and hair was real ivory. And the furniture was French, ivory-colored too — like in some of those great houses they had seen abroad. And overhead pink cherubs, with ivory ribbon streamers from their waists, played with ropes of roses — dull pink roses against a pale blue sky.

Vance was there, on a satin sofa — a kind of long French sofa, with a pillow back of her; in some creamy kind of dress; some fluffy ivory-colored lace thing. But I was noticing most her eyes and hair — black against the whiteness. And her eyes. But I saw her eyes just only for a second.

" Vance," I whispered, on my knees beside the sofa. " Vance, why don't you look at me? "

" I'm ashamed," she whispered back.

" Ashamed? " I asked her. And with a quick motion, she hid her face upon my shoulder.

" Ashamed? " I asked her again, after our silence. " Of what? " and turned her face where I could see it.

" Last night," she said, " last night, last night."

" Don't say that, Vance, again. Never again," I told her. And we were still again. Until once more I felt her shuddering — that nervous shuddering that I feared passed over her again.

" What! " I said sharply to her. " Not that again! "

" I was so lonely," she whispered, and stopped.

I waited.

"That day," she went along, "that awful day that woman laughed so!"

I could see her — when she said it — I could see her there in her room alone, not understanding; and Death screaming down there underneath her windows; watching it all day and night with those great eyes of hers — and filling out and peopling the darkness, and all she didn't understand, with her imagination — that restless imagination of hers.

"That day," she said, "you didn't speak to me!"

I begged for her forgiveness then — what I could — for the share I had in it. "I don't understand it now," she said —" all that row and shooting!"

And I told her what I knew — about that half-nigger.

"It was a thousand years," she said, "that day, and those two nights. I feel a thousand years old, at least. And that night — that night you shot! And that pistol smoke in the hall! My father!"

She stopped.

And all at once I knew that old shuddering had caught her again.

"I won't," she said, when I spoke sharply to her. "I won't again. But it seemed to me I could see him," she went on — as if she couldn't stop. "It seemed to me I could see his face just the same — and his hand, just like—"

"That dream?" I said.

She nodded and was still.

"And now," I said, "you've got to tell me about it — you've got to tell me about that old crazy dream."

She wouldn't tell at first; but I teased her and teased her — and told her it would be better to tell me — better for her.

" They say if you share a thing like that, it's easier
for you. If two can carry a secret," I said, " with less
worry than one can, maybe they can a dream."

And I smiled and laughed at her and encouraged her,
until finally she told me of that wild dream of hers —
drawing away from me, back into a corner of the sofa;
and sending her eyes far off behind me in the distance.
And talking — after a while — in that still, hushed voice
of hers — that still secret voice the children tell each
other those old nigger ghost stories, as the winter night
comes on.

" It seemed to me," she started — lying very still and
whispering, almost —" like we were all in this great place
that I was never in before. All three of us in this place,
in danger like we are here —" she said, and stopped.

" Oh, I don't want to," she said. " I know you'll say
it's just plain silly."

" Go ahead," I said.

" And outside," she went along then, stretching out
her hand, " outside, I thought there was something there.
Something there — we wanted to get away from — and
couldn't.

" Smoke," she said suddenly. " I thought it was just
something hiding inside a lot of smoke. You couldn't see
it. You didn't know what it was.

" And I thought we'd go to the window and we'd try
to get out — and try and try! But there was something
there, invisible, something monstrous.

" And when we got there — to the doors and windows
— we couldn't get out, it wouldn't let us! I don't know
why, but we couldn't. We were afraid, afraid of that
thing, that thing there in the smoke.

" And so we sat there, and sat there, and sat there.
And by and by," she said, and smiled, a quick little ex-

cusing smile and moved restlessly, " you know how it is in dreams — it seemed like all at once we were back here in this house.

" And Clang! something went shut, and a nigger's voice, a great thick voice like a nigger saying: ' There! You stay there till I come and get you!'

" And outside there, I thought," she said, her eyes growing deeper and her body tense. " Outside it was all smoke now. All around us in a ring. Only nearer now! Only a lot nearer! And my father and you were walking up and down, walking up and down! But we couldn't get out. For it was still there — only nearer."

Her voice grew lower and shakier, and she caught up her knees to her, and sat there, her great eyes staring out just like a scared child, just like those children telling stories in the dark. I shivered, just a little myself, sitting there. I couldn't help it.

" It came and came and came," she said. " And it was all around us. Smoke! And all at once one of the windows — for we'd had them all closed — like we do here; all of a sudden this window swung back very slowly. Oh, so monstrous slow — a whole lifetime. And the smoke poured in! And then all at once I heard this dreadful cry, my father! Right back of me crying — dreadful:

" ' It's got me! It's got me!'

" And there he was! There he was! There he was!" she said.

And stopped, panting — pushing both her hands away from her face, her fingers spread out stiff; and her face drained white, with her deep eyes staring at me.

" Quit it, Vance," I said, " quit it!"

For I saw she shouldn't be doing that again.

" But I heard him. I heard him say it just as plain as I hear you," she said.

"Why shouldn't you?" I said, "after this — all this. All this worry."

"Oh, I know it's wrong — foolish," she said.

"But I saw him. I saw him there — just like I see you. I saw him lying there on his face. I went over where he was — and he was lying there on his face — and his hand — his hand was under his head — so. His hand —"

"Vance," I said, getting up on my feet, and standing over her. "Vance, will you stop this!"

For she was shuddering miserably through her whole body; shuddering and sitting up, and staring down — as if she saw him there, right there before her on the floor.

"Yes," she said, and stopped right away.

"Anybody'd think you were crazy," I said, for I thought I had to talk her out of it.

"Yes, dear," she said. "I will. I'll stop."

And I, kneeling down beside her — she took me and clasped me, and clung to me, like a child afraid of the dark.

And outside, while we sat there, I thought I heard — I certainly did hear, the "creak, creak, creak," of that damned Dead Wagon, go by our windows.

And after a while — after a long while, she said: "It *was* a good deal better to tell you."

"I believe so," I said, pushing back her hair, and comforting her, like a child — just like you would a child.

"I won't do that again," she said finally. "I won't — you'll see!"

"It worries me so to see you, Vance," I said. "It'll tire you all out again."

"It won't; you'll see!" she said. "I'm going to get up this afternoon. Get up and get ready to go to-morrow. You'll see. I'm old now. I'm a thousand years older now after these last two days.

" Older than that great turtle they found over there in the river," she said, and looked at me and we both laughed.

For after all we weren't, either of us, very old yet.

And right away after that, she was back again. Her spirits were as bright and lively as they ever were.

But outside there, we knew — we both knew — the Fever was all around us. The street below us was full of it. And now and then, if you listened, you could hear the voices of the sick folks — one or two of them — very faint, moaning and muttering. And I kneeled beside her, scared and wondering, both of us wondering whether or not we ourselves were going to escape it. But I, especially, kneeling there by her, wondering secretly, and worrying over what the doctor had said about her, the warnings he had given; scared and wondering whether that next day, or week, or month, I would still hold that dear body in my arms; or whether death, creeping and crawling outside our windows there, would have her at last; take her forever from me — before we could escape, escape and get her out of there.

And then, after a little longer, we heard my Uncle calling out in the hall and saying, I'd better come and let her sleep some more.

" You'll see," she said, when I was going. " I won't be like that again. I'm through with all that foolishness of that dream. I'm a woman now. It's been a thousand years now since I was a girl."

And the strangest part of it was, she told the truth. From that time on she was a woman — stronger and firmer, and a lot more sensible, and steadier than any of us.

CHAPTER XIX

THE GREEN FLIES

MY Uncle looked up once during dinner. We were alone yet; Vance was still upstairs resting. He looked up at me, once.

"There's one thing," he said. "A lawyer's bound to know something about Property."

I had to grin when I answered him. But he didn't see that — he wouldn't — about " Property "!

It was all mighty serious to him —" Property "; something that you feared and bowed down to, and worshiped, with candles, almost.

Then he looked up a second time, after a while.

" It ain't much I got now," he said. " But what there is will be all for her."

There was nothing for me to say. I looked up at him, curious — and waited.

And then finally, he said to me again, after a long wait — sitting there, motionless, head down, between times; waiting for Arabella to bring in the dessert:

" If anything happens to me — if anything should happen to me, there's some things, I expect, I'd better show you. Pretty quick! " he went on.

I looked up at him quick, for naturally, I thought of " Hagar's Hoard." But I told him we'd better wait till to-morrow. It was kind of crawly, listening to him, talking with those dead eyes on his plate — as if everything was done and over with — like he was dead and buried already.

" To-morrow," I said, " when we're going. You can tell me to-morrow."

I don't know whether I did right or not; I never was quite sure. But anyhow, he didn't answer, or try again, and right away Arabella brought in the dessert, and he gobbled it up and got up from the table.

The next thing I remember, now, as I look back to it, was Arabella, standing out there on the sidewalk around the house, to the back door, looking down toward the big barn, muttering to herself, under the big elm tree at the corner of the house.

" What's the matter, Arabella? " I went out and asked her.

Another sign and myst'ry I expected.

" That old Gen. Sherman," she said, still keeping looking, where he lay — still lay, curled up on the doorstep to the harness room in the big barn.

" What ails him? " I said, looking.

" I don know! I don know! " she said, shaking her head, and kind of talking to herself. " Just lyin' there! Just lyin' there!

" I can't call him," she went on. " I can't git him away from there; he won't come! "

" Why don't you go and get him, then? " I said.

" I dunno; I dunno," she kept answering.

She seemed so like a fool, just standing there, looking, and the dog not a hundred feet off.

" Why not? " I said.

" I dunno; I dunno," she said, " I ain't thought I would. I done let him alone.

" I dunno," she said. And then, when I pressed her, " I dunno as I wan'ter go; looks to me like somethin' ain't just right there! "

" Oh, go along out," I said, mad. There it was, broad,

hot daylight. "Go on along. If you want anything, I'm right here."

And so she went dragging over there, one foot after the other, and the old dog got up as she came along. But instead of coming toward her, like he usually would, he stood with his back to her, looking up at the door to the harness room, and growled. I heard him growl, down in his throat.

And I stopped and waited before I went into the house. And the negress looked around, and saw me, and went along on, and stood up close to the door — that glass top door to the harness room.

And then, all at once, she stepped back, and called to me, and I went over — wondering what new foolishness this was. And when I got there she was talking, going this old singsong.

"Oh Lawdy!" she was saying. "Oh Lawdy! Oh Lawd! Oh Lawd God!"

"Keep quiet!" I said, for her voice was rising. "What is it?"

"See 'em, look!" she said, her eyes standing out like knobs. "Look yonder! Look at 'em!"

The dog was there at the foot of the outside stairs. He didn't want to move, so I kicked him aside. But at first I didn't see it; I didn't notice a thing.

There was a black curtain to the window in the door — closed clear down to keep the light out of the harness room.

"What!" I said, speaking sharp to her.

"Them flies," said Arabella, pointing. "See 'em! Them great fat green flies. See 'em, see 'em crawlin'!"

I saw them then. The glass this side of the curtain was covered with them — light green against the old black shade — green, and whitish wings; a gauzy veil of great, fat, lazy flies sitting there and crowding, and dragging up and down.

But then it didn't strike me either; funny too! I'd heard all about it. The negress stood behind me, twitching at my coat tails. "Come away! Come away! Come away, Mr. Beavis!" she said. "Lawd God, can't you smell it?"

The dog stood there beside me now, head down, cocking over one red eye at the crack under the door. And the coarse old yellow hair rising up along his back bone.

I looked at him, and I looked at her, and then I stepped off the step, for I smelled it — that awful sweetish smell you get going by a field in the summer — a field where those old buzzards come flapping slowly up.

"Yassuh," said the negress, reading my eyes. "Yassuh, somebody!"

Then I took my key. It was to the other door, across the carriage way from the harness room.

Lord, how I hung back, and hated to!

"Don't you do it!" said the negress, begging me. "Mr. Beavis. Don't you never do it!"

I took my key, the dog following me, and unlocked the door.

He stood right back of me; a bristling collar of hair standing out around his neck, and his front paws on the step — his little red eyes looking at my heels.

But the negress went around to the side — to the window to the harness room on the other side. I had unlocked the door and stepped into the dry hot barn when I first heard her starting screaming:

"Oh God! Oh God! Oh my God!"

She was hollering — the way the niggers do when they see Death; the way those sanctified niggers holler when they're being saved from Hell:

" God he'p me! God he'p me! God he'p me!" More like a bark than anything human. " God he'p me!"

I jumped to go out, for I thought of Vance. But she stopped then — bit right off where she was. My Uncle had come there. Just the sight of him was like a cold bath to her always.

She stopped and whispered.

So I went back. I went along through the carriage way — dark with the place all closed. And stood and waited till my eyes got used to it. Stood, and it seemed like my feet were held down, grown out with roots into the floor. The old dog was there behind me, waiting.

And then I went along, of course, and took the iron latch, and the dog crouched back of me a little, and growled down in his throat. And clack! I put up the latch, and with a jerk, snatched back the door — and

" God!" I spat it out of my mouth, that puff of thick, hot air; that rush of flies — all into my mouth and eyes and hair. I spat and waved and warded with my hands against the flies and the stench and the sight — under the light from the crack of the shade before me — of that black thing — and all those crawling, feasting flies; that black thing that had been the half-nigger, on the floor.

And slam! The door went shut again. And I stepped back, straight on the paw of Gen. Sherman. Not a whimper, not a sound out of him — except again that deep old growl down in his throat.

And the negress started hollering again — the way they do in those meetings of theirs.

" Jesus! Jesus! Jesus! I'm aburnin'! I'm aburnin'! I'm a sinner! Oh, he'p me! Oh, he'p me! I'm agoin' to die!"

I ran out again. For I saw she had got loose from my Uncle Athiel.

And already, from somewhere up the alley, the niggers had begun to gather, looking. They stood there — three or four of them — with those motionless black faces, looking. There were two more coming when I got there.

"Hyah!" said my Uncle Athiel, to them. "Take hold of her! Make her stop!"

But his voice wasn't loud enough. And he knew it — and he motioned to me, to help.

"Come here you," I hollered to two or three of them that I had seen around before. "Take hold of her! Take her way — over there to her room!"

For they were crowding in around. And my Uncle didn't even prevent them.

They took her — two big nigger women first, and then two more. She was bowing down and jerking back — like a fish jerking out of the water. And hollering and crying.

But they took her, one to each arm and leg, and lugged her, yanking and jerking and hollering, just took her with them back into the big old servants' room. And not a change, not a sound, not an expression on their old smooth faces — except now and then, when she made a jerk — jerking and twisting more than usual, and they had to strain a little holding her. They took her along, just as calm and unruffled as with anything they were all used and accustomed to — with this old common religious fit, just as natural and expected as sudden sickness or childbirth.

And then when they quieted her some:

"Judas! I'm glad to hear that chatter stop!" my Uncle said.

"She hadn't ever seen a nigger dead with it, I expect," he said, watching after them.

But the other niggers didn't look after them at all. Their soft old black eyes were looking at the old harness room, and the glass door with the shade down, and the old yellow dog standing by the doorway.

"Get 'em out of here," said my Uncle to me — asking me to do it, like it was the usual thing, instead of doing it himself. "Get 'em out of here!"

I sent one nigger off to get the undertaker — for Make Haste Mose.

"And now, the rest of you," I said, "get out of here! Git!"

And they moved away slowly, back a little way into the alley.

"I can't have 'em; I won't have 'em watchin' and gogglin' 'round. Half of 'em are thieves," my Uncle Athiel said.

But there wasn't any expression in his voice, somehow. There wasn't even any life to his fear. And I was doing it all for him — just naturally, like he was an old, old man!

We stood there waiting, waiting a little ways off; watching the old dog outside the door there — standing watching.

"He must have gone in there, that half-nigger," said my Uncle Athiel, staring toward the closed black shade. "He must have run in there hidin', when you chased him. Through a window, maybe.

"And right after that," he said, "it must 'a' took him! What time was it he came? What time do you think?"

"Most midnight, it must have been," said I.

"That's the time!" my Uncle Athiel said. "That's the time they get it! And then the old dog came!"

"Yes," I said.

Arabella had started up again, hollering — singing out and hollering, something new!

"Oh, God! Hosses and chayiots! Hosses and chayiots! Oh, my God!"

A big nigger woman — the first one that had grabbed her — came up behind us.

"She's agoin'," she told my Uncle Athiel. "She say she's agoin' away from here. She say she can't stay here no longer."

"Let her go," my Uncle Athiel said to me, without turning around. "She won't be any more good after this."

"Yassuh," said the woman.

"And you — all the rest of you — move along now!" I said, for they were coming around again by the gate to the alley — whispering, looking.

So they pushed back, stepping on each other — the front ones on those behind them. But they stood around outside there, with their old expressionless faces, still looking.

"That was it, I expect," my Uncle went along. "That was how it was. He came and stood there — that old dog. And the half-nigger thought he'd lie low and wait and see if he wouldn't go away. But he didn't, the old fool dog," said my Uncle, watching him.

There he stood, there by the door — a funny thing to look at — that poor old rambling, toothless beast that nobody thought was any good, or ever could be. But when the little dog was killed, and he saw it; and he saw, what we did not see, that night after, that half-nigger — some old ghost of a dog — some old mastiff away back there in the blood of that old mongrel dog, waked up and stood there all that time, bristling and watching at his enemy.

"If he'd a moved, he'd set the dog a hollerin'," said my Uncle, thinking of the half-nigger. "So he lay there still. And then, then the Fever took him. And then, after that, I expect, it was this way: When the nigger found that it was most daylight, and he'd knew he'd got to do something — go somewhere — and he was getting sicker and sicker all the time — why then he turned and twisted and raised himself up, and tried to climb out and get away. And the tryin' and exercise and strainin' killed him! You can't do much," said my Uncle Athiel. "You can't do much when you once get that Fever. It starts you bleeding from the stomach; it kills you."

He'd got talking as low and tiresome now, as a man talking of some Fever a thousand years ago — as if it wasn't there around us at all. And all the time my eye was on that black shade, closed; and my mind was seeing what was there behind us.

"Well, there ain't any use of our staying here any longer," said my Uncle Hagar. "Let's go on back to the house."

And when he said it, I stood and stared at him, and then I broke and started on for the house myself, for I thought of Vance, finally. It was like me, just exactly — only one thing at a time for me. And that thing out there in the barn had fastened on all the mind I'd got, I expect, and eaten it up.

And when I got there, Vance was down below, in the side hallway, all dressed as usual, cool as you please!

"What was it?" she said.

And when I started and took time telling her:

"Did they find some one dead out there — that half-nigger?" she asked me. For of course there had been a number of cases like that — in other places — like I told you, where folks had crawled in and died.

And when I told her she was right, she was as cool and collected as an old soldier.

It wasn't very long after that, before Make Haste Mose and his men had come there with their coffin. They came in front at first, but we sent them around back into the alley.

I went out part way, just enough so I could keep my eye on them. And it certainly did not take them long. For Make Haste Mose kept driving them.

"Come on — come on!" he kept saying. "Mek Haste! Mek Haste! Mek Haste! We got to be gettin' along!"

Just an ordinary nigger he was, a kind of pleasant, careless nigger. But he certainly was a driver that summer. It seemed to me like it couldn't have been more than ten minutes, all together — from the time that empty coffin thumped upon the ground, till they took it off again, with that half-nigger in it.

And after that, when I was coming into the house, Arabella was going away for good. You could hear her just as plain, going down the alley, hollering:

"Oh, Jesus! Oh, come along! Oh, Vict'ry! Vict'ry! Vict'ry!"

You could hear her just as plain way down the alley — clapping her hands together, and hollering that — her voice rising and whooping and breaking.

"Niggers' Doomsday!" said my Uncle, at the door to the side hall. "Niggers' Doomsday!

"And I don't know but they're right," he said afterward. "I expect we'd all die if we had to stay here!"

And it seemed to me his face was yellower — more like tallow; and his mouth bluer; and his eyes duller than they ever were.

BOOK VI

DOOMSDAY

CHAPTER XX

THE FEVER

AND now I've got to the last day — that day we thought we were going — and didn't. And one of us never did go! And when I think of it, I sit and wonder still, sometimes, at the devilish, infernal way it all happened.

It does seem, sometimes, as if the Devil was in the whole thing, tying us there in that invisible net, that was thrown around us, and kept us all from getting away. And certainly if old Satan owns the money, and buys folks with it, like they say in the old stories, he surely had arranged to come and take his pay — that day.

That night before was the longest night since the world began. I know; for I saw it all. I couldn't sleep a wink. For just as soon as I lay down, and shut my eyes — just that soon I saw the thing — that half-nigger lying there on the floor again. And heard the nigger woman screaming for the Judgment Day. And that day before there had been three deaths more in houses we could see from our own windows — folks we'd known or seen, or could recall when one of us would say: "Don't you remember that little short woman with the gray hair?" Three deaths on three different streets and three Fever fires lit that evening. The thing was falling all around us; striking unforeseen and crazy as death in a battle. And if we hadn't had it yet, it was only just the mercy of God, it seemed to me. For, of course, we didn't know what really brought the Fever, then.

So all night long I sat there, restless, sleepless — and every now and then half whispering, half praying to myself: "Just this one night! Just this one night! If we can only get through this one!"

For it seemed clear enough that it was now or never.

And sitting there, and watching, I saw and overlooked, and didn't even understand the thing that came to keep us.

It must have been half-past two o'clock in the morning. I know I had looked at my watch some while before, and it was a little after two. Everything was still. Earlier in the evening we had all been busy, finishing packing up — what we could; and for a while I heard my Uncle fussing around in his room. But now it seemed to me both he and Vance were sleeping; and I was the only one awake in the house — in the world, it seemed like sometimes. For the town was very still, like one of those old dead cities, I remember thinking, they found out in the Persian deserts. Then all at once, the fire-bell rang; and I heard the sound of feet drumming on the sidewalk — some nigger policeman, or militia man, I expect. They had them running to the fires.

There had been quite a number of fires lately; some set, they said, for purposes of thievery. But none very serious. I heard the noise and saw the light and the general direction of this one. And it was quite a little blaze. But I didn't pay much attention to it. And I never thought, until they brought us word in the morning, that it was Uncle Athiel's nigger tenements burning.

It was after breakfast time before we heard of it all. We were going to start away and leave the house a little before noon — to drive over and take the afternoon train out in the eastern end of the town, where they stopped and started their trains now, so as to keep them out of the Fever. And our four trunks were already loaded, when John McCallan came to go over the place for the last time with me, and see what we wanted him to watch especially; and told me the news that they were all burned up and destroyed — all our tenements gone together.

I never hated and feared to go any place in my life like I did to crawl up those stairs and knock on that old brown door of the Purple Room where my Uncle Athiel had gone back after breakfast. For I saw then what might happen.

"What is it?" he said, from the other side of the door.

I've always said he looked better that morning. I believe he'd had a pretty good night's rest. His eyes were brighter, and his voice, when I called him, was stronger, when he answered through the door.

"Open up, please," I said. "I want to speak to you."

And so he opened it finally, and stood there — and back of him, I saw, he was holding that old brown satchel he used to carry for his rents.

"Well, what!" he said sharply. For it struck him, I expect, that something unusual must have happened for me to come there and rout him out of that room.

"There was a fire down town last night," I said, stuttering.

"Suppose there was!" he said, his eyes set hard and black and still on mine.

"The tenements have gone!" I blurted out.

"Gone! Last night!" he said, slowly, like a man trying to get it through his head. And looked away from me, and licked his lips. That was all he said.

"I thought I'd better tell you right off," I said to him.

But he didn't say anything or move.

" So if you wanted anything done —" I went along.

" Done! " he said after me, in a kind of an old dead voice. " Done!   No, I reckon that's all that can be done — for me!

" No," he went on, while I stood there waiting.   " No, I expect that settles it."

And he drew back and shut the door after him, very softly, and locked it, turning the key in the lock very slowly.

I didn't like the look of his face, then; the life had gone down in it, in that minute or two, like turning down a lamp.

I went down, and out around the yard with John Mc-Callan and came back then to see Vance; and she said that all that time she hadn't heard her father moving in his room.   It must have been, then, half-past nine o'clock; and the trunks were all gone on their way.   And we were wondering what we should do next.

But a little while after that my Uncle came out, and got us both in the sitting room, and started talking to us.

" Here," he said to me.   " I've made up my mind.   You take these two tickets and this money, and take your cousin Vance and go."

His eyes were like burnt holes in a blanket, way back in his head; but there was some light in them now again, a kind of steady light that never went out of them afterwards.

" What will you do? " I said.

" I've got to stay," he said, a little quicker.   " I've got to stay; I've got to stay and watch out for my ' Property,' all that's left."

" Property! " I said, " Property!   What Property? "

" This house.   My house! " he said.   " I ain't agoin'

to go and leave it. It cost too much. I've got too much money in it!"

I saw Vance get white and bite her lips. The whole thing that we'd built up was falling to pieces again.

I was the first one — my temper — to go, as usual, under the strain.

"We're all ready! We're all ready!" I said, getting up, and marching toward him. "You can't go back on us now. No sir! You've got to go!"

I was mad and scared at the same time. The Fever was moaning and screaming all round us. You could step to that window and hear the old "*Um-um-um*," that groaning of the sick. There was a boy, a boy named Saunders — we knew him well — down the street opposite us. And up the street a woman, crying, that morning, in some house again.

"Yes, go!" said my Uncle Hagar, his voice rising, stronger. "Go, and starve to death! Go, and die in the poorhouse!"

His voice broke, and he stopped where he was — or I believe he would have been crying.

But that didn't stop me.

"Do you think it is any prettier death," I said, "to stay here and rot in this damned Fever!"

"Beavis!" said Vance.

"I ain't afraid of it. I ain't any more afraid of this Fever," said my Uncle Hagar, "than I am of sunstroke. You don't have to get it unless you want to."

"Tell that to the Marines," I said.

"I know what I'm talking about," said my Uncle.

"What are you going to do? Are you going to keep Vance and kill her?" I said.

"That's different," said he. "Vance is going with you."

"Let me talk to him, Beavis," said Vance. "Let me talk to him."

"Oh," I said, raving, and turned my back, swearing at him and his foolishness under my breath. And stood there at the window, looking down at the deserted street while they talked it out.

"I can't afford to," he told her. "I can't afford to. It ain't going to be possible for me to go."

And when she told him the house and everything in it would be well watched and taken care of, he said "No," he knew better. "Not with all the niggers in town sitting and watching and staring at it, and talking over all those old stories. No, somebody would have to stay and watch it.

"But you can go," he said, "you two. You've got to."

And so for an hour, it seemed to me, they had it back and forth; he saying that she must go, and she saying that she never would go without him; and telling him how she'd waited all this time just to get him to go; and teasing him and arguing with him, and telling him — suppose he lost it all. What then? We'd get along someway.

And part of the time she sat beside him on the arm of his chair, and part of the time she was down in front of him on her knees — sometimes — looking up and talking, and catching hold of his hand, like a teasing child.

And he on his side was just as obstinate and determined that she should go without him. And several times he patted her hand and when she was looking at him, pushed back her hair, and looked into her eyes; very clumsy — clumsy like men are who don't show their feelings that way very often. But she wouldn't move without him.

The talk went in circles; round and round, and back to

the same place — round and round, like the dogs following a fox on the hills; and you could see his mind turn
back again and again, to the center of everything to him
— to his property.

But Vance held where she was, and finally I thought —
we both thought she had him. For he stopped talking,
and she kissed him, and told him he was going, and to go
upstairs and get ready; and he got up without answering,
and went upstairs again into his room. He seemed
pretty shaky.

But when he went in there, he didn't come out again.

Half-past ten o'clock came, and I didn't like it.
Eleven, and I was getting restless, and Vance was too. I
saw her listening by the staircase. And then, quarter
past eleven, and, if we were going, we'd got to be starting
soon. And finally, Vance went up and told her father
he'd have to come down and have some lunch before he
started.

But all he said was: "I'm not hungry." And Vance
and I took a few bites together, standing up, and clearing
everything right away. I had the horse all harnessed in
the barn.

And then, at quarter to twelve, Vance went up, all
dressed to go, and knocked at the door. And her face
was flushed and excited.

"Come, Dad, come!" she called. "It's time to go.
We're all ready."

He didn't answer at all at first, and then he said again:
"You go!"

"Come, dear!" she said; kept saying. "Please, we've
got to hurry!"

His hand came on the doorknob once, she said, and
turned it, and he started to turn the key in the lock, but
he didn't, quite.

And all at once this loud voice, that she scarcely knew was his, came out from behind that old, high door: "No sir. No sir. I'll stay right here. I'm going to stay right here with my Property. You can go, but I got to stay here and keep my eye peeled for my Property."

And after that he didn't say any more, only — after she had knocked and called a lot more —: "Get away from there! Get away from there!"

By that time I was up there beside Vance, and when he said it, she turned to me and caught her arms around me, and hid her face in silence — the way women sometimes do, turning away at the end of a burial. A hundred times she has told me that her father was dead to her, really from that time on. But she didn't cry; nor sob; nor move hardly. And then she stopped, all at once; she stopped and drew away from me, and said very quietly:

"I knew that he would never go!"

I saw, of course, what she was thinking of — that dream of hers.

And we went downstairs again, and Vance took off her hat and we made our plans to stay.

There was no use of arguing now. I could see that from her face. She wouldn't go — it would only be a useless burden and torture to try to make her now. I saw that, without talking.

I saw that; and I went out to the barn, and unharnessed the horse — clenching my hands, and striking them against the side of the building to hurt and bruise them. For I knew the thing was done, that we were all done for.

"Don't worry," said Vance, when I came back. "You needn't, about me anyhow. I'm just as strong as you are now, and stronger — you'll see."

And the strange thing — a thing I never could understand about women — it was true, just as she said. In times like that, strength comes to them — a dozen times their usual strength. Where from? I never understood. But I never saw any change like that one — that frail girl, we all worried so about, when it came to the test, out-tired us all — strengthened and hardened, somehow; steel to our soft iron; a diamond against glass.

She had a lot more sense, and understanding and cheerfulness, I know, than I did. From that time on it was I who looked to her for strengthening and self-control. Fatalism, I believe they call it now; acceptance, I call it. And you know, as well as I do, that women, the best of them, have it a hundred times more than men.

We could hear my Uncle walking all that afternoon — slow at first; then back and forth; back and forth; back and forth on that floor above us.

Then spaces of silence.

" What can we do? " I asked.

" Let him alone," said Vance. " Maybe after a while, I can get him to come out."

But he wouldn't — not even after she whispered, and told him it was too late to go now; that we were not going.

And at evening we couldn't get him out for supper.

" I can't eat; I don't feel like it," said my Uncle Athiel, finally, to Vance. And she was encouraged — we both were — to hear him say something — anything.

CHAPTER XXI

TWILIGHT came finally, and the shutting of the windows. We did it naturally, now, by force of habit — in spite of the discomfort of it, and the choking heat.

For the idea, and the fear of that poison air outside, had got hold of us — and now, especially, with the Fever groaning under our windows, all around us. And that night, and the nights before it, too — I went to shut the windows down against it good and early — as glad and quick to do it as a child that shuts the door behind him on a black stairway.

" I don't believe we'll either of us sleep much to-night," said Vance. " Not anyway till we know what he's going to do. We'll stay here and wait."

" Won't you be too tired, dear? " I said.

" Not the least bit," she said. And her voice was clear and strong, and her looks as fresh and little tired as I ever saw them.

So we waited and watched and listened, together, into that night.

All over that town, I expect, folks sat watching and worrying through that night — but none in such a curious way as ours. For what we did really, was just to sit and listen for sounds upstairs; for the motions behind that old locked door, which would show what the man

266

locked up in there was doing.   And to guess from that what really was in his mind.

He might really not be well like Vance thought.   But to me it seemed that whatever sickness he had now, was sickness of the brain, and not the body.

He walked still, after supper, continually, up and down — but not so fast, nearly, as he had on that afternoon.

It darkened early — another early twilight.   The curtain of blue cloud which draws up toward night on the sky out over the Mississippi even after the pleasantest day — and especially as the fall comes nearer — was up to-night again.   The lamp-lighter came by — we heard his heels go clacking down the sidewalk; and the feeble sparks of the gas-lights twinkle out behind him.

And now, near and far away, across the town, the light of the Fever fires came out again, like evil flowers blossoming in the night.   Not lighted in nearly all the cases now. As time went by, they gave that idea up.   But now there were so many deaths everywhere, only an occasional fire, lighted here and there, made a great lot in the town.

And now one more was lighted on our street, and we knew it was for the little German woman — the last of that family the Fever had started in, down under the hill.

" The last of them," I said, " the last one of the whole family.   Once inside the house, once the thing gets in —" and I stared gloomily at the old light — the light of the Fever fire that lay like bright orange paint on the window frame, and on the face of Vance, standing watching.
ˌ   " She was glad, I expect," said Vance softly.   " I know that I should be."

Upstairs my Uncle had stopped walking — tired out, maybe.   And sat there, motionless, in the dark.

And, watching the fire down the empty street, we talked

of what had happened in those last few days — of Arabella, and of her strange ideas of the end of the world, and all that.   But, as usual, I spoiled it.

" It's likely to be the end of the world for some of us."

" Oh, you are hopeless," said Vance to me.   " Can't you ever pretend; can't you ever believe anything? "

" Can't you go — won't you? " I said, for the hundredth time.

" No," said Vance.

" Well," I said at last, " at any rate we're here together."

" Yes," said Vance, " but it's not the end of the world for *us*."   And her shoulder trembled, once more, but only a very little, in my arms.

" I know it won't be," she said, " for you and me."

When I spoke back and told her how impossible that was that she should know that, she was just as certain as she ever was about it.

" You can't explain it," she said.   " No, you can't explain your feelings — can you?   No, not any of them! Heat or cold, or gladness or light.   They must come to you, that's all.

" No," she said, " there's many a time that you and I will watch the daylight out together."

And then she turned back quickly, sudden tears in her eyes, and went out to stand a long while at the foot of the dark front stairs, listening.   And I knew, of course, that that thing was in her mind again — that premonition she had had about her father.   But we didn't mention it, either one of us, again.

There was nothing from upstairs, and Vance came back to me.   She still thought — both of us did — that it was better to leave him to himself, and not to disturb him. She had tried calling earlier, several times; and though he made no answer to her, it was plain enough he didn't like it.

"Aren't you tired standing there, Vance?" I asked.

For it bothered me, for one thing, to stand there at the window, with the light of the Fever fire before us.

And so we did not go back again. We sat down, on that old curved backed sofa that had been her mother's — the only real common, homely piece of furniture around the place — an old time hair cloth sofa, with bright worsted headrests at the ends.

We sat there waiting — talking — wondering — that long first of the night, together. It was very still — dead, silent, mostly. Outside, very faintly, the little tinkle of the mule car, now and then. And once or twice the sound of the negro militia men passing on the streets. But mostly silence. We sat there talking, silent, listening.

We all remember, all of us, I expect! We never can forget those first few times that one dear woman gave us the half-spoken, half-hidden confidences of a woman's heart — phrases, broken phrases; silences. Her hand in your hand; her dear body touching yours. But for me the thought of it brings back again a touch of fear, the sudden touch of a cold fear, lest now — now that I had her in my arms, lest I would certainly and surely lose her out of them forever. A sharp cold touch of fear — and the hush, and threat and uncertainty, of that unearthly silent night, with the fire lights, and the poison of that Fever, out beyond our windows, and the vacant, silent streets.

The man upstairs was moving finally. He'd lighted a light — for the first time he'd lighted up his light. We saw it from the windows of the Crystal Room, shining outside on the trees from underneath one of the shades. Then for a long while there was nothing more we noticed.

We talked of him naturally; and of the thing which bound him there — his fear of poverty, of fire and thieves; and what actually there was that he stood guarding there, and was so scared for. Our talk went rising up and down from silence, like a flickering candle in a dark draughty room.

Once, outside, there was a sound — the sound of a hairy body come against the side door; and a sigh. And after a scared second or two we understood that it was Gen. Sherman, the old dog, come back — as near as he could be to us — now Arabella was gone away — for company. And we talked on about the man upstairs — and about what he probably would do. We heard him moving around again then; and after a while — a heavy sound as if he had flung himself upon his bed — heavy and tired out.

" Money," said Vance. " Poor father's money. A world with nothing in it anywhere but money. Poor man!"

" 'Property,' " I said, quoting him. " Damn Property! If that was all there was in life, I'd hope to die to-morrow."

" Old folks — lots of them — are that way," said Vance, defending him.

" Oh, I certainly hope we won't be like that, when we are old," she said.

I grinned. I couldn't help it — talking of old age for us, and all the world around us full of death and danger.

" Just as sure as ever," I said.

" Just as sure," said Vance.

And then: " Listen, what's that? " she said, sitting straight.

He seemed to have got up, and to be dragging a chair across the room, slowly — very slowly. We stepped into the hall, and stood listening, waiting.

And: " Listen," said Vance again.

For suddenly, again, we heard that little bell go, jangle, jangle, jangle, in the cellarway. Not loud at all — but very plain from where we stood.

There was no one at the doors — not a soul. I rushed to both of them, in just a second or two. At the front door, nothing! And at the side door, old Gen. Sherman curled up in a dead heavy sleep!

And back I went, down into the cellarway, and Vance after me.

And overhead again, first in the light of a match I lit, and then by a candle Vance brought out, we saw the four little call-bells in their row against the back of the stair.

It seemed to me that one wire coil was still moving — still shivering and palpitating.

" What do you think, Vance? " I said. But she didn't answer.

" The one from the Purple Room! " I said.

" Let's wait," said Vance. " Maybe it may start again — if it is he — if it is he doing it."

So then we stood waiting, watching those four little dangling bells.

If that one had rung, I thought, there was only one way that it could happen. By that little dangling wire, hanging down there by the spring from which it had been disconnected. That little dangling wire, with the crook at its end, where once it had been fastened on. Then all at once — there was no doubt of it. We saw that dangling wire move, slightly — very, very slightly — just enough to catch that vibrating, sensitive little coil, and,

" Jangle, jangle, jangle," went the call-bell from the

Purple Room, there in the half-shadow from over our head.

"He did that," said Vance. "It's he that's been doing it all the time."

"Yes," I said, and together we raced back again to the front hall.

Upstairs my Uncle Hagar was dragging something — that chair again across the room; slower — slower — We noticed how very slow he went. And then,

"Bang!" it toppled over the floor.

Then I waited a while below, while Vance went tiptoeing up the stairs. And after a while she said, there were a few unsteady, tottering steps, more uneven for his lameness, and he fell heavily again upon the bed. Then she thought she heard him groan very low.

I was with her in a second. I thought I had heard it, too.

And finally she spoke to him, and he didn't answer.

But he did groan again — and then again. And finally he spoke out, to himself — not her:

"My head! God, my head!" and I knew, and she knew right away, what had happened.

"Get back," I said to Vance. "Get back!"

And: "Can you open the door?" I called to my Uncle Athiel.

"I'll manage to," he said, painfully, after a while.

"And I'll go and get the doctor," I said to Vance.

"Yes."

I went, running. It was only just a little ways; and by luck I found the doctor there, all ready.

And he came right out, and hurried back with me. And when we got there, the door was opened, and my Uncle Hagar was in bed, and Vance stood there beside him

— watchful, pale, and steady and calm as if she had been nursing the Yellow Fever all her life.

"That's it!" said the doctor.   "He's got it; that's the Fever!"

It was a little after twelve o'clock — that hour after midnight — when the Fever nearly always came.

CHAPTER XXII

THE WHISTLING DOCTOR

"THOSE windows are all closed!" said Dr. Greathouse, looking around the great high room.

I told him when he asked, that we had never changed, right from the beginning. We had closed our windows, all through the house, at night always, at sunset — since the Fever came. And he nodded his head, as if he liked it.

"But I don't believe you can stand it now," he told me.

But when he went to open the windows up, my Uncle tossed and motioned and whispered to have them closed again.

"I can stand it, I expect," I said. "If I can't, I'll sit out in the hall."

And my Uncle, motioning, showed that he was better satisfied.

And then, after that, he showed us there was another thing he wanted. He was going to have Vance kept out of there; he whispered about it, but not very plain, for it was hard work for him, naturally. So the doctor cut him short, saying, "I'll take care of that."

But I don't believe he caught entirely what my Uncle Hagar wanted. He thought he just wanted her kept out of that room of his. But what he really wanted to have him do, was to send her out of town entirely, I believe. And every time he saw her after that time, he got worried and excited, thinking she was there, and he had kept her there.

But that made no difference anyway. The doctor himself would have sent Vance if he could, but there was nothing he could do, nor I, about getting Vance to go. It was no, flat, from her, from the first. And the best that he could get was to make her promise to keep away from her father — out of his room — and that only because she saw it hurt him to see her.

It was the same old story with her; her weakness was her strength. You could press so far, but when she refused to give way — when she still fought you and laughed at you — what was there you could do? You couldn't use physical force to drive her; you couldn't drag her off in chains and irons. So there she was, and there she stayed in spite of us — like many a woman has, before and since, I expect.

And so finally, the doctor got ready to go. And I was to stay and watch my Uncle myself, for that night.

" I'll send you a nurse along to-morrow," he said. " You can't do it all."

Nursing was all there was to Yellow Fever, he said, and nobody could watch twenty-four hours without sleep.

" That's the one thing that kills them — their nurses sleeping. That's the one and only thing I've got against these niggers nursing. They just can't keep from sleeping, sitting there alone. They aren't responsible. For they've got to be watched — these Fever patients —" he said, " every minute. They've got to rest, they've got to be made to lie perfectly quiet."

And after he told me this he went away and left me there. And, as I watched him then, he looked to me like a man who had no business to be out himself — all tired and worn out.

So, I sat there alone, in the great Purple Room, and stayed awake, easy enough that night. Stayed awake and watched the faint shadows from the Purple window draperies against the wall, and the darkness and twisted shadows on the ceiling. And sat and gave my Uncle Hagar what he needed, and thought and thought. I wasn't scared, exactly, now. The thing was done. And now the Fever was in the house, all we could do was to wait, with the chances all against us, as we thought. For then, of course, folks didn't know what caused it.

We couldn't go now, anyhow. Those old, invisible ties that caught us there and bound all of us together — were stronger than they ever were now. Neither Vance nor I could go away now, and leave the old man sick there, and alone.

And so there was really nothing for us to do but sit and wait, with the chances all against us. Sit and wait, but without so much nervousness or excitement as you'd suppose. Just wait with that same kind of calmness, I expect, that a bird has lying in between the claws of a cat.

I thought of Vance, naturally, and what would happen if she had the Fever. But I couldn't think of that — I couldn't let myself think of that. So, partly to forget it, I turned my thoughts to that other thing, that other question that had been always right before us — that old secret of my Uncle's Property — of "Hagar's Hoard." And now I thought of it more easily and naturally than ever, because of what had happened; because I sat there in that room, where that old store of his — those green-backs that they talked about — was kept, if it was any-where.

So my eye went searching round that great high room for places where it might possibly be. There were the purple draperies at the window, and the canopy over the bed — all with their letter " B " in a circle of gold laurel leaves, which that vain fool, Mr. Bozro, had patterned after the great house he had seen abroad that Napoleon had had.

But after you looked at them, they seemed like a poor place for hiding. And there were not very many likely places that I could see anywhere. Except the bed, naturally; or the great thick carpet with gold threads across it. They made hiding places big enough for anything — and common enough. Too common, I believe, for him to use them.

But most of all, right away, passing over everything, I watched and examined to see about that bell that he had always been disturbing, fussing around at night. But when I looked at it, it seemed to me like there was nothing to see there. Just this flat, old-fashioned bell-rope — flat like a tape, a tape say six inches wide, with a long fringe at its end; and at the top a round brass ring — a kind of ornamental cap, where it went into the wall. It seemed the most unlikely place for him to have hidden anything. He might, though, I said to myself, have sewed paper money into the long tape. But I didn't think so; I didn't believe it; it was somewhere else.

I did notice, once, looking everywhere, that old brown satchel that my Uncle Athiel got his rents in, peeping out from underneath the bed where he had thrown it, I expect, when he had finally made up his mind he couldn't go. But when I leaned over and looked at it, I saw that it was open — gaping open with nothing in it. And I gave the cursed thing another kick under the bed and forgot about it.

And so that night passed; and morning came, and Vance brought in what breakfast I wanted — cooking it herself, of course — for the servant was gone. And we settled down to the regular ways of a house where there is sickness. Sat down and waited, through that morning, for the doctor to bring us in another nurse.

When he didn't come, at first, we said the doctor was having trouble — like he said he would, to find a good one. For nurses — good ones — were almost impossible to get now, the Fever was running on so fast. The houses right around us were full of it; and that wasn't even a little fraction of it all. I sat and waited, and he didn't come. And, finally, when my Uncle got resting a little better, sleeping apparently, I made up my mind I would go and see what was the matter. It was just a little ways anyhow, and Vance could watch, out in the hallway, for my Uncle wouldn't let her inside anyway.

And so I went over, and I saw Dr. Greathouse, for the last time.

Uncle Mungo met me there at the front door, with his face that old dead shiny color that the darkies get instead of getting pale.

"He's got it," he said, half whispering. "My Mister Willy's got the Fevah!"

It gave me a worse start, somehow, than when I knew my Uncle had it. I had just only seen the man — just those few hours before. He must have been already touched with it then. And the feeling came over me, stronger and stronger than ever before —

"Everybody's going to have it. We're all going to have it now."

I'd given up the hope of escaping. And there was the feeling with it, not so much of being scared, but just reckless.

"Well, here goes!" you said to yourself. "I'm next! Everybody else is hit."

And yet, all the time, underneath, you hoped you might not get it after all. Yourself — you and yours.

I went right in, naturally, to where he was — in that great, low, long, old-fashioned bedroom of his on the first floor — all tumbled up the way a man living alone, without women folks in the house, leaves things — and his clothes just where he left them when he threw them off.

" Hello," he said, when I came in, with as much of his great strong voice as he had left. " What do you think of this? "

It was a pretty light case, he said, so far — only —

" These fat ones are apt to have it kind of hard," he said, and tried to laugh, and couldn't — much. He was weak, naturally, and it hurt his head too much.

And when I asked him about anything that I could do, he said, " No, nothing.

" I'll doctor myself," he said, " mostly, I expect. The rest of them are monstrous busy now. I'll doctor myself. And Mungo here'll take care of me — and pull me out. You will — won't you, Mungo? "

" Yassuh, I'm just goin' to do that," said Uncle Mungo, trying to smile.

" I bet on you, uncle. And not the first time, either! " said old Doctor Greathouse, thanking him with his eyes.

And then, when I started to go, the doctor talked and asked a minute or two about my Uncle Hagar. He made himself. Told me about a nurse; and what doctor he would have; and said he'd see we got them there himself, right away. For the doctor was coming to see him the first minute that he had; and he'd send him right along over to see us.

And he spoke about Vance, and said we certainly ought to get her away. And when I said I couldn't get her to go, he said he expected that was true. Women were that way. Naturally, too.

" But don't give up too much. Don't worry too much about her," he said. " This Fever is a crazy thing. You can't account for it. It comes and goes when it wants to. And when it once gets you, you can't tell anything either. A great, strong, fat animal like I am, is in a lot more danger than a frail little nineteen year old girl like Vance. You can't tell why, but it's so.

" The fact is," he said, " they don't know anything — they don't know anything about it. It's just as much a mystery as it was when the Pharaohs lost their slaves from it in Egypt."

And then I thanked him, and told him to stop talking, and got up to go.

But he managed to ask me one more question before I got away.

" How was it —" he said, " could you keep your windows closed all night? "

And when I told him that I could and had, he thought a minute and said he was glad I did. It was just as well.

" You can talk all you want to," he said, " there's something outside there. There's something there in the night air that carries that disease." And he waited a minute, looking up at me from his pillow.

" Something," he said, and turned restlessly in his bed. " Something. God! Sometimes you think — almost — you touch it almost with your finger tips; and then it's all gone — gone! You can't quite get the thing. Lord! How I wish —"

" Lie down," I said. " You're a nice one to talk about lying quiet."

And when I went out, and all the time I was sitting there, I was seeing those old fat, sleepy mosquitoes up

there on the ceiling, and the walls. And flies, too —
bothering him then. There weren't any screens with us
those days. I wouldn't have noticed the mosquitoes, I
expect, except we had been so free from them those last
few days — those days of the Fever — with all the windows closed at night. It was the only thing that made
the great hot house bearable. And once we had the mosquitoes barred out, we kept it pretty free of them. But,
then, of course, we didn't know — we hadn't any idea at
all — what it really meant.

Uncle Mungo stood there waiting for me when I went
out.

"How's he 'pear to you? How's he 'pear to you?"
he asked, mighty anxious. And his hand was a little
shaky. The old nigger was getting pretty old.

"He'll come round," I said, more cheerful than I felt.

"I 'spect so — I 'spect so," said Uncle Mungo, agreeing with me, like he always did. "He's doctorin' himself. And there ain't anybody knows more 'bout the
Fevah'n my Mister Willy does. No sir!"

His voice kept getting stronger as he kept saying it to
himself. But he was still pretty scared and shaky. He
was a mighty frail little old darky; I don't believe he
weighed much over a hundred pounds.

"The only thing that keeps o'botherin' me," he said, low
and secret, "the only thing worries me's like this: Sup-
posin' sometime he went out of his haid. Sposin'— so he
couldn't tell me just what to do; and I was left here alone
some night, with all that 'sponsibility.

"It sciahs me. It sciahs me, thinkin' of it.

"'Fore God, Mr. Beavis," he went along, his voice
shaking and breaking a little bit, "'fore God, I rather die
and be buried a hundred times, than have anythin' hap-
penin' to my Mister Willy. Or have anybody else to —

or have any dozen of 'em to die. He's done more good-
ness in this town than any hunded folks, ain't he?
There's hundeds and hundeds of folks'd miss him comin'
whistlin' down their street, more'n anybody else on this
yere earth, I believe. Yassuh!"

The old man was getting too excited. I told him he'd
have to stop it — and tend strictly to his business.

"All you've got to do is to keep him still," I said.
"That's what he says to do himself."

"Yassuh, I will," said Uncle Mungo. "But sposin' I
was left alone here, and sposin' I didn't know what to do
and he got aloose from me all alone here some night?"

"Oh, stop your fretting, Uncle Mungo," I said. "Quit
your worrying; that won't happen. He ain't so bad."

But that was what did happen — just exactly what
did happen, finally, so they tell me.

And all around me, going home — oh, in half a dozen
places maybe — I either saw the windows open, or heard
that moaning from the houses, from the rooms where
they were down with the Fever.

It lay around us — striking down one head after another. There it was, inside that old house of ours. I
looked up from under the house when I got there, and
saw it, ugly and dreary — in that bright sunlight — with
its great thick, brick walls, and its brick eyebrows over the
windows; and the round blind windows built for statues
that were never made, and the old Tower in front, like a
great old gray owl over the sidewalk.

And there it was — the Fever inside that old prison
now, inside the house; and we knew well enough what it
did when it once got in the house.

And who were we — how different — that it was going
to miss us?

And so I went on in, slowly, and went slowly up through

the empty lower hall, and found Vance sitting at the entrance of the Purple Room.

"He's got it. The doctor's got it now," I told her. And in spite of all I could do, tears came into my eyes a little. I had to cry. He'd been a mighty good friend to me — those few months.

She'd known him ten times as long as I, and ten times as well. But she didn't let go of herself a minute. She smiled, and took my hand, and patted it.

"That doesn't mean he's got to die," she said. She had been right. She wasn't a girl any more; she was a grown woman.

"Go, Vance, go!" taking her in my arms, "for God's sake, go! We're all going to have it. We've got to. Everybody. Go, won't you! Go! — when you've still got the chance."

She shook her head and put me away from her.

"He seems quieter," she said, looking there into the Purple Room, where my Uncle Hagar lay, dozing.

CHAPTER XXIII

THE BELL ROPE

THE new doctor had gone, and I sat there, trying to keep awake. Lord! It was awful. When there was a chance, the excitement of the chance of going away, it was well enough, but now, with that all settled; with our hope of leaving gone; now, just sitting there in that sick room, it was something monstrous. Especially now, when those locusts got going! That old, hot, sleepy song of the locusts.

I opened my eyes and sat up — and my Uncle lay there looking at me — with a little brighter look than he had before.

"You don't know," he said, in a dull kind of voice. "Everything went wrong with me!"

It was the first time he had spoken for an hour or two.

And then he stopped; and I didn't know what to say. And those cursed locusts went on grinding out there, putting me to sleep.

"Twenty years!" said my Uncle, then. "Yes thirty! All wrong!"

Then he didn't talk for a long time — and then only slowly — as if his mind worked slowly, and in pain.

But it seemed to me like his mind, just as soon as it came back, always started back in that old groove where it had always been.

"Don't talk," I said. "It ain't good for you."

284

" There was one hundred and fifty thousand dollars one time," said my Uncle Athiel, after a while, " that I could count on. Good sound property.

" Now," he said louder, " I can't count more than thirty thousand! " and he tried to get up.

" Lie down! " I said. " Don't do that again! "

They mustn't talk and they mustn't move at all — like I told you. It kills them often — like it probably did that old half-nigger and the German. But after that he fell back — for he was jerked back by the pain in his head, like a great weight, to his pillow.

After a while, when he got his strength again, his eyes kept open and were on me — his face lying toward me. And it seemed to me now — though I may only have imagined it, thinking afterwards, on that fringed bell-rope beyond, hanging down the wall. His great old hickory cane stood there beside it, and somewhere, I knew, under the head of his bed somewhere, was that old time Derringer pistol that he had.

I stopped his talking for the time, but his old thoughts, waking up once more, I expect, just started boiling in him again.

They made him talk for a while, every now and then — in spite of me. In a way, I was glad of it — it kept me from sleeping. But I couldn't let him do too much, just the same.

" You wouldn't believe it," he said, " you wouldn't believe it! " and started struggling.

" Lie still! " I said, " I won't let you talk any if you do like that."

" First there was that damned war," he said, lying there with those little black eyes on me.

" You know that! " he said, after a little longer.

" Yes," I said, humoring him, " I know that."

"And then those banks — those scoundels — those banks. You know — Judas! What they cost me!"

I nodded at him, waiting to see if he wouldn't stop; waiting to see if his talk wouldn't just run out of itself.

"And now this," he said, "this town ruined —" and started moving, and stopped, looking at me.

"You wouldn't believe it, would you?" he asked me, staring. And I told him I certainly would not.

And for a while he stopped again, thinking it over, and I thought he might be resting.

"You might say I was getting too old," he started on again, "but I don't believe it was that — do you? I don't believe that did it — do you?" he asked louder — when I didn't answer, getting dull and drowsy.

"No," I said, sitting up again.

"No," said my Uncle Athiel louder, "no, you're right! No, sir! No, sir! You wouldn't believe it if I told you. One thing after another and all wrong — and all wrong! And you couldn't tell — not one single thing — in advance!

"Sometimes," he said, and stopped staring at me, with a meaning look — feverish, I expect.

"Sometimes, it almost seemed like there was something after me! Something I couldn't get quit of — following me!"

Then after that he waited a while. The work of thinking and talking had worn him down. And I sat there, listening to those locusts outdoors, there in the trees.

"Grind — grind — grind! Grate — grate — grate!"

It seemed like they were grinding holes in my brain, through my ears. And the air was still, and hot, and bad, in that room, naturally — and nothing moving, but a fly sometimes, buzzing across the ceiling. And outside nothing, either. Nothing but those damned droning locusts. And, as far as being afraid — as far as being scared, I didn't fear anything any longer, or know anything, or hear anything, but those locusts, putting me to sleep.

Vance looked in every now and then, and I sat up and appeared the best I knew how; and prayed that nurse they were going to send us would come pretty quick, for I didn't see what I could do, if somebody didn't come along.

My Uncle rested for a little while. Then he went on talking more — now and then — about his Property, about the War, about his losses — those everlasting losses he had made.

He cursed the War — both sides — and all their generals; and Jeff Davis and Abe Lincoln both — but especially Davis, and the money — all that Confederate money they left folks high and dry with.

God! If I could only have killed those locusts, outside there, grinding me to sleep! The nurse didn't come and didn't come. I got up, and walked around — as quiet as I could; and went out and doused myself with water. It was no good at all. Just as soon as I was back there I heard that old droning coming through the windows of that old hot room!

My Uncle Hagar traveled up and down again, in his mind, talking over what he'd done and lost. He talked about Vance a while — and started blaming her for staying.

"She ought to have gone. She ought to have gone first," he said. "She always was a delicate child. We've always fussed and worried for her. I'm glad she's gone now. She ought to.

"It's different with me," he said, looking toward me again. "It's different with me. I had to stay here to

take care of it — to take care of everything! To keep
care of my Property!

"Didn't I?" he asked me.

And I naturally said, "Yes."

"I'm glad she's gone," he said finally, about Vance.

"You and I can stay here now, and take care of it.
We'll keep our eye peeled! We got to keep our eye
peeled now, you understand, for fire and thieves! For
most all the white folks have gone now — most all the
rest of 'em have gone! This town is full of thieves!"

I had to quiet him on that, and let him start on something else.

"And, as far as Fever goes," he said again, trying in
a funny way to snap his fingers, "I don't give that for it.
I don't fear it any more than I do sunstroke. And
there's no more use of having it."

You couldn't tell how his mind was. That was an example. He didn't even know he had the Fever, apparently, and yet he did know he was sick. And in many
ways he seemed bright as anybody.

He seemed to take it for granted too, after that, that
Vance was gone. And we were alone there — we two in
the house. I know he lay there after that, for a while,
looking at me.

"I like the way you stood by me," he said, after a
while. And after that — it was kind of funny — he said
something again about lawyers taking care of Property,
and nodded to himself, his head all the time on the pillow.
Then after that, he let up a little bit, and relaxed himself
and got sleepy, and shut his eyes.

"All right," he said, several times. "O. K." And
then, afterwards, just before he went off to sleep:

"I got something — I'm going to show you," he said.

" Something — just as soon as I get my voice back. Just as soon as I get rested up!"

And he looked at me, then; and he looked at the wall back of me — I'm sure he did, where his old cane stood; where that fringed bell-cord hung down. Looked over there, just as he had done, I expect, every night since he laid there in that great room; and then he went off quietly to sleep.

I just remember it; I just can remember it. The nurse hadn't come, and wasn't coming, apparently, and those locusts were too much for me. The next thing I knew was Vance standing at the door, saying she would stay outside there while he slept, and I must go and rest.

I went — I had to. I just could tell her that he mustn't see her; that she must not go in, for his sake as well as hers, and I started off to my own room. And when I got there, if you'll believe me, and lay down — I couldn't sleep, I couldn't sleep a wink! I kept seeing Vance out there, and worrying; and those locusts, those dry, grating, damned locusts, outside there, still went grinding, grinding, grinding on my bare brain, and keeping me awake!

I tried for a while. I thrashed and banged and rolled around — then I got up! And from that time on I changed. I didn't want to sleep. Those locusts going still nearly drove me mad like something rasping and grating inside my skull. But I didn't want to sleep again. I just had no desire to. I had no desire on earth now — only to have those locusts stop.

My Uncle Athiel was asleep still, when I went back. He seemed to be getting along well, Vance said, sleeping quiet and restful.

And I sat there, alone, looking around, trying to keep

my mind off those droning locusts — and off from Vance. My old continual worry about Vance. My mind, that had been so dull, now got just wonderfully clear.

I looked at my Uncle lying there, yellow and old and gone, I believed; as good as gone, anyhow. And I saw him, younger, coming down from the hills, in those old rough pioneer times in the rich new country, hunting this thing — this Property; this money of his, that had turned now, these twenty years, and gone hunting him — to death.

" And us too," I thought to myself, " with him." For it certainly did seem that not one of us had much chance, now. And yet I didn't seem to care much. It didn't seem to worry me at all. I didn't care much about anything but those locusts.

And I looked around that great room — and its fool fol-de-rols; and I thought of all that great house — that old silly, self-advertising of that dead man, that he was better than his neighbors. And then about this other man who followed him.

One of them dead, by his own hand, in that very room. And now this one, too, this little, common, yellow, old man there, tucked in under that great purple canopied bed with the gold laurel wreaths on it; dying there, most likely, the same as the other had — in the same place, and for the same reason — for Property — for Money. And when I went over it, and around and around, it certainly did seem crazy enough — what they had done. That Money folks are always fighting for — crazy and little and strange! With that Fever out there, and all those people dying all around us — like it was the end of the world, as the niggers thought! And we there, waiting — waiting!

I watched around again, after that, looking around

the room; thinking of what he probably had there; and then, of what he said before he went to sleep, that he was going to tell me. And naturally, then, my eye went back again to that call-bell, and that cord to it that hung down there, to see if there could possibly be anything there which would account for his continual fussing with it, and his looking at it now. Any place there where he could hide his money, if he had it there. But there was nothing I could see.

That cord itself — that big, flat, rough purple cord, would hardly be a hiding place — I had made up my mind then — though of course it might be. It was big enough of course, to have bills sewed into it — if you wanted to. But I didn't think he'd do it. It was too handy, too easy to be looked at. And at the top of it was only that big round brass cap, or ring, where it passed up above there into the wall.

I must have been looking up at it, when he woke up.

I saw right away that he was stronger for his sleep, when I saw him waking; and I noticed, too, that with his strength, his suspicious ways had come right back again. " What are you looking at? What do you see? " he said, in a cross old ugly voice.

" Nothing," I said. " Why? "

" Nothin'," he answered me in his turn, and didn't talk any more.

Whatever he had thought he'd show me, I saw then he never would.

He seemed brighter, a lot — brighter and uglier.

" If getting better, means getting uglier, like they say it does," I said to myself, " he's getting along."

He kept his eyes open, after that, for a while, a good share of the time; always lying there on his side, looking towards me.

He felt better, himself, too, and stronger, I believe, for once he said, I remember, looking sharp at me:

" They think they got the old man. They think they got him, but he ain't through yet! "

I had given up the nurse's coming now, for the present anyhow. I didn't know what I could do that night, if there was nobody by then, but I thought that I could stand it. Those locusts would stop anyhow. Anything if they'd stop going! So I hung and stuck it out.

He got restless as the afternoon went on, and then not so ugly; and after a while, when you could see the sun was sloping down, and he was getting tired again, you could see his grip on his mind was weaker. And he started, once or twice — and then went on — explaining again, and explaining and explaining, his life, once more — and his Property — and how he lost it.

He was friendlier to me, as he got tireder, I knew; appealed to me now and then, and gave me advice — about getting old; about Property.

" Don't you never let yourself get old," he said, " never, without something put by to take care of you! "

And then, I remember too, his saying: " What's an old man! Think of it yourself! Nothing, nothing, more'n what he's got. That's just all! Just what he's got.

" Did you ever see 'em? " he said to me. " Did you ever see 'em sitting around a poorhouse yard?

" God! " he said, " you didn't know it — but my own father died there — in the poorhouse! There's where your folks took me and raised me from! "

It made him worse, thinking of it.

" Have something laid away, Beavis, my boy," he said, advising me, " and be mighty careful what you have.

Money — legal money — that's the best. I've tried 'em all. That's best."

His mind was getting cloudy now, I expect. " That's the best," he went along. " They can't get it away from you. They can't get it from you when you're old!

" Legal money!" he said, getting cloudier.

" But keep your eye peeled! You got to keep your both eyes peeled! All the time — all the time when you get old."

The shadows were growing longer, from the trees in back; evening was coming; those locusts in the trees — I expect the shadow was falling on them — were running down. Thank God! Thank God! It was like passing into heaven!

He didn't talk again; he went to sleep. I got up and looked out doors.

It had looked to me — and Vance thought so too — like that boy, that Saunders boy down the street who had been moaning, had died during the day. And I could see now that was right. Those men had been there — the undertakers — and I saw the pile of stuff — of bedding — in the road before the house.

There was a little wind. As the night came on, it looked a little like a thunder storm. A little wind had started up, whirling in the corners — papers and those little old, light, dry leaves of the elm trees. And the locusts were all still — everything dead, exhausted, still — except this little rustling of those leaves sometimes.

My Uncle Athiel roused a little, grew restless; and once or twice he whispered that pretty soon the windows must be closed. But I waited — just as long as I could. That breeze, that little breeze — after all that day — it was like a spring of water in the great African Desert.

I don't think I kept them open longer than we had before — I don't believe I kept those windows up any longer than I should! I certainly couldn't have known anyway!

But while I turned away for the last time to go back into the room and look at him, those fools outside there had lighted up the Fever fire in the street, right there, right under our windows. I didn't see it — not at all, until it was too late and the fire all going.

They lighted up that fire, and just then the breeze grew stronger — those whirls of wind that spring up before a thunder shower. It was blue, and darker, and it seemed now that we would get rain at last.

The wind came up, and came whirling. I could hear it in the dry trees. And before I knew it, the puff of thick, black smoke came blowing in the window — and a leaf or two — and one little piece of paper.

"What's that?" said my Uncle, starting from his drowse. "What's that?" and sat up straight.

And I jumped my fastest for the window.

But not quick enough! Too late! For:

"Fire!" cried my Uncle Athiel. "Fire! Thieves!" and yelling and crying out, he jumped up on his feet, carrying the light bedclothes with him; and stood, and half-reached and half-stumbled out; and pulled at that fringed cord. And when he took it and pulled, the thing gave way and pulled out on him from the top.

And he toppled and fell upon the floor, face downward; the bellcord in his hand; and with his fall came the sharp clatter of a little box at the top of the cord — a little round box behind the round brass ring, where it went into the wall — the clatter of this little box as it struck against the wall and on the floor. And with it, over him as he laid there, came down this shower of money —

greenbacks, packages of it, and some of it just loose bills. And it lay there over him — on his back, and his head, and even on his outstretched hands, where he lay there face downward on one hand, with his sheet upon him like a shroud. I sprang to him; and looking over, as I sprang, I saw the figure of Vance Hagar looking from the doorway.

And I knew before I touched him, that he was dead.

I don't say that she knew exactly. I don't pretend or expect to explain it. I don't say that she was sure beforehand how he would die. I only just can tell you what I saw. But he lay there, Vance has told me a thousand times, exactly as she'd seen him in that dream — one hand under his forehead, and one hand outstretched.

Of course you'll say they died that way, in the Fever, often — from those sudden starts like that — and of course it was not just exactly as she saw it. The money wasn't there for one thing. She hadn't seen the money in her dream.

But there he was, at any rate. Dead like she had seen him. And there, over him and around him, was spread " Hagar's Hoard," the remnants of the old man's fortune, that he had fought so long and savage and ugly for.

And I know that I hope that I shall never see such a sight again. Or pass such another night as that.

It had killed him — that hoard of his — just exactly as much as if it had drawn him in and strangled him.

CHAPTER XXIV

FUGITIVES

THEY came for him that night, very late — almost midnight, I remember. It was pretty hard for Vance — so soon, and in the middle of the night that way — and that one lone, tired, white man that could come; and the dim lights of the hearse outside there, waiting.

She couldn't go with him, of course, when he went away. She could not go in there — into the Purple Room, before they took him. I saw to that.

But she was very quiet and very reasonable about it all; she'd thought it out herself.

"It isn't like it had come unexpectedly," she said. "Like I hadn't known!"

So, whatever you think about that dream of hers, it did one thing. It really did prepare her for the thing that happened. Nobody can deny that.

She was a lot more quiet and reasonable; and cheerful too; a lot more use in planning what to do next than I was. She's told me many and many a time just how she felt about it. She had given him up. He died for her that night, when it was finally settled that he wasn't going. And now there was only just one thing left for her to think of, so she says — myself. Women are so, I've always thought — practical in their feelings — the best of them. Made to love and fight for us that are living —

open and public; and love and mourn for us when we are
dead — in secret by themselves.

And so, by midnight, it was all over. My Uncle Athiel
had left his old brick house that he cursed and loathed,
and guarded so, forever. And the next thing for both of
us — we both understood — was to escape. That old
Hoard of his — that old Succubus, the doctor had talked
about, had held my Uncle there until it had his life. Now
that he was gone, the question was, had it held us there
until it had our lives, too — or would have them both
before it was done?

I had gathered the stuff up — the greenbacks — before anybody else had come in — the doctor, or any of
the rest and crowded it into that little old brown satchel
of my Uncle's — that I remembered seeing under the bed.
It wasn't counted up of course. All I did was to crush it
in there — into the bag. But there was a lot of money,
I was sure. And funny, right away, it made me scared
and nervous — the responsibility of it! I kept edging
around — staying around the place I had hidden it, in
my room. I slept with it that night — that early morning — beneath my pillow.

When I woke up, I remember, my neck was all lame —
all stiff and lame, sleeping with the thing there beneath
my head. But I slept just the same. I had to — like
lead. And I woke up clear, bright as a dollar — ready
to fight out and run; get Vance out of town somehow.

She was ready, now. She would go anytime. We
started talking of it the first thing in the morning, when
she came down from her room.

But the trouble was, now we wanted to go, could we?
The Fever had been in the house, now, with us. We
might, more than likely, have it coming on ourselves —
who knew? They couldn't cast us loose into any other

place now — especially now with the whole country —
with places right around there, in particular — up in
arms against Memphis, like they were. In arms really,
too; " Shot gun quarantines," in every direction on the
roads — north and east especially.

And it was going to be mighty troublesome for us to
get out of town by railway. I could see that, more —
even than by the roads. They could watch the railroads
closer.

" We could drive," said Vance.

What we wanted to do, was to get up in the country
— up into the middle of the State, where my folks came
from.

" Would old Dolly stand it? " I said.

" Certainly, she would," said Vance. " And a lot better than leaving her back here!

" It wouldn't take us but a week or so," she said, explaining. " We could go south, where they aren't so
careful — Toward where they've had it themselves, and
then turn — turn east gradually."

" We could try it," I said.

" Yes, we must," said Vance, jumping up. " Let's go
out and look at Dolly now."

So we went out there to the old barn together — to
where the old horse was. She looked right well; she
hadn't had a thing to do for all those days. And when
Vance came in — with sugar in her hand, like she usually
did, the old mare turned her head, and whinnered at her.

And Vance stepped in her stall, feeding her. And
directly she put her arms around her neck, and kissed
her, and cried a little — thinking of her father, I expect,
and stopped right away again.

When we came out together, walking back to the old
house — I remember, I said to her:

"But even south they have those 'shotgun quarantines,' out on the roads. Supposing, supposing, right away, you ran across one."

For most of them — of those places around — were deadly against Memphis the first few weeks.

"Suppose you did," I said. "You might. Suppose you ran across such a town the first thing where the roads were barred."

"That's just the town we want," said Vance, and looked at me.

"Want!" I said. "Why? How'd you get in? If you met one of those guards of theirs, how would you get in?"

"Oh, we'd get in," said Vance.

"No, I want to know," I said. "What'd you say?"

"Say?" said Vance.

"Yes," I said. "I want to know before we start. There's no use going, and getting held up right away. Do you know one thing," I went along, "that you could say to get us out with?"

"Yes, I do — I believe," said Vance.

"What is it?" I kept on asking her.

"If I met a guard," said Vance, slowly —"If we do meet one," she said —"the first thing I'd do, I think, before he said anything — I believe I'd ask him if they had the Fever there — first. I'd ask him that," she said, "before he could say a word to me!"

"Yes," I said. "Then what?"

"And then, right away, before he'd get after us," she said — and stopped a minute. "You'd ask him for a minister!"

"A minister!" I said — my heart starting going.

"Yes," she said, and wouldn't look at me — and started talking on again.

"We'd tell him," she went on — talking a little faint, but like a person who's saying something that they learned by heart. "If we had to — I'd tell him — you'd tell him!" she said, turning those big, deep, honest, childish eyes of hers on me at last and dropping them right away again, "that we were running away to get married. And we didn't want to tell him where we came from."

"Get married!" I said, my old heart battering at my ribs, urging me forward. And my old pride, still holding me back. "Get married — we can't. I can't do that. You know I can't. I haven't got a dollar. I haven't any money in the world!" I blundered out.

"I have," said Vance, her eyes on mine.

"That's it!" I said.

"Money!" said Vance. "What's money!"

"A good lot," I said, and thought right away how funny it was — after all my cursing of it.

"Now?" said Vance, still looking at my eyes.

I didn't answer her.

"Between us?" she said, coming nearer.

There was no use arguing — and holding back with her. My old pride was no use. I had her in my arms right away.

"That's settled," said Vance — staying there, still.

It would be much better of course; in a way, it was almost forced on us, you might say, by our running off that way we did together.

"You see," said Vance, moving and looking up, after a while, "you see, it would be kind of a passport — being married in a place like that; where they were very strict against the Fever — wherever everybody knew they didn't have it! Why, the certificate from there, when we went along — you see, the certificate from there —"

"Yes, I see," I said, kissing her.

"So then," she said, after a little, "we'll go — to-morrow morning, early. And we can take that old leather trunk, that smallest one."

"Yes," I said, my pulse racing up again.

And so I went out to do my part, getting ready.

You wouldn't believe how burdensome it was — that money — now I had it. How hard it was to decide what to do with it.

I thought first that I'd put it in the bank — leave it there. Then I couldn't — I couldn't do it. All that talk of my Uncle's against banks wouldn't let me. Besides, I was nothing but a boy anyhow. What did I know about banks myself? So finally I decided I'd just take it with me — where I could keep my eyes on it. Then I'd know.

There was thirty thousand dollars of it — just about, I had counted it, finally that morning roughly. And afterwards I found I was right. It was about that; and that was all there was, I believe. I've had folks say to me since, if I'd only look further — in other places! They think there was somebody else in the house after-wards — got more. They say there was more; that there must have been! But I never thought so. I knew what my Uncle said about it, that last day. And I don't think, knowing him, he'd have it anywhere else, anyhow. It would all be right there — where he could watch.

But then for that matter, thirty thousand dollars un-der my hand there at night, in bills! A million dollars wouldn't worry me so now.

Then there was the house too. You wouldn't believe how careful I was in leaving that house, how I went over everything with John McCallan, leaving it.

"Remimber this, sor," said John, "I never saw you go. I never knew you left the town, out of a house with a faver in it! How long would they kape me on the force if they knew it!"

"Don't fret about that, John," I said.

"I don't, sor," said John. "Not a nickel's worth. And if I did, 'twould make no difference. I'd get that little girl of yours out o' here, if it cost me my job on the force this evening."

"God bless you, John," I said. "I wish that you were going too."

"Me!" said John.

"There's plenty of them have gone," I said —"police, and doctors, and ministers, too."

"I know that, sor. An' I'm very sorry to have t' say it t' you. I know that," said John, standing square footed in front of me. "But me!" he said, and stopped. "Lit me ask you somethin'," he said: "If I got away now from here — from what I have to do here. If I got away and saved myself, why then — after thot, where'd I spend the rist of my days? Where'd I go — what'd I be after thot? Let me ask you thot!"

"I don't know," I said.

"I don't know," said John — and shook his head.

"But you can go," he said, "and they'll all be better off to have you goin'. All the white folks that can," said John, "have their first duty to git away from here. For them that stays'll git it now," said John. "Make up your mind to thot. All thim that stays'll only feed the Faver. They'll all have it. And most of 'em will die. This ain't no Yeller Faver now. It's some old plague, some black plague they used to have in them old times, come back again."

We thought that — ourselves, now — that we'd have it, all the white folks that stayed — we'd got to think that way ourselves, now — that every white man there was going to die. And it did seem worse and different from the Yellow Fever, they said. The dead wagons, droning by us, fuller every day; the folks around us going down — the folks we knew; the poor folks laid away in the trenches in the graveyard; and the niggers burying them all night — just eating there and sleeping there, and burying them — with those tar fires going around them night and day.

It seemed natural to expect then there was no stopping it at all. It did seem that finally it would get us all — all the white folks anyhow. And why not us too, like the rest — and especially now it had been there, in our own house with us. The only thing for us, we knew, was to go if we could. But could we — could we get away before it took us? And hadn't one of us, or both, right then, in our blood, the poison of that Fever?

If it hadn't been for Vance, I believe — if Vance hadn't been so sure, I don't expect I'd have taken the chance of going off just that way we did; not knowing but it might strike us later on the road, maybe.

But I don't know — I might have too. I was pretty young and venturesome those days.

And anyhow we packed up that night to go — what clothes we could and we took along, too, a couple of blankets — two old army blankets — so if we wanted to — if they wouldn't take us in, we could just camp out doors somewhere, if we had to.

It was clear weather, calm, perfectly clear and bright. And we weren't the only folks that had done it that year, I expect. But it was Vance who thought to plan it first, as usual.

" If there should be the Fever anywhere — or they

wouldn't take us in, we could camp," she said. "We could go into some farmhouse, if it is better; or we could camp."

Lord, how still it was when I woke up that next morning — before the dawn. And stole out into the yard, just after daybreak, and harnessed up the horse.

And then full daylight — the sun up long enough to purge all that old imaginary Fever poison from the air, and we started out, to go out of the city, going out south first! And my Uncle's house — old Grummit's Bank — with its old tower, and its old heavy, slate covered mass of brick walls, locked and empty, back of us. And ahead of us, the empty city.

An empty city — not yet awoke. Vacant now even in the middle of the day. A city without children or women to be seen, or the shadows of any living things moving on the streets. And then, that time of morning, nothing at all but stillness and closed windows, and blank faced houses staring on the street. All motionless — just everybody gone; or out of sight. Doctors and nurses, even, and sick too, mostly — tired out, exhausted at the last spent ending of the night.

All empty — the whole town. And in one place on the main street, I remember, especially, seeing a great squash vine, an old frail, flimsy squash vine, had grown up, and trailed along the curbing of the street, beside the sidewalk, and still went there living and uncrushed, and oats were growing up in any number of places on the streets.

We were very lucky, very lucky, going then. We could not have picked out an hour of the day that was safer — when we were less expected than in that early morning time when we went jolting out at last into the rutty, dusty, red, old country roads.

We were very lucky. We were through two towns —

and were getting into a third one — driving east already, and a little to the north — before there was anybody held us back at all.

There was a man then in the road — a fat man — with a gray mustache, that jumped out of the bushes, at the side of the road — suddenly, like he might have been sleeping — and trailing an old single barrel shotgun after him.

Lucky for us again, he was on Vance's side of the old buggy.

He looked at her a minute — where she leaned out toward him, looking eager — then drew his eyes away, and started out to talk to me.

"Good morning," Vance said to him — first.

"Good mornin', ma'am," said the fat man, most polite, taking his hat off very low, and he looked back at her.

"Please, sir," said Vance, in that big, wide-eyed, child-like way of hers — like she was very hurried and excited and scared, "will you tell me, please," she said, her voice shaking, "have you got the Fever here, sir, yet?"

"No, ma'am," said the fat man, standing there, looking with his gun pointing at his stomach. "No, ma'am."

"Oh, you just don't know how glad I am," said Vance, sighing — still watching him with those great eyes of hers. "How glad I am to hear you say that. I was so scared we might be going to some place where they'd had that terrible old Fever.

"They say it's terrible, just terrible there in Memphis!" she said, looking at him.

"Yes, ma'am, yes, ma'am, we're keeping watch of that!" said the fat man, standing straighter.

And then:

"Beavis," said Vance, but not taking her eyes from him at all. "Beavis," she said, looking quick at him, and

back again, " I wonder, Beavis," she said to me, blushing,
" if this gentleman wouldn't help you — help us! "

" Anything, ma'am," said the fat man. " Anything I
can, ma'am."

" Well, then, sir," I said, " you certainly can. You
can show us where the nearest parson lives."

And I looked at him a minute and he at me; and then
we laughed, we both laughed — and Vance laughed with
us, blushing.

So he showed us where the minister lived; and we went
along, Vance thanking him. I didn't look back at all —
I didn't dare to. But Vance did, once.

She said he wasn't looking when she looked. He stood
there in the middle of the road, thinking, looking down.

I remember the minister — when we first saw him; a
tall, old, stringy codger, with one of those old long beards
those country ministers used to wear those days, sometimes. It was quite early in the morning yet; he was
out hoeing in his garden, I remember — shirtsleeves and
galluses, and carpet slippers on his feet. We had to
wait while he dressed up. I remember how wet and slick
his hair was, and how his old white tie stuck out. When
we came to pay him, I know, I had to pay him in those
old " shin plasters." I had found quite a lot of them
in some of the drawers of my Uncle's old secretary — the
only other money that I found.

There was nothing in between those, and those great
bills in the little box at the end of the bell-rope — those
packages of big bills in Hagar's Hoard. And:

" We can't give him a hundred dollars," said Vance.

For that was the smallest we could find.

I remember the old man looking down at that great
fist full of those old " shin plasters "— and I stammering
and apologizing.

"I ain't seen any of those for a number of years," he said, watching them.

He wasn't quite sure, I expect, whether they were good or not.

So then we went along, Vance and I, man and wife, driving out in that hot summer morning. The red dust inches deep on the road, the old locusts still crying in the trees, and the woods dry and rusty, and yellowing toward the fall. And the persimmons tree standing golden in the fields.

We went on and on, through those old country roads, Vance and I — in that old high buggy, with that little leather trunk strapped somehow on behind. And Dolly poking on along; and I with that old satchel of my Uncle's — with Hagar's Hoard in between my feet — guarding it.

You've got no idea how that thing bothered me and kept me watching. I'd got me a Colt's pistol that day before — a real pistol, not that old Derringer my Uncle had. And everybody that came along got a sharp looking-over from me, now, let me tell you.

But the main thing, of course, that I never could forget, was the Fever — and Vance. Did we have it? Were we carrying out with us that old Fever poison in our blood?

We rested in the middle of the day, or Vance did, after eating lunch, at the edge of a grove — one of those old high groves we have in our country, with the soft fine grass under them; and the big high lofty space below the branches. Vance rested, and I sat and kept my eye — kept my eye on Hagar's Hoard — and thought about its first owner, and his constant watching, while I did.

I thought quite a lot of him, then — my Uncle Hagar as I was sitting there. And what he'd done with his own life; and of his money, and what he said to me that last day — that yesterday that seemed so far away already. And especially I kept hearing him telling about old men. What they were.

"An old man — what's an old man?" I kept hearing him, "nothing but what he's got! Nothin'. Nothin' but what he's got!"

And if that was so, I kept thinking, there was all that time left of him to be remembered — that mussy wad of greenbacks in that little old handbag of his, beside me. And when I did get thinking of it, I knew, already, there was no great grief or memory of him in me — and I was sorry and ashamed. But it was true.

Already those days of Fever — that monstrous yesterday, were fading from me. I was tired out, I expect, just weary with the awfulness of it, till at last the feeling had just dropped off of me. And every step we went, the hot golden weather and the soft, hot, lazy silence of the day rose and rose around us, and washed the memory of all that — the Fever and the dead man from my mind. I was forgetting it, for I expect I was sleepy, and tired and happy again. Yes, very happy!

"If only now we have escaped it!" I said to myself, with a start. And it seemed then, for the first time, to me, that maybe we had. I had that feeling beginning then. That maybe, by our good luck, by accident, somehow, we had escaped it.

And when it came to me, when I thought of it, I started somehow almost believing it. And suddenly I leaned over, from where I sat, my back against a great tree, leaned over Vance and kissed her, where she lay peacefully asleep, resting on one of those old army blankets we had brought.

And then, along toward evening, we went along again, drove along through two or three more towns — around them rather, when we could. They didn't make us any trouble with their quarantines — only in one place. And then we just showed the guard our certificate from this place where we'd been married — when he started arguing. And left him there behind us in the middle of the road, laughing. But that was all; nobody bothered us after that; and the further away we got from Memphis, naturally the easier for us.

It was seven days — six days and a half in all. For we got through of course; we were safe. We didn't have the Fever, of course — by the grace of God, it all came right for us.

Good luck it was principally, I expect — the luck that young folks have somehow. It was youth of course; and that great house that saved us — that great old house, and the shutting out of the Fever at night — of the things we didn't know that went carrying death around at night. How foolish we would have thought it, if they'd tried to tell us what it was then really. And yet we saved ourselves by what we did — not knowing why. And many thousand folks besides us, too, I have no doubt, one time and another, with that old time custom of fearing the night air — the night air and its poison, out beyond the other side of the closed windows.

Yes — anyhow — we escaped — Vance and I —

That afternoon, I was telling you about — that first afternoon —!

We stopped, I remember after a while, at a farm house, thinking to get a bite to eat; thinking maybe if it was good and clean, that we might ask to spend the night there. But after supper, Vance shook her head at me, and I didn't ask. It wasn't a very pleasant place to think of stopping at. There aren't very many in that back country, like that was.

So we went along — we drove ahead — and the shadows

got right long at the eastern edges of the woods. The sun was going — and there would be a moon, Vance said.

We went by quite a number of those farms, with their bare, trodden yards, and barns and corn cribs — the dogs and pigs and chickens — unclean, ugly — more like lairs of animals than homes of men.

The rusty sun got lower and lower back of us, and the great still yellow moon swam up into the old violet colored sky above the eastern trees.

" It's getting late, Dear Heart," I said. " We've got to decide what we're going to do — pretty quick."

" Yes," said Vance, and sighed and was still.

We rode in long stillnesses, with the squeak of the traces, and the grating and filtering of the dust from the buggy wheels. And the freshening smell of evening in the air.

" I don't expect," said Vance, at last, " we'd better try to look at any more of those farmers' houses. They're all so crowded — so unpleasant. All these strangers —"

And she stopped, and we were still again. Everything on earth was still — so very still, like it is always, somehow, when one of those great yellow moons first comes swimming up there in its violet sky. A miracle, a still wonder, like God creating a new world for you, before your eyes!

" It's getting late," I said. " We must decide where we are going."

" Yes," said Vance, again.

And after a while she spoke again.

" It's so pleasant here," said Vance, softly — after a long sleepy grating of the wheels. " So pleasant out here in the night. These great trees here — some of these great groves. These great old silent trees — and the moon! It will be light — all night — almost. . . .

" We could tie the horse out somewhere, tie out Dolly somewhere. She'd be safe enough," she said. " There'd be no more danger at all. All safe," she whispered, " all —" and stopped — trembling.

" Yes," I said, my heart beating in my throat.

" But this," I said, and touched the satchel between my feet, the old, brown satchel, with Hagar's Hoard locked up in it.

" That too," said Vance, " safe. Yes, safe enough!"

" Yes," I said, finally — and was still again.

" Money!" said Vance, softly. " What's money?"

. . . There was a little brook, with just a little water running in it after all that dry summer heat. It flowed in through the edge of a great high oak woods, a wonderful dry high-roofed place to camp. And a cornfield came up — came up, one corner to the trees. A cornfield — rustling, stopping in the faint wind; with that sweet, warm weather smell of corn.

We tethered the old horse beneath the trees, a little ways away from us.

The wind came up — and fell again — like something breathing — shaking and shivering in the oak leaves, up there, over us — and dying down again.

The great fall moon came rising, rising in the sky — the violet sky — the milky autumn sky — across that old fragrant field of corn — rustling — lisping — still.

THE END